P9-DNR-393

PRAISE FOR
The Feral Detective

"The first *GREAT NOVEL*
about the Trump era."
—VULTURE

"*HYPNOTIC*.... Lethem leads
us to the limit of our conventions,
then drags us past them."
—*LOS ANGELES TIMES*

"*HILARIOUS* and
TERRIFYING and *WRENCHING*....
Phoebe is one of the grandest, funniest heroes
I've come upon in a long time."
—MEGAN ABBOTT

"[Lethem] gives the missing-girl
genre his own *QUIRKY, ENTRANCING*
spin in this paean to SoCal noir."
—*O, THE OPRAH MAGAZINE*

"Menacing and allegorical....
FULL OF PLEASURES."
—*THE NEW YORK TIMES BOOK REVIEW*

"*Feral*'s desert politics and *DYSTOPIAN WIT* cast a sort of spell."
—*ENTERTAINMENT WEEKLY*

"*LETHEM [IS] A MASTER* of the genre-bending detective novel and eccentric characters."
—HUFFPOST

"A *WILD, URGENT, VERY FUNNY* book. . . . In his ever-more-electric prose, Lethem illuminates both the barbarity and the beauty."
—DANA SPIOTTA

"Super-entertaining. . . . Lethem's writing is *SO GOOD*."
—*AARP THE MAGAZINE*

"I want to read a shelf of Heist. I want to make him my new Travis McGee, and that's, seriously, the *HIGHEST PRAISE* I know."
—JOSHUA COHEN

THE FERAL DETECTIVE

Also by Jonathan Lethem

NOVELS

Gun, with Occasional Music

Amnesia Moon

As She Climbed Across the Table

Girl in Landscape

Motherless Brooklyn

The Fortress of Solitude

You Don't Love Me Yet

Chronic City

Dissident Gardens

A Gambler's Anatomy

NOVELLAS

This Shape We're In

SHORT STORY COLLECTIONS

The Wall of the Sky, the Wall of the Eye

Kafka Americana (with Carter Scholz)

Men and Cartoons

How We Got Insipid

Lucky Alan and Other Stories

THE FERAL
DETECTIVE

A Novel

JONATHAN
LETHEM

ST. JOHN THE BAPTIST PARISH LIBRARY
2920 NEW HIGHWAY 51
LAPLACE, LOUISIANA 70068

ecco

An Imprint of HarperCollinsPublishers

This is a work of fiction. Names, characters, places, and incidents are products of the author's imagination or are used fictitiously and are not to be construed as real. Any resemblance to actual events, locales, organizations, or persons, living or dead, is entirely coincidental.

THE FERAL DETECTIVE. Copyright © 2018 by Jonathan Lethem. All rights reserved. Printed in the United States of America. No part of this book may be used or reproduced in any manner whatsoever without written permission except in the case of brief quotations embodied in critical articles and reviews. For information, address HarperCollins Publishers, 195 Broadway, New York, NY 10007.

HarperCollins books may be purchased for educational, business, or sales promotional use. For information, please email the Special Markets Department at SPsales@harpercollins.com.

A hardcover edition of this book was published in 2018 by Ecco, an imprint of HarperCollins Publishers.

FIRST ECCO PAPERBACK EDITION PUBLISHED 2019.

Designed by Renata De Oliveira
Photo by Liz Stepanoff / Shutterstock

Library of Congress Cataloging-in-Publication Data has been applied for.

ISBN 978-0-06-285907-5

19 20 21 22 23   LSC   10 9 8 7 6 5 4 3 2 1

In memory of

MICHAEL FRIEDMAN

ARDEN REED

DAN ICOLARI

Only too well do I know the Yahoos to be a barbarous nation, perhaps the most barbarous to be found upon the face of the earth, but it would be unjust to overlook certain traits which redeem them. They have institutions of their own; they enjoy a king; they employ a language based upon abstract concepts; they believe, like the Hebrews and the Greeks, in the divine nature of poetry; and they surmise that the soul survives the death of the body. They also uphold the truth of punishments and rewards. After their fashion, they stand for civilization much as we ourselves do, in spite of our many transgressions. I do not repent having fought in their ranks against the Ape-men. —JORGE LUIS BORGES, *BRODIE'S REPORT*

Granted there is no artifice here, no trickery, what motive has this man for having no motive? —DAWN POWELL, *TURN, MAGIC WHEEL*

PART I

THE WASH

1

I WAS TWENTY MINUTES LATE FOR MY APPOINTMENT WITH THE FERAL Detective, because I drove past the place twice. In daylight, broad flat morning, in a rental car with GPS that only sort of betrayed me. It was the feeling the place inspired that betrayed me worse. The feeling, specifically, that it was a place for driving past, and so my foot couldn't find the brake. White stucco, with redwood-clad pillars and a terra-cotta tile roof. A deck ran around the second floor, accessible from stairs on the parking lot side. The windows were all barred.

The signage at the various doors was either crappy plastic or just banners printed vertically, nailed through eyelets to the pillars. One said only TATTOO, another SPA. Upstairs, WARRIOR SUTRA BODY PIERCING. In the window of SPA, in front of closed curtains, neon bulbs in red and blue said OPEN. I assumed I knew what *spa* meant in this case. It was nine on a Saturday morning, January 14, 2017. Or nine twenty, since I was, as I said, late. It seemed impossible to be late for an appointment with anything at a building such as this.

To make an appointment here was to have dropped through the floor of your life, out of ordinary time. You weren't meant to be here at all, if you were me.

Having missed the destination, I drove a ways on Foothill Boulevard before figuring it out. The malls and gas stations and chain restaurants took on the quality of a single repeated back-drop, such as Fred Flintstone would motor past. Space was different here. I doubled back and slowed. The building wasn't dark, exactly—nothing could be, in this glare. But it had a warty density that made it easy to miss.

The problem was also the immediate surround. Beyond the parking lot, a wide-strewn trailer park. On the right, behind cyclone fence, a tundra of pits and heaped hills of gravel, in a lot the approximate size of Central Park. Maybe I exaggerate. I do. Half the size of Central Park. In this wasteland the building seemed fake. It claimed a context where none was possible. I mean, human beings, ones you'd want to be or know. The power that had caused me to drive past was more than unappealing. The building made you aware of mental blinders. To park your car here was to not be who you thought you were. Maybe I wasn't now.

Plus, the blue was killing me. I don't mean *the blues,* as in *the white girl blues.* (I did have those, though I'd never resort to such bogus shit aloud.) It was the blue of the sky that was killing me, that and the way, across the street, with no sense of proportion or taste, snow-capped peaks argued intricately with the flat galactic blue. Beneath the peaks, white bandwidths of fog clung to the contours of rock. There was nothing like these in the sky itself.

If I stared at the places where the blue met the white, it freaked me out. It was a thing you only saw in the movies, with actors costumed as dwarves running up a CGI mountain, except here there was no black frame, no exit sign floating in the periphery. Just the blue. I considered the word *unearthly* and then discarded it as stupid. This was the earthly, precisely. I parked in the lot behind the building and looked for suite number eight.

I had to go up the stairs to find it. The second-story deck

put me in a new relation to the expanse of trailers, the suburban vacuity beyond. It didn't solve the mystery of what was tucked inside those gravel arroyos, though, or how the white fluff could be stuck to the mountains when there wasn't a cloud in the sky.

Lady, you did this. You went west. Now, suck it up. I knocked.

2

IN CASE IT ISN'T OBVIOUS, THERE'S A DETECTIVE IN THIS STORY. BUT I'M not it. I had myself halfway cast in the role when I got on the plane, but no. Sorry. Then again, the story does involve a missing person, and it could well be me. Or you or practically anybody. As he said to me once, who's not missing? He was prone to these low-ebb oracular remarks. To my surprise, I learned to like them.

3

A VOICE BEHIND THE BRASS #8 CALLED, "IT'S OPEN." I PUSHED IN. THE usual law of glaring sunlight applied, so I was blinded in the gloom. There wasn't a foyer or waiting area, let alone a secretary screening his appointments. I'd lurched into the so-called suite, a large, cluttered, murky space that grew darker when the voice said "Close the door" and I obeyed. In the instant I'd had to discern outlines, I made out the boat-sized desk, the figure behind it, the shapes along the walls, all inanimate. No other bodies waiting in ambush, I felt reasonably sure. I could be back through the door before he'd be around the desk. I had pepper spray and a tiny compressed-air klaxon horn in my purse. I'd never used either one, and the klaxon was maybe a joke.

"Phoebe Siegler?" The only lamp in the room sat on the desk. All I saw was jeans and boots. The lamp had for company only a landline, a heavy black office phone. No computer.

"Sorry I'm late," I said, just to say something.

He dropped his feet from the desk and rolled forward in his chair and my eyes adjusted first to find his worn red leather jacket, cut and detailed like a cowboy shirt, with white-leather-trimmed vest pockets and cuffs. The leather was so stiff and dry, it was as if a cowboy shirt had been cast in bronze, then spray-painted. An absurd jacket, though I came to take it for granted. More than that, as an emblem. I've still never seen another like it.

Above, his big head came into the light. His eyes were brown under bushy, devilishly arched brows. His hair streamed back from his wide forehead, and his sideburns were wide and beardy enough to seem to stream from his cheeks too. Like his whole face had pushed through a gap in a web of hair, I thought absurdly. Where the burns stopped he needed a shave, two days' worth at least. He resembled one of those pottery leaf-faces you find hanging on the sheds of wannabe-English gardens. His big nose and lips, his deep-cleft chin and philtrum, looked like ceramic or wood. Somehow, despite or because of all of this, I registered him as attractive, with an undertow of disgust. The disgust was perhaps at myself, for noticing.

A minor nagging mystery for me had always been what did Meryl see in Clint anyhow? I think I caught that movie on cable when I was eleven or twelve, and I'd found him only baffling and weird. So maybe that was the mystery I'd come all this way to solve. Realizing I find someone attractive is often like this for me, a catching-up of the brain to something as remote as if on some faraway planet. I guess I could cross it off my bucket list: I'd now felt a jerk on my chain for a fiftyish cowboyish fellow. Go figure.

That didn't mean I wanted to flirt. I was terrified, and showed it. He said, "I'm Charles Heist," and moved farther into the light, but didn't stick out his hand. My eyes adjusted enough to tabulate the array of stuff along the walls. On the left, a narrow iron-frame bed, with heaped-up blankets, and pillows lined the long way, against the wall. I hoped he wouldn't suggest I consider it a couch. On the right, a battered black case for an acoustic guitar, a two-drawer filing cabinet, and a long blond wood armoire, one I couldn't keep from noting would have been a pretty swank piece of Danish modern if it wasn't ruined. But this was my brain pinballing to irrelevancies.

He helped me out. "You said on the phone you were looking for someone." I'd called a number the day before and been called back—from the phone on the desk, perhaps.

"My friend's daughter, yes."

"Sit." He pointed at a folding chair between the file cabinet and armoire. While I took it and scissored it open for myself, he watched, seeming frankly unashamed not to show any gallantry. I preferred the desk between us for now, and maybe he felt this, so that in fact the deeper gallantry was on view.

"Jane Toth sent you?"

"Yes." Jane Toth was the social worker whose name the local police had given me after they'd finished shrugging off my expectation that they'd be any help in my search for Arabella Swados, whose trail had led to Upland. Eighteen-year-old Reed College dropouts three months missing didn't meet their standard for expanding their caseload. So I'd gone to find Ms. Toth, a local specialist in destitutes and runaways. After subjecting me to a sequence of expectation-lowering gestures herself, she'd jotted Heist's name and number on the back of her card and mentioned his weird nickname. She'd also warned me that his methods were a little unorthodox, but he sometimes produced miraculous results for families with trails grown cold, like Arabella's.

"You bring some materials?"

"Sorry." I would try to stop saying that. I dug in my purse for Arabella's passport, with a photo taken just a year before, when she was seventeen. "I guess this means we don't have to look in Mexico."

"We're not that near to Mexico here, Ms. Siegler. But if you wanted, there are places you could cross the line with a driver's license."

"I don't think she has one."

"Is she using credit cards?"

"She had one of her mom's, but she's not using it. We tried that."

"Or you wouldn't be here."

The passport I'd slid onto his desk was clean and tight, and the tension in the binding snapped it shut, not that he noticed. Heist—I should call him Charles, only he wasn't that to me, not yet—didn't look at the passport. He stared at me. I've endured my share of male strip-you-bare eyework, but this was more existentially blunt, souls meeting in a sunstruck clearing. For an instant he seemed as shook that I'd entered his office as I was.

"I guess you don't work along those lines so much, tracing documents and so on." Duh. I was blithering.

"Not at all."

"In high school she worked on an organic farm in Vermont." Saying this, I found myself flashing on the mountains, the blasted expanses I'd just ducked in from. The blue. Arabella and I, we were an awfully long way from Vermont's village green rendition of the rural now. "She got onto a kind of off-the-grid idea there, I think. You know, from similarly privileged kids who didn't know any better than she did."

"Off-the-grid isn't always a terrible idea." He said this without venting any disapproval my way, as much as I'd invited it.

"No, sure, I didn't mean that. So, that is the kind of thing you do?"

"Yes." Now the blue light of his stare was the same as that sky: killing me. Perhaps in mercy, he broke the tension, opened a desk drawer at his right. Of course a gun could come out. Or maybe this was the part of the script where he produced a bottle and two shot glasses. Perhaps I closely resembled the woman who had broken his heart. I leaned a little forward. The drawer was deep, and scraped free of the desk heavily. He scooped his hand down low and brought out a furry gray-striped football with a cone-like white snout and soft pink claws like the hands of a child's doll. I surprised myself knowing its right name without even trying—an opossum.

The creature's legs and thick bare tail dangled on either side of Heist's arm, but it wasn't dead. Its black eyes glistened. I sat back a little. The room had a warm woody smell, like underbrush, and now I credited it to the animal I hadn't known was hiding in the drawer. Heist stroked the creature with one blunt finger, from between its catlike ears, down its spine, seeming to hypnotize it. Or maybe it was me that was hypnotized.

"Does it work like a bloodhound?" I joked. "I forgot to bring a scrap of clothing."

"Her name is Jean." He spoke evenly, still unaffronted by my flip tone. "She's recovering from a urinary tract infection, if it doesn't kill her."

"Just a pet, then."

"Some people thought so, but they were misinformed. I took her off their hands."

"Ah. So now she lives in your desk?"

"For the time being."

"Then what—you release her to the wild?"

"If she lives. She probably won't."

It all sounded a little righteous to me, but I didn't have the zoological grounds to quibble. Still, I couldn't keep from the impression that Heist cuddled the animal not for its own sake, and not even to impress me, but to salve his own desolation. Maybe just hearing about lost girls was too much for this person. I'd begun kicking myself for imagining he could locate one.

"What do you need to go forward?" I asked. "I mean, concerning Arabella."

"I'll ask around." He stroked the opossum, who blinked at me.

"Should I pay you?"

"Let's see what I find, then we'll talk. Are there other names?"

"Other names?"

"Other names she might go under. Or names she's thrown around, part of this time in her life. Friends, boyfriends, enemies."

"I think she quit throwing names around. Quit calling home entirely. But I'll check with her mom."

"Anything is better than nothing."

"There is one name, though I hesitate."

He and Jean waited, all eyes on me.

"Leonard Cohen."

"Go on."

"She was a bit of a freak about him, I think that might be worth mentioning. Even before he died, I mean. It could be that's the point of this, ah, general destination." Not to add that I couldn't think of one other fucking reason in the universe a thinking, feeling teenage vegan would migrate to this locale, but I didn't want to insult the precinct Charles Heist and his little friend called home.

"You think she went up the mountain."

"I couldn't dismiss the coincidence." Here was exactly as far as my sleuthing had gotten: Mount Baldy, one of those mountains Upland lay at the foot of, was home to Leonard Cohen's Buddhist guru, had been for a decade or so his place of retreat. I couldn't pick it out of the lineup of white-topped peaks, but for that I had the rental's GPS, or maybe now this guy.

The prospect seemed to trouble him, and he waited a long time before producing his totally unsatisfying reply. "Okay. I'll put it on my list."

I wished he'd actually exhibit a list, even if it were scrawled on a Post-it, but it was at least good to hear him invoke the word. Action items, procedures, protocols, anything but this human freak show in a red leather jacket soothing or being soothed by his comfort opossum.

Well, wasn't I the judgmental Acela-corridor elite? The bubble I'd fled, coming west, I actually carted around on my back like a snail's shell, a bubble fit for one. As my fear abated, in its place a kind of rage coursed through me, that I'd come to this absurd passage, that I'd placed Arabella in hands such as these. Or that Arabella had placed me in them; it could be seen either way. Seeming to read me again, Heist lifted his free hand from Jean's ears long enough to palm the passport into an interior pocket of the jacket. Too late for me to take it back. I was an idiot for not making a photocopy and for letting him near the original.

"Where can I find you?" he asked.

"I'm staying at the Doubletree, just down Foothill—"

"Under your own name?"

"Yes, but what I was going to say is could I come with you? Maybe I'd be able to help describe her—"

I'd stopped at a sound of clunking and rustling, directly behind me. I almost shit my pants. Another rescue animal? The front panel of the armoire slid open, and two filthy bare feet protruded sideways into the room, their ankles covered in gray leggings. The feet twisted to find the floor, and the rest of the person attached came writhing out, to crouch like the animal I'd mistaken her for.

A girl, maybe thirteen or fourteen, I guessed. Her black hair was lank to her shoulders and looked as though it had been cut with the nail clippers no one had taught her to use on her raw-bitten fingers. She wrapped her elbows around her knees and watched me sidelong, not turning her almond-shaped head completely in my direction. She wore a tubelike black sundress over the leggings. Her bare arms were deeply tanned, and lightly furred with sun-bleached hair contrasting with the black sprigs at both armpits.

"It's okay," said Heist. He talked past me, to the girl. "She isn't looking for you."

She sat that way, quivering slightly, pursing one corner of her mouth.

"She thought you might be an emissary of the courts," he explained. It was nice he felt compelled to account to me at all, I suppose. I'd half risen from my chair. I sat again.

"Go ahead," said Heist.

The girl scurried up and into the mound of blankets on the low bed. She took the same position beneath them, huddled around her knees, her eyes poking from the top as if from an anthill.

Was it a message to me, that I should remember some lost don't wish to be found?

Heist lowered Jean gently back into her drawer and slid it shut. "This is Phoebe," he said to the girl. "She's looking for someone else, someone who ran away. We're going to help her."

We? I might cry now. Did the girl ride on Jean when they searched together? No, she'd need a bigger animal, a wolf or goat. Or maybe the detective carried her under his free arm, the one that wasn't holding the opossum.

"I'll find you at the Doubletree," he said to me now. It wasn't curt or rude, but I was being dismissed. I felt as though a trap door had opened under the chair.

"You sure I can't go along?" I heard myself nearly pleading. "I'd like to get the lay of the land, actually. I'm only here for one reason."

"Maybe after I make a few inquiries."

"Great," I said, then added lamely, "I'll work things from my end in the meantime." The words we exchanged seemed credible enough, if they'd been spoken in a credible atmosphere. Here, they seemed a tinny rehearsal, something having no bearing on what was actually being enacted in this room, a thing I couldn't have named and in which I was an unwilling player.

Could I ask him for the passport back? I didn't. The girl

watched me as I went for the door, opened it to the blinding glare. For the first time, I noticed the water dish and food bowl in the corner—Jean's meal station. Or maybe the furry girl's. It occurred to me that Heist had introduced the opossum by name, but not the girl. I felt demented with despair, having come here. My radical gesture, to quit my privileged cage and go intrepid. Take the role of rescuer. Yet it was as though I'd been willingly reduced, exposed as nothing more than that opossum, or the girl in the blanket. My mission had defaulted to another surrender to male authority, the same wheezy script that ran the whole world I'd fled. All the lost girls, waiting for their detectives. Me, I'd be waiting at the Doubletree, to contemplate all the comforts I'd forsaken. And yet I felt also the utter inadequacy of the authority to whom I'd defaulted, he with not even a gun or a bottle of Scotch or a broken heart in his drawer, only a marsupial with a urinary tract infection. I was confused, to say the least. I got out of there.

4

BLAME THE ELECTION. I'D BEEN WORKING FOR THE GREAT GRAY NEWS
organization, in a hard-won, lowly position meant to guaran-
tee me a life spent rising securely through the ranks. This was
the way it was supposed to go, before I'd bugged out. I'd done
everything right, like a certain first female nominee we'd all relied upon, even my male friends who hated her, as a cap on the
barking madness of the world. Now she took walks in the hills
around Chappaqua, and I'd checked into the Doubletree a mile
west of Upland, California.

I'd grown up a pure product of Manhattan, secretly middle-
class in Yorkville. My parents were both shrinks, and their
marriage was a device for the caretaking of my mother's jittery,
wrecked romanticism. An only child, I might have been one too
many. I spent a lot of my childhood farming myself out to the
houses of families with siblings, houses with a raucous atmosphere in which I could be semi-mistaken for just one more. It
wasn't so much that my parents discouraged my bringing friends
home. When I did, my parents were always delighted, and, putting out tea and cookies, sat us down for what I imagined—still
imagine—couples therapy might be like.

I saved my parents a calamitous sum by getting into Hunter
College High School, then forced them to produce the calamitous sum by getting into college in Boston. The summer before

my junior year I interned at a literary magazine, and when I returned to New York after graduation I worked there. It was a place that encouraged the nonsurrender of certain radical feminist-theoretical attitudes I'd cultivated at college, even as I prospered in an atmosphere of lightly ironized harassing "mentorship" in an office full of men ten years older than myself. From there to NPR, where I did research, prepping the one-sheets that made interviewers sound like they'd read books they hadn't read. And then Op Ed, my foot in the door of the citadel.

The notorious day in November when my boss and all the rest of them sat deferentially with the Beast-Elect at a long table behind closed doors, to soak in his castigation and flattery, I conceived my quitting. At the start of the following week, I actually opened my yawp and did it, made a perverse stand on principle, stunning myself and those in range of hearing. The hate in my heart was amazing. I blamed my city for producing and being unable to defeat the monster in the tower. I already had my escape charted out, and I gave exactly zero of my accumulated mentors, or my parents, any say in the matter. For my thirty-three-year-old tantrum, I was patronizingly dubbed The Girl Who Quit. I think I won Facebook that day, for what it's worth. I mean, of course, inside the so-called bubble.

Roslyn Swados had been my supervisor at NPR. Twenty years older than me, a public radio lifer, she was recently divorced when our friendship began. I was fresh off a juvenile breakup myself. She had me to her perfect Cobble Hill duplex for a dinner consisting of a bottle of white wine and a baguette and a giant hunk of Humboldt Fog, a cheese I'd somehow never tasted until that night. We polished them all off in an orgy of commiseration, then moved on to a bar of Toblerone.

Roslyn's life ran along the lines of the New York I'd idealized growing up, one increasingly unavailable to those of us coming along after—the one implicit in a thousand short stories from the

'80s and '90s issues of the *New Yorker* still stacked in my parents' bathroom, some of which I'd memorized. It was only likely that her address was Cheever Place, a landmarked, tree-lined block that formed my sanctuary and ideal.

Neither of us were lesbians, so I couldn't be in love with Roslyn. It didn't make sense for me to want to be her, since there was no one for me to divorce yet. I wasn't Roslyn's daughter, either, since I still had a mother, and she had Arabella, who was a high school sophomore when I entered their lives, still living at home, though she had in some ways already grown elusive to Roslyn. It was more like I'd farmed myself out again, as I'd done before college. In this case, to a family where I could be a younger sister to the mother and an elder to the daughter. I'm sure Roslyn hoped I'd glue the two of them together at least a while longer. I never blamed her for making this calculation. Our friendship was real, and the calculation was wrong, as it happened. I couldn't glue mother and daughter together, not even briefly.

But I did get close to Arabella. She trusted me. Soon I enjoyed two uncanny familial friendships, upstairs and downstairs in the same duplex. This was a kid who'd become a vegetarian at twelve, after reading Jonathan Safran Foer's book, and who had three posters in her room: Sleater-Kinney, Pussy Riot, and Leonard Cohen. Her sexuality was unclear, but I got the feeling the sexuality of the entire high school at Saint Ann's was unclear, so she had company. She no longer spoke to her father. She played guitar, badly. I worried when she told me Cohen's "Chelsea Hotel #2" was her favorite song (*giving me head on the unmade bed*), but took heart when it became apparent she identified not with the female subject but with the male singer.

Arabella and her friends were those who couldn't recall a time before 9/11, or only barely, an evil channel glimpsed before their parents dug the remote from the cushions to switch it off. Though they made me feel old, I rooted for her and her compatriots with the dumb devotion others reserved for sports teams. I frankly envied Arabella when she declared her disinterest in eastern colleges and applied to Reed. I thought she'd thrive there.

One night in September, I went to dinner with Roslyn. We met at Prune, on First Street. We sat on either side of a stew of mussels and leeks, our favorite, only nothing was right that night, and it was more than the nothing-is-right of foreshadowed electoral doom. Arabella hadn't been calling home. Her texts were minimal, their tone hostile and defensive. Roslyn didn't know what to do.

"Did you call *your* mother from college?" Roslyn asked bluntly.

"My mother wasn't one you called," I began. I said it with a glibness I regretted immediately.

"Arabella thinks of me the same way."

Of course. Something obscure came clear, the reason I'd inserted myself so deeply in this family. I'd been free to behold and adore a mother and a daughter equally, even if they couldn't themselves. In the system of my own family, I could only choose one side.

"I'll reach out," I said. The thing I knew she hoped I'd say.

I got Arabella on the phone, once. She didn't like her classes, or Portland. She repeated a promise from before, that she would drop out and head down to Mount Baldy, to find Leonard Cohen. I treated this with skeptical amusement—a big mistake. And Arabella probably sniffed me out; she was too smart to fool. For the first time ever, I'd agreed to act as a go-between or mole for her mother.

Then came the week in November when, accompanying the national calamity, Leonard Cohen dropped dead. When Roslyn rang Arabella's cell, she got only a text in return: *I'm fine.* Somehow, I thought, *I'm fine* never means what it says.

I urged Roslyn to contact the dean of students. She'd already been contenting herself, it seemed to me, with too little word from her daughter. Arabella was a New York kid, I reminded her. It meant she was equipped, sure, but also that the rest of the country, even funky Portland, would be an alien wonderland to her—never more than after November 8.

But Roslyn was a New Yorker too. Distracted, stoical, and now, like all of us, a little or a lot wrecked. She'd been hitting the white wine hard, without enough Humboldt Fog and baguette to soften the impact. I didn't blame her. She satisfied herself with a few more flat-affect texts from Arabella until the day in mid-December when even those quit coming, and when calls to Arabella's number resulted in a "Mailbox full" message.

Roslyn woke from her trance and bought a plane ticket to Portland. She was distraught enough that I offered to join her. We flew out on a Friday night, and we were together when Reed's security let us into Arabella's dorm room, the single she'd fought for. The mess there included unopened mail dated as far back as September, masses of untouched schoolwork, and her abandoned passport, the one I'd now handed over to Heist. Like most New York eighteen-year-olds, Arabella wasn't a driver, so she'd fled without an ID, which set off alarms. We talked with the dean of students on Monday before flying back east, but Arabella hadn't made herself visible to their system of counselors and advisors. She'd been discreetly failing out from the start, and no one knew her.

Back in New York, I tried to help a nearly insensate Roslyn with some rote sleuthing. A credit-card record put Arabella on an Amtrak to Union Station in Los Angeles. Leonard Cohen, it didn't take much to learn, had been recently living not on Mount Baldy, but in Los Angeles proper, among the Jews and pop stars, as would anyone with a brain. Well, not Arabella. The last thing the credit card's trail revealed was a purchase—a bunch of groceries—from a supermarket called Stater Bros. in the Mountain Plaza Shopping Mall in Upland, California, fifty miles from the Pacific Ocean. It pointed to a pilgrimage to the Zen mountaintop, just like she'd promised. So, having sworn to Roslyn I'd find her daughter, I arrived in Upland for a look around.

Harvard, Hillary, Trump, the *New York Times*. Names I hated to say, as if they pinned me to a life that had curdled in its premises. Those might be summarized as feeling superior to what I hated, like the Reactionary White Voter, or the men who'd refused me the chance to refuse to marry them by refusing to ask.

Well, unlike the helicopter-raised people around me, I could look in a mirror without someone else holding it—or so I liked to think. If there was an outside to my fate, I'd locate it, or be damned inside the self-referential system of familiarities. Maybe I could bring back Arabella, and with her, a report from the exterior.

5

MY HOTEL WAS ONLY A MILE FROM THE DUSTY YELLOW MYSTERIES OF Upland, but it might have been a million. Claremont was a town that presented itself as an implacable fortress of non-native shade trees and well-kept craftsman houses, fitted around a college campus as empty and perfect as a stage set. In this cheery simulacrum I discovered nothing I could get a purchase on, apart from a lively record store, but I didn't have any way of playing a record. So I took my phone to a bakery and coffee shop called Some Crust and read Elena Ferrante at an outdoor table and hoped for some amusing college student to hit on me. I got hit on by amusing senior citizens instead. Perhaps they, like the Klan, had been lately emboldened. I retreated to my hotel.

My room reminded me of a gun moll's wisecrack, in some old film I'd seen, on entering an apartment: "Early Nothing." I was left with Facebook, where my friends had responded to the election by reducing themselves to shrill squabbling cartoons. Or I could opt for CNN, where various so-called surrogates enacted their shrill hectoring cartoons without needing to be reduced, since it was their life's only accomplishment to have been preformatted for this brave new world. Television had elected itself, I figured. It could watch itself too, for all I cared. I read my book.

On the second day without a call from Heist, it began to

rain. There was dramatic promise in the storm's beginnings, with a three A.M. lightning strike that might have been right over the Doubletree. It shook my room with a sound like a sonic boom just an instant after the flashbulb flare that had woken me. Could the world be saying no thanks to 2017, to the latest outlandish shithead cabinet appointment, after all? Maybe I'd come to California to join it in sliding into the sea.

But the lightning was mere overture to a dull steady rain that fell unceasingly through the day and night that followed, unimpressive except if I stepped outside the door of my room. The hard-baked desert ground, which exposed the lie of all those shade trees, didn't soak the water up but refused it. The rain gathered in torrents coursing downhill, away from the mountaintops, which were no longer visible through the roof of gray mist. These gouts made every sidewalk crossing a white-water rafting opportunity, only I didn't have a raft. Southern California wasn't made for pedestrians, needless to say, but today it wanted amphibious vehicles.

I retreated to my room to write e-mails, except the one that mattered, the one I owed Roslyn. I knew my friend was in tatters, waiting for me to deliver a miracle. Instead, I'd reduced myself to her West Coast equal, for the moment: a woman in a room, alone. I might be nearer to Arabella; likely I was. But I couldn't prove it.

So my thoughts turned to my appointed savior. I Googled a few combinations of *feral*, *detective*, and *Heist*, but, surprise surprise, he didn't have a website or Wikipedia page. Nor did it help that his last name doubled as an improper noun. Most of the results not involving crime movies were links to heartbreaking and lurid newspaper accounts of children abused by their caretakers in Florida and elsewhere, which pushed me off the search in disgust. I played some Leonard Cohen on YouTube through my computer's lousy speakers. A fairly weak gesture in Arabella's direction, but maybe it would somehow summon her up.

The third morning, I couldn't take it anymore, and I tried Heist's phone. I got his voicemail. "I can't answer the phone. Please leave a message." I called twice but left no message. Unlike the first time I'd heard it, I now had a face to go with that strange calm, flat tone: a strange calm, flat leathery face, bordered in extraordinary hairs. I couldn't purge it from my thoughts, nor could I quit picturing his office. Was the furry girl wrapped in her blanket on that cot, jumping at the ringing of the phone? Or was he? Whose bed was that, anyhow? Were the girl and the opossum lapping together from the water bowl in the corner? I felt I might be obligated to bust in there and free that child, but I was paralyzed with uncertainty, and the absurd hope that Charles Heist was suddenly about to deliver Arabella and make sense of my dereliction of my own life, my own trajectory. I longed for my cubicle, for another Tinder date at the Bourgeois Pig.

I sent out a Hail Mary e-mail to my only actual Los Angeles acquaintance, a high school friend who'd Liked my quitting on Facebook and invited me to get in touch. Now, hearing my location, she broke the news that Culver City, where she worked in a gallery, was a nearly two-hour drive on a weekday, even without the rain. Still, I had nowhere else to be, unless I set out up the mountain to poke around the Zen Center on my own—the location was plain enough on Google Maps. But no, I'd give Heist at least one more day. So I told her I'd treat her to dinner at the best restaurant she could show me in Culver City. I needed the hell out of the Doubletree and the whole Inland Empire.

6

THE GPS INSTRUCTED ME TO "MERGE ONTO INTERSTATE TEN WEST, TOWARD LOS Angeles," but in the robot's voice it sounded like *lost and jealous*. The sea change from the suburban desert interior, of which there'd been stunning miles to traverse before I'd seen downtown passing on the right, was unaccountable. As the miles peeled beneath the tires I thought of Arabella, the western distances she'd had to go to make her disappearance—how many, exactly, I had yet to know.

Last I'd seen Arabella in person she'd been musing on what I then thought was her little joke, about finding Leonard Cohen. "Don't you go hitchhiking now," I'd said to her. "It isn't 1972 anymore, except in your heart."

"Don't worry, I won't," she'd said, with a teenager's glum exasperation. I hadn't forced her to promise. Now, each mile ticked in me, a metronome of self-reproach. If I could have Arabella back now, I'd have tried to insert a tracking microchip under the skin at the nape of her neck, like they do with cats and dogs at the adoption shelter.

7

I MAY HAVE BEEN TO BLAME, BUT BY THE TIME OF OUR MEAL'S SECOND course, I figured I'd never call Stephanie again and might even block her if I didn't have the brass to unfriend. Of course that's when the conversation got interesting, at least a little.

"Everyone's trying to get out of New York," she informed me, in what I suppose she intended as a kind of congratulation. "You're not even ahead of the curve. Out here it's like, what took you so long?"

"I don't need to be ahead of the curve," I said. In fact, I was a little stunned to find myself in an outrageously expensive restaurant, one with a low glow of orange light at each table and an actual fourth-tier—but identifiable—movie actor at the bar. The sheer urbanity, in the decor and clientele, had actually thrown me for a loop. Nothing in Upland or Claremont had challenged my New Yorker's sense of superiority. But Stephanie had me meet her at the gallery first, where glam-bohemian staff and collectors, women in leather jackets and heels, men in beards and T-shirts, browsed what seemed an entire city block of white walls and unfathomable objects, making me feel by their blasé fabulousness very much the poor little match girl by comparison.

"You become yourself out here," said Stephanie now.

"How so?"

"In New York, that caffeinated neurotic atmosphere guarantees you think something important is happening every single second of your life. In fact, you're just eating shit. I mean literally so unhealthy you can't even look at yourself in the mirror. And you ride the subway to some job that barely pays your rent and the only reason you don't know it sucks is that a thousand other people are telling you how lucky you are."

Stephanie could look at herself in the mirror, I'd wager that. She wore a sleeveless black dress showing gym-sculpted arms so teenage-boyish they made me a little hot. I braced myself for an infomercial on the benefits of a diet of sheer avocado.

Instead she said, "With the space around you here, you can't kid yourself. You have to wake up every day and you have to decide who you are in a total void."

She might have been talking about me in my room at the Doubletree after all. I put down my fork, which had been continuously employed in the cause of departure. "Funny you should say that," I told her. "I think I've been undergoing a sort of void encounter myself these past couple of days."

Stephanie shrugged. "It's impossible not to."

"I felt like the mountains were too close and too far away at the same time."

"Wild edge," she said enigmatically.

"What's that?"

"L.A. has more of it than any other city in the world. Wild edge, city right up against whatever, the sea, the mountains."

"That's crazy." I couldn't gratify her with anything less equivocal than that.

"You can feel the civilization as this kind of thin layer that's just been troweled onto the landscape. It's, like, everything's provisional."

Well, on the one hand there's mansplaining, and on the other, there's the sound of a woman quoting the mansplaining to another woman. She confirmed my guess. "This artist we're working with, that's actually the title of his upcoming show, *Wild Edge*."

And whom you've fucked or are about to be fucking. Stephanie turned red enough that she didn't need to say it.

And I suddenly wanted everything she had, practically including the portobello and groats on her barely fussed-with plate. Her head start in fleeing to Los Angeles, her Culver City version of the void encounter, so much less tawdry than my own. I'd been calculating how soon I could get my rental car from the valet and drive east to the Doubletree. Now I wanted to leverage a night on her couch.

"There's plenty of wild edge," I said. "But there's a surplus of everything else too. A boggling amount of *San* and *Los,* with a side order of *Rancho*." I was getting defensively goofy. I felt we'd come to that juncture where you allude to the man in your life, in order to claim you've got one. A life, that is. I thought, absurdly, of mentioning Charles Heist, or asking if she'd heard of the Feral Detective. Knowing Heist had something in common with having a man in my life—he never called.

"Where are you again?"

"Montclair—I mean, Claremont." I was too embarrassed to say Upland, for some reason. "It's, uh, a really different scene." I waved my hand in the approximate direction of the movie star.

"I've never had any reason to go." I felt it as a sudden withdrawal of her sympathies.

"If there's a Midwest of Los Angeles, I think I've found it." Earlier I'd mentioned I was looking for a lost friend, nothing more. Now it occurred to me she might think the "friend" was myself, and not be entirely wrong. I tried another joke. "There's nothing but there there." Stephanie wasn't buying.

After this glance into each other's voids there was little left for me and Stephanie to do but to deplore the orange monster for a while and say no to dessert. We crossed these items off the list, and I kept my promise and picked up the check.

8

THE RETURN DRIVE ON INTERSTATE 10 IN THE DARK, AND STILL IN GUSTS
of rain, was baldly terrifying. It was hardly less crowded than at
rush hour. If the six lanes of red taillights were a video game,
it would have been called *Chute of Death*. In fact, at the crest of
an ear-popping hill I came to a famous cemetery, one with its
own freeway exit, on the other side of which the Inland Empire
spread before me, looking like the proverbial blanket of tinsel.

As it happened, not much later, crouching around a fire in
the desert, I'd hear it explained that the hill crowned by the
cemetery marked the point at which, in a future of rising sea
levels, the Pacific would be exhausted in its encroaching from
the west. These immaculate gravestones littered a chunk of future beachfront.

Suck on that, Wild Edge.

9

I WAS AWOKEN IN THE DARK. NOT BY MY PHONE, WHICH I'D ALREADY learned to switch off, having discovered how rarely my New York friends seemed capable of conjugating western time zones. It was by a rap at the door. I rolled from bed to pull the window's heavy curtains and discovered only more pounding rain streaking the glass. But technically there was daylight behind it somewhere, not night.

I croaked out some stalling sounds while I wiggled into clothing I'd discarded in a trail from the bathroom to the bed. Lacking eyes on me, I'd descended to dormitory squalor pretty rapidly.

Charles Heist stood in the hotel's corridor, his black plastic poncho glistening with rain. His hair was swept back under a soaked Dodgers cap.

"You ready to make some rounds? I could use you now."

Rounds? Was he a feral doctor now? "Sure, sure. Just let me—" I indicated the room behind me. I was barefoot, still blinking in the corridor's light.

"You have rain boots?"

"I went to the airport in my winter stuff."

"You'll want it."

I didn't know whether to invite him and his dripping work boots in or shut the door in his face. So I split the difference, left it ajar to the corridor while I went into the bathroom to brush my teeth, found my boots and coat, then corralled my phone and handbag—Pepper spray! Klaxon!—and joined him.

"Should I follow you in my car?"

Heist shook his head. We passed through the lobby, where I helped myself to an umbrella from their supply. I also shot the young woman at the counter a dark look for having succumbed to whatever gambit Heist had employed to cause her to surrender my room number. She didn't blink. I tucked myself into the wind and gale of the front lot, where Heist steered me to his pickup truck but left me to open the passenger door myself. So much for cowboy courtliness—Heist was as unmannerly, as dour and self-enclosed, as an emo guitarist packing in after a poorly attended gig at a bar in Greenpoint. That being my sole point of personal reference for riding shotgun in the garbage-strewn cab of a pickup.

Heist had started the engine before I tucked my knees and umbrella inside and slammed the door. The vinyl of the seat and the plastic of the dashboard were cracked, yellow foam insulation bulging in both cases. The windshield too had a hairline network extending from where a stone or bullet had impacted it on the passenger side. The wiper blades glided unimpeded, though, carving and recarving windows through the rain.

I eyed the glove compartment, wondering if it would fit an opossum. Maybe some smaller creature.

"Are we going up the mountain?" Those white crowns were purely theoretical now, battened somewhere high behind the gray ceiling of the storm.

"Not just yet. I want to take you to the Wash."

I tried not to find that ominous. "Who or what is the Wash?"

"The San Antonio Wash. It's the alluvial fan for Mount Baldy, or what's left of it." In the grip of the phrase from his own mouth, *alluvial fan*, I heard Heist begin dreaming of some incommensurable distance, not really addressing me at all. It was a sound I would grow used to from him, this ready unaffixing from the time and space we were meant to be inhabiting, like the cab of his truck. In fact I'd grow needy for it, even if in a given moment it seemed to erase not only me, but him too.

In this instance, he tore himself free without my help. "You probably drove past without noticing. Everyone does. It's hidden in plain sight." We were headed east on Foothill, out of Claremont's trees. "That's one of the reasons this zone between Upland and Claremont is what's called unincorporated."

"Unincorporated?"

"It's neither town. It's between."

I suffered a lurch of intuition. "The gravel pit, you mean."

"There's a gravel pit at the north end, yes."

"It's called the Wash?"

"Most people don't know it has a name."

"Listen, I'm a slow starter. I'm better after my coffee."

He turned toward me and drove with one hand, like people do in the movies. All you can think is how they're about to crash and it drives me crazy, even in the movies. "If you don't want to go into the Wash, I'll take you back to your hotel."

Now Heist wasn't distant at all, though I might have preferred it if he was. We were nearer than when seated across from each other at his desk, and I felt pitched into the fractal-like whorls of his nostrils and lips, the leonine sideburns and eyebrows. He resembled a breathing woodcut. His eyes were soft, though, and his voice unthreatening.

"On the contrary, I was wondering when you'd ask." My yammering wasn't entirely under my control. Again, I had to see that within my fear was fascination, and more. I wanted to confirm my ability to anchor this man's drifting attention. Before he found Arabella, I thought, he ought to find *me*.

Unless I stunned him with my pepper spray, the only method

available was my nervous riffing. "Only what's the frequency, Kenneth? Seems like a rainy day for a hike."

"It's not so much a hike I had in mind. The Wash people need help. Word is three more days of rain."

"What kind of help?"

"If they sleep in the pipe they might drown. They don't know they need to be rescued."

"I might be your first customer. I wasn't sure I could keep dry for much longer in the Doubletree."

Heist was already qualified to be at least my temporary boyfriend, inasmuch as he'd learned the art of ignoring a percentage of what came out of my mouth. But the next thing he said silenced my joking for a while.

"Plus, there's someone in the Wash who might know your friend."

"Someone's seen Arabella?"

"A young woman. I could be wrong. She's pretty spaced out. If I'm right, Arabella's going under another name. Maybe you'd want to talk to her and see what you think."

"Yes." The possibility that he'd actually advanced Arabella's case reduced me, if not to tears, to syllables. "Just let me in on the plan here."

"Try not to come on like the police, that's the main thing."

"I can do that, sure."

"Great." With his free hand he rolled something closer on the long seat between us. I felt it as electric when he closed that distance so casually, then disappointed when he reapplied his eyes to the road. I took up what he'd nudged against my leg—a battered aluminum thermos.

"Go ahead."

It was black and hot. I wasn't discreet in my slurping. The bracing effect helped me shake off the aura of dream that clung to my waking the way the raindrops clung to the pickup's windshield. That coffee was a wiper blade, cutting a window for my brain to peer through. I wanted to ask him who was looking after the marsupial in the desk drawer and the tween in the armoire, but the answer was obvious: they were looking after each other.

Heist parked us on the south side of Foothill, just behind the sign marking the edge of San Bernardino. He took the truck off the boulevard's shoulder, into the muddy gravel seam at the top of the cavernous margin of earth and gravel, now gushing with wide rivulets of runoff, this thing he'd called the Wash. Tearing past this nullity the first few times in my rental, I'd thought it impressively huge, if also uninviting, not an entry point into anything. Stepping from Heist's truck, onto the layer of desert mud, I took the true scale into my body. The faraway buildings and trees seemed to recede as I surrendered myself to the earth's surface. I unfurled my nerdy umbrella.

Heist went to the side of the pickup's bed, covered with what I now saw wasn't a hard cap but a fitted tarp, snapped tightly onto the bed's walls. He unfastened it from the corner nearest the driver's door and repeated his disconcerting magician's stunt, that of disclosing animal life where I hadn't thought to look: a trio of dogs' snouts nosed through the gap he'd widened.

He tore free another few snaps and the dogs scrabbled over the bed's wall and leaped clear of the truck, one after the next, flowing like train cars on an invisible rail. Brownish husky-type dogs, with raccoon eyes and ridged backs and curled, banner-like tails. Laughable that I'd spent my vigilance on the glove compartment when Heist had *The Call of the* Freaking *Wild* conveyed behind us the entire time. If it hadn't been for the rain I liked to think I would have heard their whining or smelled their fur. Maybe, though, these weren't whining or fur-stinky dogs, were instead only ghost clean and silent, on point. They circled the truck, skirting the roadway, and went down into the ditch, seeming to know we were to enter the Wash.

The rain had eased just enough that I couldn't cite it as an excuse to balk. It had been a day since I'd witnessed a lightning strike. Heist, the dogs coursing around his boots, beckoned me down toward a gulley where the fencing had been peeled up to form an easy entrance into the pit, which continued to seem to expand in my sight, as if it wished to swallow me. I had to half collapse my umbrella before I limboed under the fence. Heist waited just long enough to be certain I was clear. In his poncho, with his arms outthrust for balance on the grade, he resembled a black kite that had touched down and grown work boots.

The palm of the storm-laden sky pressed down to meet us as we descended the bank on the far side of the fence. Within a few steps, I couldn't see back over the ridge to Heist's truck. I had to keep my eyes at my feet anyhow, to navigate the muddy gutters rushing underfoot. The dogs surged in and out of my peripheral vision. One curved to me and I held out my hand for him to sniff in greeting and he endeared himself with a hasty sandpaper lick, then resumed scouting. Either the dogs had already been muddy beneath the pickup's tarp, or they'd instantly found puddles nearly up to their shoulders to plunge through. At either side of the bulge along which Heist had led me, I saw now, runoff gushed as if from a ruptured main.

"Holy hell," I said. "This thing is like a bathtub filling up."

"It might get there."

"Is this the runoff for the entire mountain?"

"There's a reservoir between us and the mountain, or we'd be underwater already."

I picked my way after him and the dogs, teetered as if on a high wire with my umbrella. My city boots slid on the slick gravel. Soon enough I learned to do as Heist was doing, seeking footings on the clumps of tall reedy grass, jamming my heels into their exposed roots. God knew what figure I'd cut with the inhabitants of the Wash, but I felt the opposite of any manner of police, unless it was a meter maid. The dogs surged ahead, braiding like a strand of DNA. The cavernous embankments of mud, ice plant, and wet shale rose higher with every step, the high thin perimeter of fencing now barely in view. I wondered if I ought to be scattering breadcrumbs or pomegranate seeds or Advil to chart a retreat. Was the rain beating harder against my little bumbershoot, or was it that the wind had died as we descended, so I noticed the sound?

I called to Heist, giving full benefit of my wishful thinking. "You think it's leveling off?"

He let me catch up. "Should get a whole lot worse, which is in our favor."

"How so?"

"We want to evacuate them. The rain makes our case."

"They won't believe in water they can't see on a moment-by-moment basis?"

"No Californian does." Here Heist offered me a short smile, an admission that he saw I lived to banter, and that he thought he'd bantered back. Maybe he had. The suggestion was that Heist not only knew I wasn't Californian but maybe wasn't himself. But if he wasn't, what was he?

The dogs had woven together to nose at a heap of wreckage, a house-of-cards pile of ragged slabs of white concrete, its edges scored with rusted stubs of rebar. Though it would have taken a bulldozer to shove it together, the assemblage suggested a lean-to or tent, a temporary shelter. Now I saw it *was* a shelter. A gray hand emerged from its entrance to chafe at the snouts of the dogs that had been pointed together there.

I observed the sawed-off plastic gallon containers set out to collect rainwater and the bed of an extinguished fire, also the refuse of fragmented materials—twisted-off lengths of car-radio antenna, stray shopping cart wheels—that lay fanned on the ground before the entrance in an order implying use value, like hand tools mounted in a suburban garage. Heist had slowed not to allow me to catch up, but because we'd entered the Wash's first encampment.

The hand scumbling at the noses and skulls of the wet dogs featured white skin coated with grime and tipped with black half-moon fingernails. Now the dogs retreated, spines buckling with an excitement that mimicked fear, as the hand grew an arm and then an entire body, which unfolded itself improbably from within the concrete slabs to stand nearly bare in the rain. The body was smooth, everywhere neatly muscled and utterly filthy, in dirty white sweatpants cut off raggedly at mid-thigh. Considered as a diaper, the covering needed a change. It took a quick soaking instead.

The man didn't seem to notice or care. His head was smooth too, or not quite, when I looked harder—it had been recently shaved, and featured perhaps a week's shadow. Heist was tallish, but not beside the nearly nude giant who'd slid from the hole. We stood on uneven ground, sure, but gazing up at him, I felt like one of the dogs, or as though I'd stepped into a sinkhole. I guessed at six six or six seven. Everywhere, it seemed, Heist reenacted his trick of conjuring mammals from floorboards or heaps of rubble. Or again, I might be dreaming, and here was my White Rabbit.

"Laird."

"*Hola*, Charles."

"You still got that shortwave radio?"

"I keep fiddling but it's out of juice." The giant knelt to sweep the three dogs into one embrace, permitting them to lap rain from his knees, his bowed thighs.

"You know what I'm going to tell you. They're broadcasting alerts."

Laird tapped his head. "Alerts I hear plenty with no radio. That's what got me down here."

"You might need a raft."

"Who's this one? She brought me an umbrella? I could turn it upside down."

"Phoebe's searching for a lost girl."

"I don't have any to spare."

"We're going to talk to Kate. The folks in the pipe need higher ground, at least."

"Kate had everybody building a levee yesterday. She calls me Tractor."

"Kate likes to make up nicknames."

"Tell her I'm not her fucking tractor."

"I'll put in a word."

"Spirit if not the letter of my remarks."

I'd been struck dumb, I saw now, by the fact of Laird's immensity, and the fact of any kind of voice coming out of that body. I imagined him standing again, taking with him all the dogs clutched to his chest like a bouquet. Yet it was Heist's ease with the giant that stirred me more. His adeptness with the animals and the people-animals of the world. I was beginning to yearn to be counted among them, to be under his care as well.

Now Laird stood but left the dogs on the ground and they darted off, seeming to know we were proceeding past this lurid sentry, farther into the Wash.

"Bye," I said.

"I'll catch you on the rebound, Mary Poppins," said Laird.

10

WE FOLLOWED OR WERE LED BY THE DEEPENING STREAM—HEIST AND I
navigating higher ground, the dogs splashing through the
depths—before descending into the midst of a tiny settlement,
a town, perhaps, made of tents and sheet-metal lean-tos, all of
them shiny with rain. The lanes between the twelve or fifteen
shelters were strewn with packrat evidence: pyramids of irregular
firewood, disassembled bicycles, a stack of computer keyboards,
and more rainwater-collecting containers, some full. No sign of
life at first except for a pair of childish feet sticking, Diogenes-
style, from a tall segment of concrete pipe, and a puppy sniffing
at an empty can. The three huskies surrounded the puppy, which
squirmed onto its back in submission, then batted at their noses.
Heist waved me into the midst of this largely abandoned village
only to move through it, and beyond.

At the next rise it appeared below us, the tunnel. The rough
mud had given way, abruptly, to an angled concrete aqueduct, a
channel directing the runoff in an accelerating course toward a
dark-overhung aperture in the stony bank beyond. As we neared,
I could see into the flat-bottomed tunnel formed by the sheltering roof. The wings of the aqueduct were dotted with pup tents
and sleeping bags, deep into the dark alcove, maybe thirty or so
visible from the rise where we stood. The population had clambered up onto these tilted planes, dragging what they could of

their shelters and belongings. These were the tunnel people. The structure that housed and hid them, that roofed them from the demolishing steady sunshine and surveillance helicopters that made their ordinary enemies, had betrayed them in the storm.

At the mouth, visible once Heist and I descended, a woman directed the effort the giant Laird had given the name of levee. It was a work in progress, to put it generously. A rotted couch had been placed in the center of the flow, to make a bulwark the water had to work under and around. Despite the sizable stones and chunks of shattered pavement that had been added at every breach, and the soaked clothes and rotting blankets, the tarps and tenting employed to cement between the stony stuff, the water did. There was nowhere for it to go but into the tunnel— the engineers had had the essential geological fact of the planet on their side when they placed it there.

The woman—Kate, I supposed—waded in the streaming, jeans rolled to her knees. The jeans, and her down ski jacket, were wet through. Kate's two helpers, both shirtless black men, one with nubby dreadlocks, took on the unwitting air of players in an avant-garde political-theatrical tableau—they'd only need an actor in a plantation hat with a bullwhip to complete the picture. One of the two hoisted a cinder block but had nowhere to go with it, stood bewildered. I had already begun to see the cinder block as he might, an asset not to be spent in error. These fighters of the sun had despoiled their village fighting water, and gained nothing.

"They ought to leave the tunnel," said Heist.

"We live in a free country, Charles." Kate spoke without turning from her effort, in a weary bark that cut above the whirr of torrent and low whistling wind. It was a voice I could have put to a middle school principal or the bailiff in a courtroom drama.

"Let me talk to them."

"That's included in *free*." Now she turned to look. The voice emerged from a face like the top of a caved-in pie, more ancient than her sturdy body. "A gentleman, however, would get into the trenches and help." She noticed me and made a swift assessment. "Ladies are counted as gentlemen in this case."

"Phoebe needs to talk to that girl Sage, if she's still around." Heist's dogs had waded in to sniff more hands, and now one stood atop the couch.

"Well, there's your task, then. Sage and Martin are on the hill with a hand truck." She gestured off to her right, the vast crumbled slope. "They could use some help. Laird quit on me."

That's because he's no tractor, I wanted to say, but didn't.

We found the pair called Martin and Sage halted in frustration nearly at the top of the grade. They looked near weeping, maybe were, the rain made it hard to tell. The two of them resembled all-American teenagers, it seemed to me, only weeks removed from Glee Club when their careers as homeless persons began. At Kate's instigation they'd broken a porta-potty out of the construction site across Monte Vista Avenue and worked it through a torn section of fencing. Now, with the hand truck, they'd mired it in a gulley, the wheels sunk where gravel turned to mud. Heist and I threw ourselves at the problem, abandoning my umbrella and all pride, making our own avant-garde theater now, something more Beckettian, I think: *Figures Shifting a Toilet into a Crevasse.* Kate received the offering of the porta-potty grudgingly. She and her helpers, including Martin now, turned the blue plastic shed on its side and began to work it into place in the levee, while Sage and I followed Heist into the tunnel at last, having earned our waiver from Kate.

"You two go warm up," said Heist. Deeper inside, a poured-concrete stair led to a dry platform. There, smoke furled from a metal drum. "I'm going to talk to some people."

Sage and I joined three others at the fire. I'd managed to

keep my handbag wedged in my armpit, and now I foraged in
it for some tissues to dab at my dripping hair. My coat kept me
dry underneath, but one of my feet had immersed completely,
my toes squishy within my boot. Sage was worse off, her dirty
green army jacket a thing you could have wrung like a sponge.
She huddled, looking at me expectantly. Heist had told her I
came with questions.

"Charles thought you recognized a picture."

She nodded fearfully.

"Her name's Arabella." Vowels echoed in the grotto of the
aqueduct.

She shook her head, mousily firm. "She never said that."

"You remember what she said instead?"

"You're her friend?" Now I saw Sage turn, as if willfully, to
the part of her that was inward and strange, that which had
driven her so far and so irreversibly from Glee Club. The task of
shifting the porta-potty had glued her to the real, but the glue
wasn't meant to hold. "Do you have a cigarette?"

"Sorry."

"I don't want one anyway."

"Oh."

"I'm just really sorry you lost your friend. I wish I could help
you." It was tra-la-la time.

"Maybe you are helping me. Did you see her—here? In the
Wash?"

"We came down together. With a guy."

"With Martin?"

"No, a different guy, older."

A shudder went through me. "You mean—Charles? My
friend who helped us just now?" A wary part of me still thought
of that furry girl in Heist's office. If I was in search of a villain
or abductor, the Feral Detective remained the only suspect before me.

She shook her head again. "The man isn't here now. A Buddhist."

I grew excited. "You mean from the place on the mountain, on Baldy? The retreat?" I wondered why Heist hadn't wanted simply to drive up with me and check it out, if he'd heard this. Maybe he hadn't. "Is he a monk?"

She tittered. "He's friends with the monkeys. He's friends with the rabbits and bears. He knows everybody."

"Is he a monk? Do you think she's with him now?"

"Uh-uh. Where'd Martin go?"

"He's helping with the levee."

"This rain isn't helping with anything."

"No," I agreed.

"Not even the drought."

I wanted to fiddle her radio dial, get her on the right station. "What about the man with my friend?" I said. "Where did he go?"

"He has Chinese friends." She laughed. "I don't mean Phoebe. She isn't Chinese at all."

"That's me," I said. "I'm Phoebe."

"Not you. That's her other name, your friend. I just remembered."

"What are you talking about?"

"Phoebe. You're *both* Phoebe."

11

HEIST HAD WORKED ON THE COMMUNITY PROJECT FOR A WHILE, SHOE-
horning the porta-potty into the levee, earning his brownie
points. By the time I emerged from the depths, back to the tunnel's mouth, having concluded there was no further purpose in
conversation with Sage, he'd sweet-talked Kate and borrowed
the hand truck. Now he was busy with a supply of bungee cords,
lashing aboard several refugee properties, their bindles and pup
tents. A few of the tunnel's tenants had seen the light and would
make an exodus, be following us back to the truck. I think they
were all Mexicans, several making up a family, it wasn't clear.
Grime and desolation and my own discomfort made their faces
difficult to read.

This was Heist's way, I'd begun to know it. He worked in
and through contradiction, rarely pitting himself, nothing done
by wholes, little ever given a firm name. A partial evacuation,
an inadequate levee, a smidge of investigation, an airing for the
dogs. Soon enough I'd feel handled the same way, which was
infuriating and enthralling both. For now I put my Manhat-
tanite ass to the wheel and got drenched again dragging a shopping cart of plastic bags full of who-knew-what out against the
muddy current, up to the lip of the Wash, where we loaded it all
under the tarp. Three rode underneath too, with the dogs. Two
more in the cab between me and Heist, humans soaked through

with disarrangement, chagrin, remorse, exhaustion. I was one of them. Maybe Heist too.

I had no idea where Heist meant to take these people. They surely couldn't all live in the armoire in his office. Yet as we began to drive, I felt thrilled at what we'd accomplished, whatever it was. Freeing humans from the Wash. Though there were now two bodies intervening on the long seat, I thought I *felt* Heist, pulsating with his brand of implacable, mellow intention, the two of us making a bracket of what I believed was called *caritas* around our rescuees. Call me naïve or selfish, but I'd never contemplated the erotic potential in altruism until now. It had always seemed like Mother Teresa stuff to me.

So it came as a shock when Heist unceremoniously dropped me off first, swinging into the Doubletree's loading zone, beneath the protective awning, and waited for me to dash inside.

"Talk later?" I said. My voice squeaked. Our passengers looked at me.

"Talk later," said Heist.

"All righty, then."

I got out of his truck, feeling dumped. I treated myself to another one of the greasy, hot, fresh-baked chocolate chip cookies from the lobby, and also to a spanking new umbrella, daring the clerk to notice it was my second of the morning.

12

THEN CAME A STRANGE TIME. IN THE HOURS BEFORE CHARLES HEIST RE-
appeared and took me away in his truck again, I entered a kind
of spell or pall, as if the small hotel room were a kind of tunnel
too, and I'd been left behind instead of rescued. I stripped off
my soaked clothes and took a hot shower, and while one part of
my mind urgently wished to scrub off the mud of the Wash, the
rank smell of the tunnel and of my homeless companions in the
cab of Heist's pickup, another part mourned some loss I couldn't
specify. I felt I'd been allowed to taste Heist's world, teamed with
him in pursuit of abjectly hopeless tasks in a pit in the rain. And
then I'd been expelled.

I sat in the Doubletree robe, picked up and read a magazine
called *Inland Empire* cover to cover. I flipped channels. Sweating, brow-knit, lips-pursed Bruce Willis negotiated on a very
large mobile phone for the lives of terrified hostages. On another
station a baby-faced senator smirked and stonewalled around the
implications of his lifetime's jolly bigotry. The television glow
didn't warm me the way the barrel fire had done, and I turned
it off.

The faces at that fire, where I'd stood and talked with daft
Sage—I couldn't shake them. Why hadn't Heist persisted, I
thought now, and commanded everyone from that tunnel? They
could have come here and piled into this room and used the

supply of fluffy towels. We could have stolen all the cookies from the lobby. Meanwhile, Heist and I could have gone off up the mountain, so that I could play Bruce Willis, achieve my rescue, deliver Arabella and myself from this absurd landscape, though not before he and I had spent a certain amount of time in some rustic cabin on a fireside pelt rug. My thinking ran along such stupid and self-mocking lines as these, but I couldn't switch it off like the television.

Thanks to a room service tray bearing a "pole-caught American tuna melt," I had the privilege of wallowing in my dissolved state in that robe and on that bedspread for a nice long interval. It was only by dumb luck, therefore, that I was dressed and even wearing some makeup when Heist returned to my door. Or not luck so much as a depraved turn within my fugue: I'd made a decision, at the most crass and dismal level, to find the Inland Empire's nearest singles bar and get laid. If Heist wasn't interested, someone else would be.

The carnal impulse I'd conceived, the first since the election, wasn't a bright and happy one. It was morose, a product of the sensory deprivation chamber of the hotel room and the whole field of disturbance that lay outside the room. I thought for a minute of calling Roslyn. Despite time zones, it still wasn't too late. She'd be up, I was pretty certain, drowning her fear in white wine and binge-watching *The Crown* or *Pretty Little Liars*. She'd have gladly talked me out of my destination, as she'd talked me off any number of Tinder cliffs over the past year. But then I'd have had to explain where I'd gotten, and hadn't, in my search for Arabella. I would have had to explain Heist. I didn't call her.

It didn't take much Googling to discover my target. A bar called PianoPiano, billed as a scene of raucous X-rated dueling-piano novelty songs, perfect for bachelor and bachelorette parties, also the hub of Claremont's otherwise tepid pickup scene. Yelp reviews termed the place, specifically, a "cougar bar"—I might hope to be one of the younger cougars on the premises, and drag something back to the Doubletree with me.

It also didn't hurt that PianoPiano happened to lie just walking distance across the hotel's parking lot. I could learn how the Inland Empire fucked, and show it my stuff in return. The well of despondence I'd fallen into seemed to demand it. So it was that I was dressed to the nines, or at least the sevens, when Heist knocked on my door again.

The rain had tapered a little, the sun long since given up somewhere behind the storm. It could have been six in the evening or four in the morning, deepening the sensation of limbo that had overtaken me. Heist had shed his rain poncho. Perhaps the absurd red leather cowboy jacket had been underneath through our whole adventure. Perhaps it was part of his body.

"Where are we going this time?" I said.

"We could eat and talk."

"My winter coat is drying in the shower."

"We'll stay in."

On the truck's seat between us, in place of the coffee thermos, sat a steaming white paper sack, foil lined, crimped at the top. Takeout Indian, hugely aromatic. I was made ravenous. We pulled in behind the spa and tattoo building. The prospect of returning to his office was dreadful and fascinating, and I made myself ready for it. But he left the motor running, removed a pint container from the sack between us, and said, "I'll be right back."

"For the girl?" I asked when he returned.

"For Jean."

"The opossum?"

He nodded. "She can only handle plain stuff, white rice."

"Until the infection clears up, right? Then back to the prime fare, lamb biryani, glass of chardonnay."

I drew a smile. Heist wasn't stone impervious to my dork charms. And he recognized the word *chardonnay,* apparently. This I could work with.

The rain had quit. He switched off the wipers, leaving just the engine rumbling our little steamed-up space capsule.

"Where are we going?"

He'd put the truck in gear and swung back out around the building. At the entrance to Foothill Boulevard, we held for a break in the traffic, those glistening lights barely visible through the windshield's kaleidoscope.

"My place, to eat. Unless you want to eat in the truck."

"Who is that girl?" I needed an answer, suddenly. "Doesn't she eat? Why don't you say her name?"

"Her name is Melinda. I found her a place. She's staying with some people now."

A place, some people. It wasn't quite good enough. "A foster family?"

"Not officially. That system wasn't doing her any good."

"So, a nonofficial foster family?" I am the Lorax. I speak for the runaways.

"Melinda isn't much for moms and dads. She needed another format."

"What format?"

"I helped her to go off the grid. You want to eat?"

"The traditional term is 'kidnapping,' Mr. Heist."

"Then I guess that makes me untraditional." It would have been a snappy comeback, if Heist were capable of those. Instead he uncovered each word as if coining it, groping toward his tautological reply. The man was unprovokable to an almost autistic degree.

"So, you installed her in a drainpipe somewhere? Or no, you're relocating the drainpipe people. Where'd you take them, anyhow? Off the grid?"

"There's a shelter in Pomona. They might still be there, if you need proof."

"No, I need dinner. I'm dying for a drink, actually."

"I think there's some wine."

"What are we waiting for?"

We curled onto Foothill only to perform a wide U-turn back to a gravel roadway, through a gated opening in a wide fence, where lay the trailer park I'd noticed earlier. My heart, or my gut, endured another quiet pitch. Dinner in his office, which fronted to Foothill Boulevard, now seemed the civilized option. This was another Wash, a dark woods I hadn't banked on stepping inside. I wasn't dressed for it, for one thing.

I might be more than a little wrought up, still turned on by our mission of rescue in the flooded arroyos and the concrete tunnel. Now that Heist was back in my sights, my craving for a random piano-bar pickup began to look like sour grapes. The frisky feeling easily reattached to my smoke-free Marlboro Man. The special air between us in the truck had brought it back, or maybe it had never gone. I wanted to stay dry, sure, and I would have been happy to be taken inside a good restaurant or even a gaudy bar. But I wanted to be soaked again too. Then again, more simply, I was terrified of the trailer park. I didn't want to have to rescue *myself*.

I said nothing, and we rumbled inside, past trailers both lit and dark, some on blocks and others looking as though they'd pulled in more recently and could get back on the road if they needed to. What had seemed a road disintegrated into a maze unmarked by curbs or street lamps, to the far edge of the grounds. There, Heist pulled up at an Airstream cocked at the edge of another gravel canyon, across which the lights of civilization glittered only distantly. In the sky, a plane sagged toward the shadowy southern mountain range. We left the truck. Heist grabbed the food and made for the Airstream. The bloated silver thing resembled a foil party balloon or toy zeppelin that had sunk to earth, then grown heavy and tarnished in its crater. I had no voice.

The dogs were happy to see us. I took it as a sign of something. Inside, everything was warm and tiny and curved, fitted blond wood and pale-painted walls, like a ship's cabin. The surface on which Heist laid out the Indian food was made by a hinged chopping block that swung out across the small rangetop. The dogs thronged on the covers of the bed, which formed the entire near end of the Airstream and was the only place to sit. So I sat there, and removed my coat, and they nuzzled my armpits. Behind the savor of the food, I smelled man and dog, a concentrated aroma. It wasn't a bad one. Heist removed plates and silverware from a compartment tucked above eye level. He also pulled a cork on a bottle of red wine and poured it into two juice glasses. I drank half of mine, and began nosing around with the dogs. They got excited and tried to French me, in rounds and all at once.

"Who's this?" I said, without turning to Heist. "I don't do tongue until properly introduced."

Heist reached over me and crowned the dogs with his hand, each in turn. "Jessie, Miller, and Vacuum."

"Vacuum?"

"Vacuum likes to clean up. You'll see."

"What's for dinner?"

He stood to the counter, pulled a paper carton nearer with a finger and peered inside. "I don't know."

"What do you mean? Didn't you order it?" I went for a teasing tone. Five minutes earlier, in the parking lot, I'd wanted to be a supervisor or district attorney to Heist's rogue cop. Now I'd be his trailer girl.

"A friend owns the restaurant. It's called The Blessings. He drops meals off when he's got extra."

"Handouts for you and your strays?"

"He likes to feed people. I helped him a few times."

"Oh, I didn't mean anything." I swallowed down more wine and Heist refilled my glass. I felt a little crazy already, or still. "Once, in college, my friends and I got really high and crashed a Hare Krishna feast. That might have been the best food I ever tasted."

Heist raised his furry eyebrows but said nothing. He only seemed to measure me again, to see if he could fit my lability and sarcasm into the frame of his stillness. The rain was inaudible from within the Airstream, or it had stopped. It was as if we'd been pressure sealed against the outside. Jessie, Miller, Vacuum, Heist, and I, playing sardines, except no one searched for us. The surroundings were impossible now to keep in mind, the labyrinth of identically boxy trailer homes, the barren moonlit darklands extending around and beyond us. I supposed the Airstream's tiny windows must glow like beacons, but the accordion curtains were sealed tight against any prying eyes. There was at least that. Heist made plates, heaping saag paneer and tikka masala around a long crisp dosa, and handed one to me. As with the coffee, I slurped the food gratefully.

"You know why I'm dressed like this?" I said with my mouth full.

"No."

"I was going to see dueling pianos. Like, two guys playing two pianos. It's supposed to be a pretty corny scene—corny but pornographic."

"I've never tried it."

"We could go now!"

"Maybe it's time to discuss your situation."

"Right, right." Vacuum shoved his snout under my armpit to scarf a grain of long basmati rice from my cleavage. "My case, you mean. Arabella."

"Yes. You had a chance to talk to Sage."

"The girl in the Wash, you mean. The one with the toilet."

"Yes. What did you think?"

"She mentioned a man, maybe an older man. A Buddhist."

"Yes."

"She also, if I got her meaning, said Arabella had been going by my name."

"I wanted you to hear that for yourself."

"Well, I did." Apparently it required both Nancy Drew and a Hardy Boy to nail that down. I didn't say this aloud. "Could I—" I reached past him, to pour myself more red wine. Airstream living was arm's length living. You could grow drunk and fat in a place like this, if you never needed to walk the dogs.

"Did it mean anything to you?"

"What do you mean, did it mean anything to me? You sound like a shrink." I left my parents out of it, for the moment. "You think Arabella's my imaginary friend or something? Or I'm hers?"

"No."

"She's a runaway. She didn't want to be found. I thought you were good at that sort of thing."

He didn't reply. Unlike Vacuum, Jessie and Miller had remained on their bellies and haunches, front paws sphinxed outward, their brows furrowed as they watched us eat. Now Heist began forking up sauced rice and vegetables and feeding the dogs. They patiently waited their turns—even Vacuum—as Heist went around twice, three times, treating them to samples of the several flavors on his plate. I had to admit the dogs were neater eaters than I was, I who'd relied on my leaned-over plate to catch what had dripped from my fork.

"Buddhists means up Mount Baldy, right?" It was the destination I'd had in hand before walking into Heist's office, before even getting on the plane.

"It could mean that."

"So, we'll go there?"

"I guess so," said Heist. "It's not my favorite place."

At this I felt maximum irritation, but it wasn't as though he'd taken my money, or promised much in particular.

"Tomorrow?"

"Sure. It's too late tonight."

"Is there more for us to discuss?" I tipped back my glass, found I'd emptied it.

"Not if you don't want to."

Something had dissipated, or curdled, in my lascivious mood. Curdled, I mean, between me and myself. For Heist? Beholding that hieroglyph face, there could be no way to be sure whether anything of my flirting had landed in the first place. Maybe I'd imagined all reciprocity. My pride bristled.

"I should have driven my own car," I said.

"If you had, I wouldn't let you use it."

Heist didn't think I could hold two juice glasses' worth of merlot? *Chuck you, Farley.* Then I felt my hand, which had been patting absentmindedly at Jessie's neck and ears, covered by Heist's. His large rough fingers slid between mine, our hands' twinned weight resting on the dog's fur together, barely moving. I looked at his crooked knuckles covering mine, not at his face. Nested in Jessie's swirling nape, our hands were as complicated as Heist's face, like an Escher drawing or a sleeve tattoo. There was no relief to be found.

"I like Jessie best," I said. "You know why?"

"Why?"

"His fur is the reddest." Maybe I was drunk. "And the softest."

"You sure?"

"Of course I am. And he's the noble one. He's having the deepest thoughts. The others don't hold a candle to him."

"What's he thinking?"

"He's wondering why you don't have any music around here." I pulled my hand free of his. "Give me some more wine." Heist obliged, his eyes wide but also kind. I drank, drooled, all of a sudden utterly looped, having eaten barely anything. I wiped my lips with the back of my hand and Vacuum licked my knuckles clean. I tore off a portion of dosa and tried to eat it, got a few bites in, fed the remainder to Jessie. "I like dogs."

"Yes."

"I mean, I'm a cat person, but I like these dogs on an individual basis."

"They're good dogs."

"I have a klaxon in my bag."

"I'm not sure I understand. Is klaxon a drug?"

"A drug?"

"I don't mean anything illegal. It sounds like an antidepressant."

"No, stupid, it's, you know, a little horn."

"A little horn?"

"Forget it. It doesn't matter."

"Okay."

"I don't kiss men with facial hair."

"That's fine."

I kissed him. In the company of the dogs, anything short of tongues struck me as pathetically Victorian. I couldn't keep mine in my mouth anyhow. The dogs rose, adjusted to our positions, settled again. They nestled near to form a hairy life preserver. The exception was Vacuum, who, following his own script, went to the floor for my plate. Heist had set it there. He'd moved entirely onto the bed without my being certain when.

"It's too bright."

Heist switched the lamps. I took the moment to smooth down my skirt but also to undo the top button of my blouse. I had boobs, after all. He'd never once glanced to see, or I'd never caught him.

I put both my hands into Heist's fascinating hair, the radiant waves of his temples. It felt coarse, not greasy. My fingers sank in to caress his skull. His eyes were closed. I kissed his eyelid, turned his head with the pressure of my palms, put my nose and lips to his strong-cabled neck. At last his hands found me, stroking my shoulder and back as if I were one of the dogs. I blew wine breath in his ear, bit his lobe. I might be steaming up the whole Airstream like a bag of takeout. I wished for Heist to uncrimp my foil.

"Who did you vote for?" I whispered.

"Sorry?"

"Don't answer, never mind, forget I asked." It might be as germane as asking the same question of the dogs. I ran my hand inside the famous red jacket. Shifting toilets into levees and corralling strays of all species apparently kept Heist perfectly muscled, not a phony cowboy with a pickup. I smelled him, put my nose close and licked his clavicle.

"Say something."

"What?"

"Practically anything, words, just so I don't have to listen to my own heavy breathing."

"You feel amazing."

"You haven't even really felt me yet."

"So far."

"You're okay so far too." His stomach was bumpy, like an underwear model's. I'd usually scorned the look, but to smooth his furry terrain with my hand was just now my favorite thing. Before I knew it, I was under the waist of his jeans and held his hard cock.

"You don't have to do that," he said.

"I want to."

"You're drunk."

"I'm not. I mean, I could be drunker."

"Oh god."

He was uncircumcised, another thing I didn't like before and now did, this splendid unshucking of his oyster-pink, rubbery self. I covered him with my mouth, just embraced the pulsing head. Then nursed, really suckled for a minute, while he twisted his body and moaned into Jessie's fur, ending with a sudden mouthful for me.

So often I'd turned away, used my hand. Not now. I wanted what he had, or was drunk enough. Sweet behind the salt; a vegetarian, I found myself guessing. Vacuum sprang for my face, but I shoved him off. In my journey down Heist's length I'd slid to my knees, off the bed and onto the floor. Now I climbed back into the dogpile.

One hand covered Heist's face. "I'm sorry."

"Sorry for what?"

"That was sudden."

"Listen, if you hadn't been responsive, I'd be pretty sure I'd raped you." I pried a finger, like a starfish from a rock. Underneath, his cheeks were tear-streaked, trailing into his sideburns. "What's the matter?"

"Sorry. It's been a while."

"You don't always cry when you come, do you?"

"No."

"Okay, because that would be weird. Kiss me." I shoved the hand I'd peeled from Heist's face between my legs and put my mouth to his. Predictably, also honorably, he tried shifting south. "No," I whispered. "Just touch me with your hand." I was swamped, totally awash, could imagine him drowning there. Anyway, I wanted to see his face. If he'd gone below my horizon and begun licking, I'd have thought too much of the dogs.

"I understand."

"I don't need understanding. I need to come." I scooted my skirt up around my waist, guided his hand into my underwear. "That. Yes." I really was oceanic. "I just want you to see what you're dealing with here." It wasn't going to take much. I could draft off his rhythm, follow him right across the finish line, if he could only keep his blunt fingers from slipping off the right spot. I closed my eyes, licked my lips. One of the dogs began whining. "Oh fuck oh fuck oh fuck—"

"What?"

"No, don't stop, oh fuck!"

I clutched his arm, felt the muscles twitching through the leather jacket as his fingers worked not too inexpertly. I climbed it like a tree and screamed at the top. The whining dog—Vacuum, I think, feeling left out of things there on the floor—barked sharply once. The Feral Detective cradled me as a parent does a child, until I brusquely pushed him off.

"Now you're crying." He spoke softly. He always did.

"So?"

"I—"

"Shut up now."

He knew how to do that. So the five of us breathed there, in that space capsule to nowhere. The Airstream hadn't even had to launch and crash-land to find a ruined planet. It had only needed to be parked at the rim of a pit in the unincorporated zone between Upland and Claremont. What was I doing with my life, that I'd come to come here?

"Are you okay?" Heist whispered after a while.

"Yes."

"You were beautiful."

"I don't know about that. But that's my first since the election." Did I exaggerate? Sure, I might have managed a few desultory one A.M. or morning-shower wanks in the zombie weeks of the Obama administration, without taking much notice of it. But my orgasms weren't small occasions. The journey to being a person who entertained them in the company of others had been a private epic. It hadn't been obvious that such pleasures would be available to me on the far side of the Neoliberal Dream.

"Okay," he said, rather stupidly. The flood of tears unleashed in me was, in fact, a flood of rage. Heist could hold me, but I could hate him while he did. Vacuum licked my cheeks clean. I let him. Men had trashed the world that women and dogs had to live in, and at that moment I counted Heist among them—the men, I mean, not the dogs. I thought of Arabella again, out there somewhere in the company of her possible abductor, the so-called Buddhist with his Chinese friends. Was she in a trailer at this moment? Were there dogs to warm her?

"Do you have cigarettes?" I said. "Or is this a vape-only zone?"

"I'm sorry. I don't have either one."

"You clean-liver, you." I went groping for the wine bottle, drank from it directly this time, a deep gulp. He said nothing.

"I've figured out why there's no music. It's a holding action. Because you're only a turntable and a collection of vinyl and maybe a personal brand of artisanal foie gras away from being just another fucking Bernie Bro, aren't you?"

I was pretty pleased with myself, but Heist had no idea what I was talking about. My bile had nowhere to land. It was as misplaced from its context as I was, here in the Inland Empire, in this zone between, where I could no longer glimpse the world that was anyhow irretrievable. Inauguration was in two days, if I counted right.

"I can go get cigarettes, or music, if you need it," he said pathetically.

"No."

"Okay," he said again, to soothe me or himself.

"No, it's not okay. Don't forget what brought me to you, Mr. Heist." My thickened tongue had to struggle not to call him *Heisht*, but my brain was suddenly acute, wide open and enraged. For a moment, anyhow. I could feel it wishing to snap shut into blackness. "There's a missing girl."

"Yes."

"And tomorrow we're going up the mountain like we should have done today, and we're going to find her, and I'm going to take her back to New York City, and I'll never see this fucking place again."

"I understand."

Heist had to show me how to flush the tiny built-in toilet with the pedal on the floor, and he had to keep me from tumbling over as he took me there and back to the bed. And then I in my disheveled clothes and he in his, minus the red leather jacket, swam into the bedclothes, and were covered by the three dogs, so that I couldn't tell one from the other when I groped in the furry dark. And there we slept, the five of us.

PART II

THE MOUNTAIN

13

THE BUDDHIST STUMBLEBUM KEPT APOLOGIZING FOR THE WIND WHILE HE showed me around the premises of the Zendo. I ought to have been grateful to him, since I'd given no advance notice of my arrival, but then again it didn't seem he'd had much to do before I'd appeared. Maybe he should've thanked me. Maybe he had, in his way, with his exhibition of enthusiasm, the little hop in his step, and his apologies for the wind.

The skies were clear up here on Baldy, the wind incessant. I shuddered, feeling it cut through my coat and pants. My legs felt naked to it. What had fallen as rain down below had apparently landed as snow here in the mountain village. Melt, or freezing rain, had made a crust atop the snow and black sheets on the paved walkways, on which a last dusting had fallen in a flurry overnight, perfect for slipping and cracking your skull. When I'd walked through the gate onto the grounds of the compound, the man in robes had been sweeping the grainy stuff off the walks and watching it blow just as quickly back across.

He'd parked his broom and welcomed me warmly, assuming I was some kind of pilgrim, and I hadn't corrected him. A pear-ish man, no taller than I was, with black alert eyes and such a heavy salt-and-pepper goatee that I couldn't see his lips. I might have taken him for a waiter at a Barney Greengrass brunch, an impression only deepened when I made out a Queens or Long

Island accent beneath the tone of plodding sincerity he'd obviously cultivated to go with the robes, and with the pointless
sweeping. It was then that he'd told me his name was Nolan.

The road to Baldy Village had even less to do with any image
I'd maintained of Los Angeles than did the valley below. The
wind had begun to impress me during the winding drive up
from the flatlands, my rental hugging the curves behind Heist's
pickup. It moved my car sideways a couple of times. I tailgated
Heist, as if tethered to his car and therefore to the road. I drove
near enough to his bumper that I could watch the dogs' heads
rustling beneath the tarp, now that I knew to look for them.

There wasn't that far you'd want to go sideways on that
winding two-lane, which on the sharper turns allowed views of
valleys like chasms behind the low rock barrier at the passenger
side. The landscape had altered completely in a matter of minutes, once past the high reservoir. The signs promising lodges
and warning of bear and fire danger gave off a whiff of Aspen,
where I'd spent a weekend skiing once—or rather, a weekend of
falling on my ass and struggling free of snowbanks.

At the Zendo, I'd parked my rental beside a weird vehicle, a
Ford Econoline van with a cracked windshield, like Heist's, and
wooden two-by-fours replacing the bumpers, jacked up on too-
big wheels. It was painted a drab matte green, like something
military, or paramilitary. There wasn't sign of another soul besides Nolan in the compound. The atmosphere evoked a mountain resort after the neutron bomb. I couldn't see the white top
of Baldy anymore. I was too near to see it, here at the Zendo. I
only sensed it, up where the wind was screaming.

"You don't hear it after a while."

I looked at Nolan, startled to have my thoughts read.

"Much like the noise inside," he added, tapping his skull to
make certain I understood. His stance was ostentatiously wide,
weight distributed evenly on the white old-man running shoes

poking from beneath his robes. Or maybe it wasn't ostentation, merely a good idea on this ice.

"I don't have noise inside," I said. "Only modern jazz. Saxophone solos, mostly, sometimes Muzak when I get lazy."

He didn't reply, only radiated a smug amused delight to have me land in his world. Maybe they didn't get so many lady pilgrims since the sex scandals broke up here, and after Leonard Cohen took a powder for the flatlands. Worse, the big Zen Poobah himself, who'd founded the place, had departed this world for the next. Possibly they didn't get many pilgrims of any kind now, only gawkers.

I'd been reading about it on Wikipedia, and it seemed impossible to me that Arabella hadn't done the same. I was barking up the wrong tree. Well, barking might be too strong a word for it. More like letting some of the noise out of my head in the direction of another person, that same noise I'd just claimed didn't exist.

Possibly this wind could blow it all away, and that was why they'd put the Zendo up here.

"I'm looking for a girl. A young woman. She might have called herself Arabella, or Phoebe."

"Recently?"

"The past month."

"Those are nice names. I think I'd recall."

"I think so too. She could have used some other name." I thought of suggesting her mother's, or some female variant of Leonard, or the names of the women in Sleater-Kinney, but I couldn't remember those.

"Yes," he said. "People often get renamed up here. Me, for instance. Roshi told me I couldn't be Nolan anymore."

"I'm sure he had his reasons."

"Oh yes."

"Is there anyone else I could talk to? Someone in charge?"

"In charge of what?"

In charge of Nolan, I wanted to say and didn't. "Do visitors sign in somewhere?" In my head I tried on some rock and roll song I'd heard in the car, hoping it could drown out the wind and how I wanted to strangle the stumblebum.

"If you sign up for a *sesshin,* a retreat, you fill out a form. Also it costs money. But sometimes people just stop by, like you."

I thanked him and asked if I could walk the grounds.

"I'm not supposed to let you go alone."

"I won't bother anyone."

"It's very snowy." The former Nolan's brain seemed to work sideways. I almost envied it. He resumed sweeping while I puttered along the paths he'd never clear if he swept a thousand years, but there was nothing to see. I returned to the warmth of my rental car and drove back down into the center of Baldy Village, to wait for Heist at the Mount Baldy Lodge bar, where he'd said he'd find me.

14

MY BAGGAGE WAS IN THE TRUNK. I WAS READY TO GO. WHEN I'D AWOKEN, bathed in sweat and straitjacketed in dogs, in Heist's Airstream, I'd first turned my face back to the pillow in shame, my mouth swollen and chalky with alcohol and semen. Heist was up and brewing coffee and I'd taken some from him without speaking. When the coffee spiked my brain and opened my lips, what rushed out was more fury. I told him to return me to the Doubletree and that I wanted to go up the mountain to retrieve Arabella in my own car. Heist was quietish. He did as I asked. He'd said he had to take care of Jean the opossum and see to a few other things. Whether this meant his office or the stray girl Melinda or more of the People of the Wash, I didn't care. He said he'd come back to the hotel and lead me up Baldy in a couple of hours.

By the time I'd showered and had about a gallon of water and more black coffee to wash down a hotel sticky bun, I looked over my little dungeon there and began packing my Dopp kit and suitcase without another thought. Whatever else, I was done with this room. Arabella was up the mountain, which Google Earth and human logic told me was as good as having her treed like a housecat. There was one road up to Baldy Village and the Zendo, and it topped out at various wilderness trails and finally the ski lift. Unless she'd helicoptered or astral-planed her way off the mountaintop, I'd find her. Should my search require staying overnight, there were the lodges, but I preferred to believe I'd pull her off the mountain this afternoon and load her onto a red-eye at LAX. Virgin Atlantic, ideally, with lots of lovably hateful Manhattanites in first class. I'd get home with a California story or two in my back pocket. No, sorry, I didn't ever set eyes on the ocean or the Hollywood sign, but did I tell you the one about the porta-potty levee? The trailer park blowjob? *Oh, What a Manic Pixie Am I!* I pictured telling this over late lunch at Elephant & Castle. So I'd thrown my stuff into the trunk of the rental and checked out.

Now I ordered a coffee at the lodge, untempted by the balloon glasses of merlot certain mountain-dwelling creatures were already crouched around at barely noon. The Zendo had been too utterly a contemplation of the void at the center of my scheme and self, my rescuer's vanity. My phone showed no signal—Heist had already shunted me off the grid, without my even noticing. I was at his mercy again, as much treed up this mountain as Arabella. My suitcase in the trunk of the rental could be destined for an LAX baggage carousel, sure. Then again, by removing my traces from the suburban Doubletree, I'd made myself convenient for abduction, to wherever Arabella had gone, or wherever Heist wished to lead me.

15

I WAITED TWO HOURS, EVENTUALLY RESORTING TO A GLASS OF THE MER-lot. Then a second. When Heist came in, around three thirty, he didn't join me straightaway but stopped to talk to a grizzled prospector type who'd been sitting at a table near the door nearly as long as I'd been at the bar, guarding a tall glass of beer and squinting at the roadway as if expecting someone. I considered joining them, to catch a hint of what was exchanged, but before I could, they'd shaken hands and parted. Whatever words had passed between them were yet more that was beyond my ken, possibly strands of the trap into which I'd fallen. Too, I felt sulky, left out of the fun.

"Phoebe."

I punched his leather-clad shoulder. "Hey, old buddy," I said. I felt the onset of my own preemptive daftness. I'd been in his bed the night before. Behaving idiotically, I might disguise how idiotic I felt. "You crack the case?"

"Not exactly." I saw him glance at my wineglass.

"Care to join me?" I said.

"Not right now."

"You want to ask me how was the Zendo?"

"How was the Zendo?"

"I met the cutest little sweeper."

"I'm sorry?" Heist looked strained, which reassured me,

actually. If it disappointed my faith in his prowess, at least my paranoia was assuaged. The so-called Feral Detective was nothing much, not avenger nor conspirer, not boyfriend material, and likely only a pair of weird weepy orgasms away from being forgotten by me completely. Most likely when I got back within range of an Internet signal, I'd find an e-mail from Roslyn waiting, explaining that Arabella had returned to New York or the Reed campus under her own steam.

"There was nothing to find," I said. "Not even one of Leonard Cohen's lost sandals. I've been sitting here for hours."

"Did you talk to anyone?"

"Nope. Why?"

"Nothing in particular. Just—"

"You can't imagine me not talking for two hours, can you?"

"I didn't say that."

"What's the matter? You look nervous. I thought you said this was a dead end." He'd begun side-eyeing the lodge bar's population, one of the more detectively moves I'd seen from Heist, actually. Yet a more innocuous assortment of alcoholic mountain coots could scarcely be imagined. I was even beginning to like them, two hours and two glasses of wine into my vigil. I'd fallen into a world of facial hair having nothing to do with Williamsburg, Brooklyn. It put Heist in an attractive light. Here he represented a clean-cut young man of the West. And I'd felt only the passingest of urges to collar these gents and demand they tell me who they'd voted for. I had a feeling they'd tell me they'd written in one another's names, if they'd voted at all.

"I didn't say it was a dead end either." His voice was low. "I think we ought to drive further up. You want to pay and we'll talk in my truck?"

"Sure."

I reached for my purse, but he said, "Here, let me."

"Really? How gallant!" I pronounced it the French way.

"I just don't want you to use your credit card," he said tightly. He threw down a twenty and took me by the arm. His grip I kind of liked, but I pulled free of it once we were through the door. We walked past my car to where his truck was perched on the shoulder, a bit up the hill.

We climbed into the cab, but he didn't put the key in the ignition. I said, "What gives? You yourself were glad-handing around that place when you came in."

"My face is familiar, your name isn't. It might be better not to leave such an easy trail."

"I don't care if they know my name." I pushed back, by instinct, at what seemed to me off-the-grid bullshit. "Hey, come to think of it, maybe I should scatter a few breadcrumbs around."

"Better not to."

"Explain yourself, detective." I still worked to keep it playful, but there was no one batting the balls back across the net. Though the pickup's engine was dead, Heist spoke with his hands on the wheel, staring straight ahead, presumably in the direction of whatever concerned him, farther up the mountain. After so long in the lodge bar, my eyes had some difficulty adjusting to the late-afternoon glare off the snow, so I turned my head down too and waited through one of his deliberative intervals. In profile, his absurd sideburns looked like some Russian count's high collar.

"If we understood Sage right, Arabella's been using your name some places. Possibly including this mountain."

"And?"

"Have you considered that she might have gotten into something illegal?"

This stopped me cold. I considered, not for the first time, that I might be the one lost, cast as the dupe. Only now it was Arabella who'd ensnared me. She'd sent my name journeying into the world ahead of me, to what purpose I couldn't guess. My name might have learned things I didn't yet know.

"Illegal like what?" I heard myself croak.

Heist didn't speak at first. When he finally did, it wasn't to acknowledge my question. His gaze remained stuck on the road, the lengthening mountain light.

"You good to drive?"

"Sure," I said, a little insulted.

"Because I'd rather not leave your car here in the middle of town. Follow me a ways into Goat Ridge Canyon, to where there's a place we can stash your ride." His use of the corny slang was too evidently native to mock. I readied to mock it anyhow, but I found myself struck dumb by all the grim implications. "Then you can jump back in with me and we'll go further up."

"Okay."

Now he glanced at my feet, which were clad in green suede loafers, already lightly stained from the lodge's parking-area rock salt. "You ought to be prepared to hike a bit."

I'd wrapped my still-soggy boots in a plastic dry-cleaner's bag from the Doubletree closet and buried them in my luggage while dreaming of check-in at LAX, what now seemed a thousand years ago.

"I'll dig out my boots."

"Good." He waited, I understood only slowly, for me to exit his truck.

I grabbed his shoulder instead. "Charles, goddamn it." The moment my hand found his form through the jacket it was way more detailed and interesting than I'd expected. I wanted him to look up from my feet.

"What's wrong?"

"Tell me what the hell is happening here." I made it commanding and yet open-ended, in case Heist wanted to ply his troth. In fact, if the wheel weren't in the way, I might have climbed up to straddle his lap. I endured a crazy oscillation, between scorn and amusement on one side and lust and terror on the other. Either Charles Heist was a bore and a joke, his mountain a total waste of time, or he was monstrous and irresistible, and plotting to savage me beneath frozen cliffs.

Now he met my eyes, but his gaze was a wasteland. I could crawl across it for a lifetime pleading for a glass of water. And his reply—well, it was the reply I deserved, one effortlessly splitting the difference between our two unnamed topics. "I can't say yet."

"You can say where you were for the past two hours."

"We'll lose the light," he said. "Let's talk when you're back in the truck."

16

MY COLLEGE BOYFRIEND WAS A BORE ABOUT MUSIC, BUT I MADE SOME OF
his stuff mine. Then I painstakingly peeled off the memories—
the discovery of sex, mostly—afterward. He couldn't haunt me
when I played his favorites, because I'd stolen them. (Later I
dated someone else with his same first name, another good era-
sure move.)

There was one CD, a live recording, by a singer I'd regarded
only as a pudgy bearded crooner, a joke. Nowhere near as hand-
some as Arabella's idol, L. Cohen, he also had a name I mixed
up with some other hippie lover boy. But when I played the live
recording one night while that same boyfriend was out fucking
someone else, I stole that record, most particularly. The actual
CD, but the idea of it too.

On the CD, the singer climbs into the corny tunes to find
extra space, secret rooms. Yet he climbs them from inside, like
the bars of a cage. The limits of the cage are those of the singer's
life: his hunger for ecstasy, and his terror of it too. At the top of
the cage of practically every song, the singer screams, or barks,
or howls, "It's too late to stop now!" The message might have
been damning me to my life, the secret cage of my autonomy. I
was nineteen.

At this point, I could have turned and descended that

mountain. Heist had no control of "my ride." But then, there had been a dozen exit doors, beginning with not getting on the plane, or not quitting the job for which, to fit myself to it, I'd whittled off parts of my soul for a decade. This was the thing about *it's too late to stop now:* it always already had been.

17

LESS THAN A QUARTER MILE UP GOAT RIDGE ROAD, HEIST DIVERTED TO
the left. The snow hadn't fallen here, or had melted—this might
be the sun side of the mountain. So much for having Arabella
treed, or thinking this mountain was as simple as its repre-
sentation on Google Earth. I followed onto an unposted dirt
road that soon became perilously steep; just as quickly, past a
curve, there appeared a cabin, barely more than a shack. The
windows were dark, and one was broken.

Heist pulled into a rut up ahead, then stepped out of his cab
and waved me into the cabin's ragged, overgrown driveway. I
steered in, and he ran up alongside, giving encouragement, as I
got the rental out of sight of the road we'd turned from. Then
I retook my place in the passenger seat of his truck. Heist had
stolen a moment to unbutton the tarp and run his hand underneath, giving comfort, I supposed, to the infinitely patient dogs.
I could have used some of the same. But he only pushed a water
bottle across the seat to make it available to me, then backed
into the drive and returned us to the road that climbed Goat
Ridge. By contrast to the dirt path it seemed a positive highway.

"You know all the nice out-of-the-way places," I teased.

"It's impossible to know them all."

"Who owns this land?"

"Nobody owns it. The Forest Service runs it."

"Then whose cabin is that?"

"Right at the moment it belongs to your car."

"That's my absolute limit, Charles. If I hear one more Zen koan, I'm going to barf."

He looked at me oddly.

"Talk to me in the King's English, Tarzan, just like they taught you in finishing school."

Heist knew to keep his promise. "Sage wasn't making a whole lot of sense, but she kept repeating that part about Chinese people on the mountain. There's a property up here, a portion sold off to foreign investors before its designation as a national monument shut down any mining rights. I think they're Koreans, not Chinese. She's hardly the first to get that wrong. They stuck out like sore thumbs when they showed up, long strings of black SUVs and a private surveying company. People up here enjoy a live-and-let-live atmosphere. 'Wild West' is another word for it. These folks put up a high fence topped with razor wire across a popular foot access to the peak. It didn't seem they'd picked up the vibe about right-to-pass. The Forest Service conspicuously wouldn't touch it, which set off a round of the usual grumbling about payoffs. Some said they're building a survivalist compound up there—apparently somebody flew a low plane and spotted a number of large water storage tanks."

Heist leaned forward as he drove and talked. His voice was as deliberate as ever, but I could hear some resonance, some melody, even, as he for once placed a few sentences end-to-end. His left forearm lay across the top of the wheel, his eyes squinting into the prospect before us, except at the tight switchbacks, when he'd ease back and lift his right hand to help him steer. The rest of the time the right rested lightly on the shift knob, like I wished it was resting on my knee. The sky around the peaks had begun to glow, hazy yellow beneath bands of pink. I was hearing a lot about things I didn't think could possibly concern

Arabella—*mining rights?*—but I didn't want to stop the flow, not even to insert a joke like *It speaks!,* though this discovery certainly did float my boat. Nor did I stick my tongue in his ear.

"Nobody here's too quick to put a nose in anybody's business, but when I asked around today, I learned somebody'd struck a deal with the compound people, for access to that old trail. It set off some alarms. This mountain has a certain allure for people who like to go off and do their own thing. Mostly loners, hermits, sure."

He faltered here, once again unaffixing from his present situation, shifting off toward an interior horizon. Or maybe it was that he couldn't decide what he wanted to tell me, how to put some bad news.

"But also . . . groups. People who want to do rituals. Stuff attaches to this place. Did you know it was Baldy where they measured the speed of light? By beaming it from the peak here. And it's the only place to mine lapis lazuli in the fifty states. You never know when you're going to run into five people in white sheets with twigs in their hair, reenacting a Greek play. You hike in here, you'll often find fruits and gourds, squashes in the creek beds, sometimes tied with colorful ribbons. Sometimes animals too, killed differently from how a hunter would do it."

I clapped my hands. "I *knew* this story was going to have animals in it." This joke I'd swiftly regret.

"The people going up here might be some I'm familiar with. They're gleaners, of a kind. I'm pretty sure they swept up Sage at one point, maybe some other kids down in the Wash. They need bodies, extras for some of their . . . ceremonies. Maybe they scooped up Arabella."

"You think there's one of these ceremonies tonight?"

"I don't know."

"But that's the hurry, isn't it?"

"I don't want to waste time."

"You wasted a lot of it, Charles. You knew about this and you didn't tell me. Why don't we call the police?"

"The jurisdiction inside the monument is federal, they don't answer calls up here very fast. It's often days before they come. They wouldn't climb to the peak on some hunch."

"Plus, that wouldn't have put you in the driver's seat, would it?"

He ignored this. I wanted to slap him, but I might have damaged the tender flesh of my hand on his die-cut features, his Brillo sideburns. Instead, I put on my Nancy Drew hat. "So, these mining rights are for lapis? Isn't that just some semiprecious, kachina-doll crap?"

"Some people would say it's more than that. I think the Egyptians used it for the eyes of their mummies. Anyhow, there's gold up here, and a vein of tungsten too. Baldy was about ten years late for the gold rush, and a certain amount of panning still goes on."

"Like those Japanese soldiers who don't know the war is over?"

He shrugged. "The war for gold is never over."

"You make this place sound like the Mountain of the Damned."

He didn't respond. I'd either touched a nerve or bored him. I wondered if I'd stick around long enough to learn to tell the difference.

Then again, it might have nothing to do with what I'd said. We'd rumbled up a sharper grade and around another sickening swerve, and now were presented with the razor-topped fence of recent legend. From a padlocked gate across the road it fitted itself to the contour of the rocky bare clearing and on into the trees on either side. Heist shifted into reverse and backed us a few yards from the NO TRESPASSING signs and off to one side, but in no way hidden.

"Aren't you afraid they'll see the truck?" But he'd stopped, and I followed him out, however reluctantly. I watched him put his nose to the air, whether in concern at my question or for some other reason, I had no idea. For my part, I thought I smelled far-off smoke, but it could have been my imagination. My ears had popped, climbing this high, and the oxygen had a sharpness that might have mimicked smoke.

"They can't exactly call and have me towed. Anyway, from what I've heard, the people who built this compound aren't always around, and when they are, they're not necessarily patrolling the perimeter. It's a lot of ground to cover."

"You keep calling it a compound, like you know something." Another nonstarter. My prodding grew desperate again. I wanted reassurances, but Heist had none. He was busy freeing the dogs, who snouted up through the first gap and over, then half vanished into the shadows of the darkening roadway. Miller and Vacuum took up the natural path of investigation, to the padlocked gate. There they began sniffing and whining. Jessie came to acknowledge me, to push under my hand, enabling my wish to believe the dogs were Heist's arms and legs, a vehicle he'd employ to reach me when incapable by other means.

Heist scrabbled in the truck bed until he came out with a battered red plastic torch light, the kind that took eight or fifty batteries. When he tested it, I was surprised to see it worked, and then I wished he'd leave it on, but no. He clipped it to a leather loop at the back of his jacket so both his hands were free.

"Where from here? Do you have a bolt cutter for the lock?"

He pointed with his chin at the tree line. "There's supposed to be a gap, for those in the know."

"That wouldn't include you, huh? This is all just chatter you happened to pick up this afternoon?" I couldn't quit taunting him with my own fears. If Heist himself was one of those gleaners, he'd gleaned me good.

"I took this trail a few times, before the fence went up. It should connect after the bypass."

He was right, of course. A few dozen yards through the trees and underbrush, the Koreans' fence was breached, peeled from below, much like that earlier fence, the one delimiting the San Antonio Wash from Foothill Boulevard. It wasn't hard to scramble beneath, ignoring the razor wire high above, ignoring the razor wire's implications too. Then, within a few paces marked by snapped branches overhead and leaf-muddy footprints below, we cut back to the clearing, only long enough to discover a well-beaten trail, off from the fence and the paved roadway, upward through the trees. The dogs examined everything for us as they threaded back and forth across our path.

"We'll be sheltered from the wind," said Heist. "It'll be darker, though."

"What wind?"

"It's sundown. Also there's a storm that might reach us."

"Who needs the Weather Channel when you were raised by wolves, huh?"

"That's right," he said, so squarely I felt ashamed. After that we were silent for a while. I needed my breath for climbing, my eyes lowered to navigate the roots and stones. I got stuck inside my own head at that point, a little diorama with me and Heist like doll figures in a tiny gleaming Airstream, and another figure of Arabella-Phoebe wandering outside somewhere in distress. She'd begun to merge with me in my own conjuring, not a good sign.

Then I felt Heist abruptly grip my arm, and I realized he'd kept me from falling. We stopped on the trail, deep in the trees, halfway to nowhere—at least I hoped it was halfway. The dogs, concerned, swarmed close.

"Did you have anything to eat today?"

"A sticky bun at the Doubletree."

"There's a place to rest just up ahead."

"I'm glad I have you to look out for me." It was a thought I formed sarcastically but all sarcasm stripped off en route to speech, like one of those joke guns that sprouted a daisy when you pulled the trigger.

18

HE MOVED HIS HAND TO THE SMALL OF MY BACK AND KISSED MY FORE-
head and some shudder moved through me, like a shadow moving across the moon, or some kind of quasi-orgasm. Maybe it
was the thin air—maybe I should look into erotic asphyxiation
techniques when I got back to civilization. Heist held me still
there for a moment, probably thinking he'd saved me from faint-
ing. Maybe he had.

"We should keep on," he said, infinitely gently.

"Absolutely."

The resting place was a turn atop a large jutting rock that
seemed to form out of nowhere beneath our feet. At the high
edge of the turn, before the path resumed among the cloaking
trees, we emerged to a view of the moon, three-quarters full and
throwing light behind some cloud cover that intersected nicely
with the remains of the sunset. Below, an inch of horizon, the
rhinestone necklace of the suburban valley, covered in fog. But
Heist pointed even lower.

Down below our feet, the road that the fence had blocked
curled into view. Beyond the tops of the trees, two blimp-like
metallic structures, each topped with a series of seals or nipples,
and with a tiny ladder to give a dwarfing human perspective to
their bulk.

"Are those the water tanks?"

He nodded. "That's why I call it a compound."

"As in, say, preparations for the apocalypse?"

"If you like. Anyhow, it's defensible ground."

"But we got in."

"We're not the only ones."

"What do you mean?"

"Signs are everywhere. Just watch the dogs."

They'd only looked like dogs to me, excitable, using their noses, shitting repeatedly. But I took his word for it: that we had company, or at least that there'd been recent passage on this trail. But then, I'd long since had to take his word for all of it.

"You know this mountain, Charles."

"A little."

"More than you've let on. Your grudge against this place isn't some passing thing. It's personal."

"How so?"

He might have humored me, but I was grateful for the invitation to haul out my Nancy Drew stuff. "It's the little things. Your undue pride in the lapis lazuli and tungsten. The way you knew this clearing was approaching."

"Like I said, I haven't been up here since the fence went up." There was nothing defensive in his tone.

"Then it's even more impressive that you remember."

He was silent a little while. "We should get to the top, if you're okay." He pointed at the trail, which now appeared a dark tunnel. He hadn't resorted to the flashlight yet, but it would soon be time. The dogs, alert to his cues, scurried into that vortex. It was colder here on the bluff, the wind was picking up as he'd predicted. I'd caught my breath from my faintgasm, whatever it was, and was ready to reclaim the shelter of the trees.

"Hold my hand," I told him, and he did. He held it until we reached the top of that awful place. The moonlight and the residual light of the day in the high layers and his hand in mine were enough, though I couldn't make out the expression on his face. That hadn't meant much to this point anyhow. I didn't beg him for the flashlight, but I wanted to hear his voice.

"Charles?"

"Yes?"

"When you came up here, before the fence, why was that?"

"A lot of reasons. I grew up partly on this mountain."

"Your parents let you run wild on these trails?"

"It wasn't so much what anyone's parents let me do or not do. It was just what I did."

"Tell me more."

"I'll tell you later."

I fastened onto *later*—that there would be one. This turned out to be all I required. I might be learning to live in Heist's wasteland, but, hey, when you looked close, it had a fauna and flora, maybe a place for me in its blasted ecosystem.

We'd ascended back into the frost now, where nothing had melted, only blown off or never made it through the canopy of trees. The crisp layer glowed in the moonlight. It compressed nicely underfoot, except where it had already been pressed into a slick boot-shaped print. The boots pointed up and downhill both—I congratulated myself for graduating into the company of the dogs as a reader of signs. I didn't kid myself, though, that I'd attained their level.

When we rose into that place, I felt it. Heist let go of my hand. We still didn't need the flashlight. The clearing was wide, ridged with dark trees on all sides, no obvious point at which the trail resumed. We were nowhere near the peak but it was plainly a destination, our destination now. The moon lit the snow and us, the glow nearly unbearable after the adjustment our eyes had made in the tunnel of trees, a day-for-night scene you'd have judged bogus in a movie. As for the plot, it was made of footprints. This investigation no longer required dogs or

Nancy Drew. A child could have found its way to the ceremonial center of that snowfield, the pit ringed with stones. Heist and I moved for it, but the dogs were first, and when they reached it, they began whining. I took the dark hole for the flat remains of a fire until I was near enough to see that it was cavernous. When Heist leaped inside, he vanished from view below the middle of his chest. Vacuum and Miller began barking. Jessie came back to find me. I touched his head with my cold fingers and trudged forward as though hypnotized to the rim of the pit.

The couple was locked in an embrace. For warmth, I supposed, given how little they wore beneath their fur costumes. This was how I understood it at first. They clutched each other and couldn't be bothered to notice us, they were so chilly and helpless in the pit there, she in her silly rabbit costume, the oversize hood with furry ears, him in his corresponding bear outfit. Their hands and feet were outfitted with oversize paws and their chests and crotches were covered with fur, but their entwined limbs were fully exposed, only smeared here and there with patches of mud, weirdly bright-dark against their pale moonlit arms.

I'd gone so far as to consider with exasperation what it would take to rouse these callow teenagers from the hole and explain to them they'd been rescued and help them down the hill before I saw that what I'd taken for mud was dark red, a kind of congealed, frosty cherry Jell-O that bunched inside the animal-head hoods. Their throats were slit. Heist had slumped down, his back against the pit's wall, sobbing, his breath torn in wretched gasps. Miller leaped into the pit, Vacuum too. Miller licked at Heist's face, Vacuum at the dead faces within the hoods, the bear-boy and the rabbit-girl, and then Vacuum began helping himself to some of the Jell-O, smearing it along his muzzle. I managed to reflect that this might be taking primal sorrow a bit far before I tumbled back from the pit and twisted around to retch bile and merlot into the snow.

I was startled back into myself by the howling. I think it was Heist who began it, first a kind of ragged keening, but joined in a chorus that rose through doggish baying to a kind of barbershop-werewolf presentation. They didn't keep it up long, but astonishment drew me up to my knees. I wiped my mouth on my coat sleeve and rubbed the ice and gravel from my palms, then unzipped my coat enough to stick my hands into my arm-pits for warmth. The rest of me was warm enough or too numb to understand it wasn't, but my hands felt bitten through.

"Phoebe," said Heist from within the hole.

"What?"

"You have to look."

"I looked already."

"Is it her?"

I groaned protest. It wasn't her, or if it was I wouldn't look.

"You have to be sure."

I crawled. Jessie crouched beside me. Heist was at the rabbit's head, pulling back the hood to show her face to the moon, while blocking the murdered throat from my view.

"No."

"You're certain?"

She was a blonde, with thin lips and empty eyes, somebody else's. Somebody else's missing girl, somebody else's demolished child in a hole, decked as a ceremonial rabbit.

"That's not Arabella."

"Okay."

The moon was pitiless, sun-like. "Take me away from here."

19

HERE, AT THE NEW SUMMIT OF MY ABJECTION AND PASSIVITY, AT LEAST in my adult lifetime, I began to disassociate. My disassociation took a particular form that was hardly useful, but may be interesting to report. In a reverie so rapidly designed by my subconscious that it was as if it had been preformatted for convenience, I had in fact not quit my job at the Great Gray Lady but instead taken a remarkable assignment. An op-ed, a special full-page intended for the first Sunday after inauguration. *You, Phoebe Siegler, are uniquely suited to infiltrate and explicate to us the Great Out There, which we at the editorial board are at last ready to admit we don't understand in the faintest.*

I should underline what horseshit this was. I'd never been asked to write a thing. As at the literary journal, I'd been a decorative editorial flunky, a limit I'd never fought my way free of. (That was partly my fault, hey—it wasn't as if I'd gone around pitching brilliant ideas for op-eds, and the witticisms that turned the heads of the men around me were more in the cause of charming self-deprecation than of carving my way out of the category of the highly dateable.) But in this fantasy, I was on a brilliant assignment into the underground that the election had in fact revealed as our nation's dominant paradigm. Sew a Pepe the Frog medallion onto your backpack, young lady, and go seduce the unspeakable and hairy, then report back. Tell

ST. JOHN THE BAPTIST PARISH LIBRARY
2920 NEW HIGHWAY 51
LAPLACE, LOUISIANA 70068

us where the hell we are. The total incoherence of this fantasy didn't blunt its consoling sweetness. Nancy Drew was defunct, replaced by Joan Didion—a female Reporter from the Outer Limit, whose meekness in the given moment would be revenged in sublime verbal retrospect.

20

I HARDLY RECALL THE JOURNEY BY FOOT BACK TO HEIST'S TRUCK, EXCEPT that he now employed the flashlight and an arm around my waist as we hustled, sometimes sliding on our heels, back the way we came. He stashed me in the cab while he rounded the dogs into the back, under the tarp. I think I passed out and missed the start of the journey, but before we reached the village again I was shocked awake by a dream of someone pelting his windshield with gravel. Actually, someone was pelting his windshield with gravel, and as I came awake I pointed it out.

"It's hail," Heist corrected.

"Hail? This is fucking Los Angeles."

"No, this is a mountain."

The arrows of ice beat intermittently against the truck as we drove the switchbacks now covered in fog. Heist pulled us into the dirt driveway to the abandoned cabin where we'd hidden my car. I never could have spotted it myself.

"I'll build a fire," he said.

"Wait, we're staying *here*?" It was so like my naughty fantasies but so useless now, and I was bewildered.

"Just you."

"While you go get the police?"

"While I go get a Jeep."

"You are so fucking deluded if you think I'm staying alone

in this fucking cabin while you—what's the Jeep for?" I couldn't stop saying *fucking,* and I couldn't displace the rabbit and the bear with their skinned-white limbs and ragged bloody throats from my visual field, not if I looked at Heist's Easter Island head, not if I looked at the cabin illuminated in his truck's headlamps, beaming through hail that was just now converting to drifting flakes. If I squinted it was almost Christmassy. Or fucking Christmassy, let's call it.

"Phoebe, those kids are warm up there. Hours old."

"Stop talking about that." I'd fished out my cell phone and was compulsively asking it to find a signal. No signal, no method, no teacher. We were out here alone, reinventing the universe.

"If we call the Feds, we'll lose hours, if not days. We might go to jail for a while. That's doing Arabella no good at all."

"How do you know Arabella's involved in—that?"

"I can't know she is," he admitted.

"Somebody's looking for those kids," I said. "They belong to somebody." Even as I said the words I knew these were the kinds of things that were far from assured in the world of the Feral Detective.

"We'll call it in anonymously once we're on the road."

"What's the Jeep for?"

"The rabbits and the bears live in the desert."

"Please, no more puzzles."

"There's two groups. The Rabbits and the Bears. They're . . . communities."

He's friends with the rabbits and bears. Sage had been trying to tell me what she knew. I'd taken it for a children's chant.

"Off-the-gridders," I suggested, proud that I could speak-a da lingo.

"Way off. They live in the Mojave, in a place nobody else goes to, a place you need a Jeep even to get to the edge of. The Bears come here to use the mountain, I told you some of it already."

"The ceremonies."

"Yes. Though they don't ordinarily leave dead bodies."

"They knew we were coming so they baked a cake."

"Sorry?"

"Nothing. You're right. We have to go to the desert, Charles. Before it's too late."

Heist moved me inside the cabin, which was unlocked, and left me there with the flashlight, to study the corners for real or demonic creatures, to examine the broken window and the corroded linoleum tile, while he got firewood out of the truck. Then he built a fire in the ancient black woodstove, faster than I'd seen a thing like that done before. He brought in a bedroll and unzipped it and put me inside, and I let him do all these absurd things to me because I couldn't imagine what else to do, and because I was immobilized by the problem of who I was, now that I'd seen what I'd seen. A lot of me was still on the hill, at that moon-blazed clearing, crawling on my knees to the edge of the pit.

"Why can't I come with you?" I whined.

"You're packed already. I need to grab clothes and get the Jeep and arrange some things."

"Feed the opossum."

"The opossum is dead."

"Oh, great. Did someone kill her too?"

"They don't thrive in captivity."

I do, I wanted to say. "Don't leave me."

"I'll be back in a few hours. We'll drive and talk, or you can sleep."

"What if the Bears come back?"

He shook his head. "They left the mountain."

"I want you, Charles." I tried to make this seductive, rather than desperate. But seduction was desperate. I'd fallen so far.

"I want you too," he said, and through the swirl of my horror and apprehension, of bears and rabbits and whatever had befallen or might befall Arabella in Heist's desert, I was still thrilled to see how it surprised him to say it.

"Then don't go."

"I'll be back," he said again.

I reached out of the coverings and pulled him to me, and made him hold and press and kiss me until he'd made me feel that the fire and the cabin around the fire were an extension of his embrace. At that, I relented. Snow whistled in through the broken window but the room had grown warm. The flames flickered through the black stove's grill and I didn't need the flashlight anymore, so I turned it off. I saw Heist as if through a hot mist. I reminded myself that I'd been the one to force him up the mountain, where he didn't wish to go. I'd been the one to walk into his office. I'd run from the great glass building in New York, and from its evil counterpart, the Golden Finger of Sauron; I'd run from the shitty old world to the bright utopian edge, the western void, to beg this abduction by a man I'd never imagined existed. He was friends with the rabbits and bears. I should change my name to Arabella. She'd adopted mine to show me who I was, to tip the script.

"Do you want me to leave you a dog?"

"Jessie," I said. "Just Jessie." I might have been dozing, I realized now.

"Okay."

And then he built up the fire and went to get a Jeep.

PART III

THE DESERT

21

I'D BEEN IN LORRIE'S COMPANY FOR MOST OF AN HOUR, COLLECTING sagebrush for the evening's fire. The stuff wasn't just lying there, it had to be crackled free of the dry underside of the living plants, twisted gray skeletal things that revealed their vitality only in the difference between the dry limbs and those which resisted, which bent and sprang back. There was an art to it, and I was improving.

Lorrie had insisted, rightly, that I wear her spare hat, a floppy sunhat, mesh dripping around my ears. Still, around the hat's edge, the sky assaulted me. The sun had tilted from its brutal perch overhead, making for the low ridge of distant bare bluffs, and the wind had picked up again. I checked my phone, which wasn't a phone anymore, but a clock, and some kind of glinty talisman too, vestige of a former life or world. The third or fourth time I did it Lorrie said, "That's not how they reach you out here."

I'd learned something about the two tribes, the Bears and the Rabbits, from Heist. I had yet to meet the Bears. Lorrie was a Rabbit. By this time, I'd met eight or nine of her kind, women and a couple of men, all sun-blazed, wiry, industrious, and what I suppose I'd call opaque. Gnomic.

I'd also been abandoned again by Heist, a humiliation that burned in me, but Lorrie hadn't been witness to it. She'd been friendly without giving me the least hint whether or not she might also be totally insane. I took this chance to draw her out.

"No? How do they reach you out here?"

"Out here they use contrails."

"Con-whats?"

She lifted the front of her hat and pointed at the sky. Conveniently—or had she clocked it in advance?—a jet's white exhaust tilted across the cloud-scudded blue canvas. The plane, long gone. If someone, let's say a JFK-to-LAX traveler like that I'd so recently been myself, had glanced down, they'd have seen only inhuman ridges, scraped sculptural vacancies. Mars. No chance they'd have imagined the two sun-beaten women fetching sticks like Bruegel peasants, let alone spotted our dire stretched shadows, speckles amid the outcroppings and sage— the plants and birds and rocks and things littering this raw distance.

"Contrails," Lorrie said again.

"Who's 'they'?"

"You know, anyone wanting to penetrate your body with radiation or advertising." She nodded again at the phone in my hand.

"I was actually thinking of calling my mom." Well, someone else's mom was in fact my intention. I wanted to call Roslyn Swados and tell her where I was and that I was still trying, that I was out here searching. Either that, or snap a photograph of Lorrie and her bundle of kindling and text it to Roslyn. So far as moms went, there was no reason not to keep Arabella and myself mixed up in my own head for the time being. It was better than equating myself with Lorrie, the option Heist had left me with when he ditched me.

"We're mostly our own moms out here. But I can be yours if you want."

So, we can pretty well settle on insane, I thought. But I wanted to keep her talking, because even the voice of an insane person may serve as a tether to the human, and I was pretty far out on the edge of things here.

"When's the last time you talked to her?" I asked. "Your own mom, I mean."

Lorrie shrugged. This was a nonstarter. Instead I pointed up, at the contrail.

"Is that one telling you anything?"

"Just that it all goes on and they're not done pretending and the bombs haven't fallen and they're not even trying to answer the question of what comes next and they're not sorry and it's our job just to be witnesses to it all, to abide with the dying planet. I don't think I can explain all of what it says, but that's a start."

Now we'd squatted in the sand to rest and study the sky, and Lorrie surprised me by tugging aside her shorts and releasing a stream of urine. It trickled its way through the ridged sand floor into a tiny ravine to begin evaporating visibly, like steam in a drying cast-iron pan.

"But there's no personal message." I knew I was being an asshole. "Nothing like 'Lorrie, phone home'?"

She looked at me with pity. "I'm sorry for your hurt."

"I am too."

"You'll let go of the people in the machine. It's a grieving process."

"I'm less into process, more into sudden procedures. Like a Botox injection, or liposuction." I felt I could say anything to Lorrie, but not in a good way. "For instance, just a few weeks ago I was working right in the brain of the machine, helping the machine to think about itself. I was practically the machine's *girlfriend*."

"Wow."

I couldn't squat as long as Lorrie, so I fell back on my ass and hands. I had no puddle of fresh pee to avoid, and was any-how already coated in the sand and desert grime that flew in the wind. The two of us continued to stare at the sky. Come to think of it, maybe a *New York Times* op-ed was pretty much like a contrail, as likely to be heeded from its great lofty perch.

"Yeah, it's pretty weird," I said. "One minute I'm Ms. Ma-chine, then, *kablooie*, I met some dogs and a possum, and next thing I knew I was here with you guys. The Rabbit people. You don't mind if I say that?"

"No, that's our right name."

"So, like I said, here I am."

"Instant karma, that's what they call it."

"Well, someone did."

At that instant, I was startled by the presence of someone approaching from behind where I sat. The insulating barrenness of the Mojave had struck me as absolute, and to find that Lorrie and I weren't alone in our contrail fugue made me feel like a dreamer, as though space had folded to make a doorway.

"Ladies."

It was Anita. Big Chief Rabbit, the one Heist had been seeking when, hours before, we'd first stumbled into the Rabbit village. It was after Heist and Anita talked that Heist had run away, deeper into the desert, and left me here. I held it against her. She was an older woman, keen and scrawny as the rest of them, but with superbly full white hair and the carriage and demeanor of a studio-bred actress, one who'd quit lying about her age.

Anita now wore a Meat Puppets T-shirt and running shorts, her feet in large muddy boots. She'd earlier appeared in a white priestly outfit I learned was designed for walking up to desert hives—Anita was a beekeeper. It was she who'd directed Lorrie to lead me out fetching sticks, so I shouldn't have been so sur-prised she'd found us. It was only that I felt we'd walked miles from that earlier point, and would need to walk miles back—yet why shouldn't our walk have been in circles, for all I could trust my internal compass in this place? I didn't trust it coming out of a Midtown F train stop.

"Maybe you should tell her less about contrails, Lorrie, and more about rattlesnakes."

"Rattlesnakes?" I said, picking up my hands. How long had Anita stood there listening? Or did she simply know Lorrie's obsessions? There might be plenty of time to delve your fellow Rabbits' minds, out here.

"She's teasing you," said Lorrie. "They're mostly hibernating around now."

"I didn't know rattlesnakes hibernated."

Anita nested her fingers together and bugged out her eyes. "In big piles all squirmed together for warmth. Though lately we're suffering signs and portents, in that regard Lorrie is correct. Nothing is certain anymore. A sun like this one might bring out some hungry confused young fellow."

"Great," I said.

Anita bent and swept up my sage branches from where I'd dumped them. She'd have been one of those older women setting an impossible standard at the yoga class—for me, always a reason to quit. She spoke to Lorrie again. "I'm taking Phoebe back. When you finish, you can start the fire."

"Okay," said Lorrie. She might be a wild-eyed off-the-gridder, obedient to none but contrails, but Anita was Chief Rabbit, and Lorrie hopped.

Anita and I left Lorrie there and strolled into the anywhere, perhaps the direction from which she'd come, perhaps not. The array of rock formations might have spelled some sense to her eye, but for me it was a page of planetary hieroglyph. I was in this woman's hands—if she had a pit dug somewhere, and a bunny costume, I was in deep shitsky.

"I want to show you a place where you can rest when it gets dark," she said. "I don't know if Charles is coming back before tomorrow."

"Okay," I said, Rabbit style. If it smarted that Anita knew Heist had shrugged me off, like a bug from his coat, I felt her flinty kindness in treating the fact so casually.

"There's a spare bed at Neptune Lodge, and a room with a closing door."

Neptune Lodge? This was the first I'd heard that name. But I gathered these were luxury accommodations—a closing door, be still my heart! I felt like the Princess and the Pea, out among these desert rats. "I'm appreciative."

Anita smiled in her quick, dry way, then said, "I never thought he'd come back here at all."

She examined me as if having posed a question. What should I say? *Lady, back in the real world, where transactions occur in denominations other than kindling, I paid him for his services?* But I hadn't, actually. *Darling, I sucked his dick?*

"I think he did it for you," she said.

He did it for you. I do it all for you, baby. I shut my eyes and felt the lowering sun on my lids. How long could I crunch along beside Anita with my eyes closed? Then suddenly I understood. It was so simple: we walked in a westerly direction. Some things organized themselves in traditional ways, sun setting in the west, for instance. Men did things for women and then vanished, and the women discussed them. I might be cracking up, here in the desert. Perhaps this was the void encounter Stephanie had predicted for me. Another in a series of them. My father had force-educated me in the ways of men and women by showing me black-and-white movies on VHS tape, all of them musicals or romantic comedies, all of them lighter than air (my mother would have meanwhile been drinking herself into a film noir fog in the kitchen). I'd spent my life waiting to be swept off my feet. A snippet of lyric floated into mind, one never far from the surface: *"A fine romance, with no kissing . . ."*

"The Bears have gotten dangerous."

"Yeah, well, I guess that much even I know."

"They've gotten dangerous in new ways. I tried warning him."

"I'm sure he understood."

"I mean to him *especially*."

Yes, I wanted to say, *it's all my fault.* It felt better to believe that than the opposite: that it had nothing to do with me at all. Eyes shut, I kept pace, walking into the sun.

"Actually, there's another reason I wanted to get you to Neptune Lodge," said Anita. "Something I want to show you. I didn't tell Charles. But I feel I can trust you. I hope I'm right."

"I hope so too. What did you want to show me?"

"We've got a downer," she said.

"What's a downer?"

"A Bear, a sick one."

"What are you doing with him?"

"We're taking care of him, of course. And then, if he gets better, we can kill him."

22

WHEN HEIST HAD ARRIVED EARLY THAT SAME MORNING WITH THE JEEP, I'd been sleeping. Light barely crept into the mountain cabin, though the sky was pale, the fire long grown cold. Jessie was pressed along my side, pinning me in the bedroll. He didn't rise at Heist's entry but looked up balefully, perfectly expressing my resistance to being roused from the covers, into the chill. Heist tempted me out with a white Dunkin' Donuts sack—black coffee and egg-and-cheese on a crappy bagel.

"Let's go," he said.

"Where?"

"The desert."

"Where are the other dogs?"

"Better they stay back. Melinda's keeping an eye on them."

"Should I follow you in my car?"

He shook his head.

"I'm responsible for this rental," I said. "No way am I leaving it out here at this murder shack. Let me drive it down the mountain and return it."

"It's six in the morning. We need to get a move on."

"I'll leave it somewhere, then. In the village, at least."

"It ought to be out of sight."

"I'll park it at the Zendo."

Heist nodded, satisfied enough. I drank half the coffee and

followed him into the village. He and Jessie waited while I pulled the rental into the Zendo's drive and around behind the main building. The drab green Econoline with the spiderweb-cracked windshield and the giant tires and the wooden bumpers was gone from the lot. I went inside to find a bathroom. Mercifully, there was no mirror.

On my way out, I bumped into Nolan, sitting in his robes on the porch, festooned in dawn steam, sipping grassy tea from a bowl. He didn't look surprised to see me, not even when I gave him the keys and asked him to watch over the car. It was a task compatible with his overall vibe, I suppose. I didn't know how to say what I'd learned since I'd met him, how the mountain had changed me, but Nolan wasn't one to pressure me. I liked him for that.

"You should eat," said Heist when I climbed back into the passenger seat of the Jeep. The sack with the egg sandwich waited on the seat between us, untouched.

"Do I look that bad?"

He didn't reply, but started out of the Zendo lot and down the hill. The Jeep sat high on its suspension and jogged easily sideways with a freedom that spoke of its readiness for irregular landscape and also offered promise of sessions of high-seas-style puking. It featured roll bars, back and front, the implications of which I'd never really considered. It was a vehicle of freedom that was simultaneously, as we left my rental car behind and diverted eastward from the familiar zone of the Doubletree and the Wash, my new cage.

I made an opening in the foil and nibbled, then tore off a portion of bagel and used it to lure Jessie from the Jeep's back seat to a place at my feet, his head in my lap. I didn't look at Heist. I didn't care for Heist so much right now. I preferred the dog, my sweet acolyte. He and I shared the egg sandwich. By the time we hit the flats, I slept again, Jessie hugged to my stomach, obliging me.

23

I WOKE AT ONE POINT TO FIND WE WERE COURSING IN FOUR LANES OF traffic, much of it massive eighteen-wheeled trucks. The landscape was flat and yellow between the billboards and warehouses. An endless freight train rolled on a parallel track at my window, boxcars from Germany and Japan. I looked up at Heist, who kept his eyes glued to the lanes. At the driver's side of the Jeep, also keeping perfect pace with us, at least for that instant, was a motorcyclist, a woman in leathers on a gold-painted Harley with flowing blond hair under a gold helmet and wide goggles. Heist sensed me looking and put his hand like a calm cap on my forehead, shading my eyes, then moved his hand lower, to touch the dog's head. I was unashamed to be put in this equivalency, to be petted. Our twin escorts, the train and the Golden Girl, traveled beside us at a fixed rate, pointed into the beyond. The ocean so far behind us now as to be unimaginable. To go east from the sea was to go deeper into the west, I understood, just before I fell back into my sleep.

Or maybe I hadn't awoken, maybe the train and the motorcyclist had been a dream. Yet the Golden Girl wasn't so easy to shake. Had she sped beside me as a taunt, or a warning? Really, the Golden Girl might have been like a piece of my desire, my self-imagining, that had broken off against my will, to become cast in chrome and leather and velocity.

I'd never been on a motorcycle, needless to say. Never once wanted to be.

When I woke again it might have been twenty minutes or a million years later, but in any case Heist still piloted the Jeep stoically into the vastening landscape, the trees growing fewer, the desert scrub dotting the dusty flayed surface with the feebleness of armpit sprigs or teenage pubes. I blinked and squinted into this distance while Jessie licked my neck and ears as if I were a puppy he'd birthed. I detected scents of bagel and egg on his teeth but behind it lay a breath not doggish but sweet and ethereal as a lover's.

The valley ahead was dotted, I saw now, with weird white looming sculptures, white sky spurs, wingless aircraft by Brancusi. First I saw five or six of these, then hundreds, as if we drove into a valley of alien towers, planted in some static invasion.

"What are those?" I croaked.

"Windmills."

"Why aren't they turning?" One or two drifted slowly around, though not enough to scramble an egg.

"The turbines go on when the grid needs the juice."

We soared on into their dwarfing midst, into the dry wastes reaching to distant moonlike ridges in every direction. I didn't understand about the windmills but it wasn't the windmills I needed to understand.

"Were you raised by animals, Charles?" I'd cleared the sleep from my throat, and I pronounced these words with a sincerity distinguishing them from my ordinary whimsicality and sarcasm, at no small cost. I knew Heist could hear the difference.

Still, he made a first move to brush me off. "Seeing how we're all animals ourselves, who wasn't?"

"That's not what I meant."

He touched my head again. "We'll be where we're going in a couple of hours. Let me know if you need a pit stop."

I pushed his hand away. "Were you raised by the Rabbits or the Bears?"

"A bit of both."

"Tell me."

24

OF THE MANY UTOPIAN-MINDED PACKS OF HIPPIES WHO'D TAKEN TO THE wilderness in the late '60s, few lasted more than a winter or two. Most dissolved, come to ruin at the crossroads of ideological dissension, venereal disease or parasites, starvation, jealousy, and sheer ignorance of the raw facts of wilderness survival. The Viscera Springs Ranch was a tenacious commune, if not the smartest, or the luckiest. Their group was served that whole menu—ideology, pubic crabs, hunger—yet held on.

Year to year their population waned, down to a core of those most resilient, visionary, or desperate. Then swelled again, as rumor of a sanctuary in the desert enticed those disenchanted with the state of things elsewhere, in the cities, in their colleges or revolutionary cells. One way or another they held on, through the brutal exposure of Mojave desert sun and wind and the scarcity of their water. For the springs that gave the name to the mining camp they'd purchased for a song had revealed themselves as a bare sulfurous trickle.

It was the bargain that sunk them: seven years in, it was revealed they'd been swindled. The group had acquired a mining claim from a previous occupant, nothing more. The claim granted no specific rights to occupy, expand, build, or smoke dope and fuck and grope in groups of three or four in the shady hollows and embarrass the older prospectors. They weren't even technically given the right to spend a night. The land was non-transferable anyway. The acres on which they'd pitched their tee-pees and erected their clay-and-wattles huts weren't theirs, but a holding of BLM—the Bureau of Land Management.

It was BLM who explained to the Viscera Springs gaggle, sixty or seventy of them, man, woman, and child, that they should vamoose. This was 1974. Charles Heist was only six years old when Viscera Springs was dislodged from its fantasy of a "homestead" in the desert, but he seemed to recall it as a fresh rupture. I suppose it was this rupture that had created his life. But there must have been something of the preternatural watchful child about him even before it. Something of the detective, gathering clues. That faintly wounded and yet un-self-pitying character, the deliberate and patient and other-directed and sometimes utterly infuriating depressive I'd walked in and discovered in the office on Foothill Boulevard must have been well under construction even before the Viscera Springs Ranch was dissolved, or exploded, and became the two tribes: Rabbits and Bears.

I filled in some of the facts around Heist's tale online later, when I had a free minute and a signal—on an airplane, as it happened. (Spoiler alert: I'll board an airplane again at least once in this story. At least once in my life.) The most useful link was a Berkeley sociology student's dissertation, *A Place Was Our First Idea: Oral Accounts of Red Bear, Breath Ranch, Evening-star, and Viscera Canyon.* Nothing contradicted Heist's story, but what came after 1974 was barely represented there at all.

So: some vamoosed. Others clawed in more deeply, arguing they'd been unwitting squatters for their whole experiment—so why not carry on wittingly? The planet was huge, especially the portion they'd lost themselves within. There were shacks abandoned practically everywhere in this landscape, and trailers, sheds, and caves where there weren't shacks. Those willing to be nomadic rarely had to build anything at all. They weren't tied to plots of land because they weren't farming, not in the high desert. They lived by nearly any other means: hunting, foraging, trading. Those who still engaged with cash might be cooking drugs or selling their bodies, selling dusted-off Bakelite artifacts at the swap meet in the old drive-in movie lot, running back to cities to clean houses or to beg on street corners. Others might quietly cash pity checks waiting at Western Union, then return in dune buggies loaded with dry sacks of beans and flour. Others detached from any nonpsychic economy, never went near the roads or trading posts, learned to eat for months at a time only dreams, clouds, rattlesnakes.

The ones who dug in deeper and continued to drag the teepees around and hold meetings and share food around the circle came to be called the Rabbits. The Rabbits were women and children and the men who, whether they'd fathered the children or not, seemed to recognize the presence of the children as a binding force, a kind of proposition for a new world, which is what they'd arrived here for in the first place. The kids who, being kids, ran wild into the landscape, but always at night returned into the comfort of the circle and seemed to give evidence of the deep human necessity for a *home*.

The others, the ones who hewed off into the higher ranges, into the dark and wild, and who returned less and less frequently to the ceremonial fires to share what they'd found out there, were called the Bears. The Bears were men.

"I know about them," I joked to Heist. He'd been talking a long time, painting a world and sometimes seeming to dream his way back into it. I wanted to yank him back into this one. "They have websites for those kind of Bears, the hairy human ones who have sex with each other."

"The name was actually Bear-Killers at first," he said, ignoring my funning. "Not Bears. The original king of the Bears, a man named Howard Burkhardt, he'd gone north and shot one and brought parts of it back on a dune buggy. Some of the Bears were wearing some of the inedible parts, the teeth and fur, and Bear-Killer shared his name with them, and later it got shortened to Bears."

"Okay, so not exactly the same thing."

"I'm not saying there might not be some overlap." I tried to catch Heist's eye when he said it, but he was still driving, and his deadpan was good.

"How many kids are we talking about?" I asked.

"I think there were at least twenty in those days. Not all midwived out in the desert, there were a couple who'd been dragged there at the start, but they didn't stay. More later on— it's in the nature of things that they kept coming."

"In the nature of rabbits, you mean? Sure. That's well known too. Especially if the Bears drop by for conjugal visits from time to time."

"They tended to do that."

"And you were one of these kids?"

"Yes. I was the firstborn."

Now he had to be pulling my leg. "The first born of—what?"

"At Viscera Springs. Well, actually there was another baby who died, I think that was part of why it seemed important. They knew they had to learn to do it right, and I survived, and they called me the firstborn."

"And you lived with the Rabbits."

"I spent some time living among the Rabbits."

"Excuse me, *among*. But you weren't a Bear, right? Because they didn't care about kids."

"Well, that's a funny thing, Phoebe."

Through his long talk we'd coursed along shrinking lanes, six, four, now just one in each direction. The desert's broken teeth ringed us on all sides. Farther off were the higher, snow-peaked ranges. I spotted my first Joshua tree, then hundreds of those knobby agonized forms, half Bosch, half Seuss. I kept my mouth shut, deciding it was a rube's move to marvel aloud that they were real.

At some point in this journey, while this tale emerged, I'd warmed to Heist again. Jessie had acted as my canine shield while I'd napped. Now he clambered into the back seat and curled up for a rest of his own. I mostly sat back and let Heist's voice caress me while I stared, hypnotized by the desert's yawning, wind-scratched contour, unfolding before us in every direction. I only stole a few glances at Heist's gnarly profile, and was for the moment relieved when he didn't glance back. It would have made things more complicated than I needed just now.

The land was the baseline here, the only reality principle. Any scatterings that humans placed upon it were provisional, and mostly in decline. Many structures were mere tatters, abandoned and even half-collapsed buildings that offered themselves back to the dust in real time, rusted hulks of cars, cyclone fencing marking irrelevant limits between unclaimed lots. Elsewhere came eruptions of slick new gas stations and chain restaurants, big box stores, the same new crap going up everywhere. More often the local reality reasserted itself, shabby pocket malls filled by outlets featuring massage and tattoo, vape and reptiles, as if the only way to make yourself right for this place was to be wreathed in lizards, smoke, and body ink.

In the last ten minutes or so we'd left most of even those marginal stabs at civilization behind us. Now, before I could interrogate Heist about his *funny time with the Bears,* he swung into a gas station, maybe the last outpost before we drove off the edge of the known. There he gassed up while I replenished with a truly abysmal cup of coffee.

My phone had a bar of signal, and while Heist went inside for his own pit stop I harvested the e-mails that had been stacking up since I'd climbed the mountain. My former reality was in a frenzy, bracing itself for the idiot's inauguration. I supposed if I were back there I'd be hand-painting a sign, organizing for the scheduled protest march. From this distance it seemed impossible to believe. It was still barely eight in the morning. We got back in the Jeep and Heist ran us up off Twentynine Palms Highway, northward, if I trusted the sun.

The cyclone fencing gave way to scribbles of barbed wire, then nothing at all. The road itself was the last human thing etched in this barrenness; the rest was behind us.

"You were saying about the Bears."

"I'm tired of talking."

I handed him the shitty coffee and arched my eyebrow. He resumed his story.

25

THE BEARS HAD A THING FOR THE FIRSTBORN. THE MANCHILD, HE WHO'D been dubbed first Baby, then Boy, then, for the color of his eyes, Brown. Little as they wanted to change diapers, forage edible cacti, stir stewpots, defecate in designated holes, or sit fireside for hours in pursuit of consensus decisions, they took an interest in the kid's progress. The Bears had begun to range farther, those days, to Cleghorn Lakes and Death Valley and the Salton Sea, some on motorcycles and some in trailers. This was also the beginning of their Mount Baldy pilgrimages, their annual ascent to the snows, to that summit of lapis lazuli and secret rituals. But Mojave government lands were still the axis of their wanderings, and they had their eye on the boy. If nobody knew who his father was, it might be all the Bears collectively, why not?

The Bears still dropped in on the Rabbits too, a ritual occurrence somewhere between a jubilee and a raid. By the time Brown was nine, he was leader of a band of Rabbit younglings that kept their own company, rock climbing and mud-bathing and killing snakes and taking secret occupancy of their own caves and shacks. It was then the Bears put their claim on him. The time had come, they informed the Rabbits by fiat. So it was that Brown went among the Bears—Charles Heist, though not yet under that name, at nine years old.

The Bears had a kind of king. I'd heard of him already,

Burkhardt, Bear-Killer. A onetime Digger, and a onetime Hells Angel, Burkhardt was the strongest and most charismatic among them. He was also the oldest, and talked constantly of his impending death, claiming he was riven with cancer, though he showed no signs of this. Burkhardt promised that any day now, with little warning, he'd walk off to some high point and let himself die blazing in the sun, to be picked at by birds. In the man-cult the Bears had been cultivating among themselves, at Burkhardt's encouragement—an unsystematic muddle of equal parts Henry Miller and Edgar Rice Burroughs, of scraps of Sun Tzu, Castaneda, and John Wayne—the boy had been projected as their totemic progeny. A pure product of the desert, Brown not only ought to live among them, he was to be raised to succeed Bear-Killer as their tribal king.

In that first year Brown ran back from the Bears to find the Rabbits. One of his favorite of the mothers (he'd never been sure which was his birth mother, or whether she even still lived with the Rabbits) taught him to read then, using an old paperback of *David Copperfield*. Less than a year after this escape he was found, during one of his wanderings, by Bears, and was retrieved to their camp; three years later, at thirteen, he crossed to the Rabbits again.

On this second return, he found the Rabbits had undergone certain convulsions, become more righteously resistant—they now defined the Bears as hardly better than rapists, and had armed themselves against them. Brown was treated in part as a spy from their camp (and, Heist couldn't deny, some of his curiosity to rejoin the Rabbits at that time *was* certainly sexual). Some mothers drew him in, others reviled his influence on the younger ones. Most of the kids he'd led no longer recalled him. He lived in a measured distance from the Rabbits, then—lived as a semi-predator, a creature of mixed purposes, yet one accepting scraps of nurture. And yes, he'd spent some nights cuddling with packs of dogs, scrambling after them on all fours, trying out their society.

Feral? Sure, that might be the word for it.

Brown had spent his coming of age this way, shuttling between the groups and the spaces between, fundamentally unhomed anywhere but in his own skin. Finally, at fourteen, he'd hitchhiked into the town of Palm Desert, a metropolis by his standards, one he'd known only in a handful of wondering visits. There, he'd turned himself in to the police for referral to Child Protective Services. His belief in the Bears' reach, their eyes on him from the dunes and pinnacles, extended to the certainty they'd drag him back unless he placed himself inside some citadel of civilization.

Arthur and Mary Heist were an elderly couple in Redlands. The Heists had raised seven foster children before Brown, who'd be their last. He lived with them for just four years, time enough to gain a name, a social security number, a GED, and a reluctant dose of Christian Scientism. From there, he'd entered basic training. Through six years in the reserves and a flop out of San Bernardino Community College, Heist endured a spell of manual labor at the Long Beach shipyards. Only then did he feel his way into what might have been an inevitable calling: dragging strays of every species out of distressing circumstances. In this, his stay with Arthur and Mary had served as a kind of apprenticeship. His foster parents' long and mutually trusting relationship with CPS provided Charles Heist a route to retrace back into the Inland Empire's infrastructure of rescue for runaways and abused children, and for teenagers snared in cults or networks of trafficking.

Only after his unique practice in Upland had been established did Heist, after ten years, return to the desert, to find what had become of the Rabbits. He went there to pay his respects to the mothers but also to spirit away any of their children or teens who told him they wanted to go. He informed the adults, as gently as possible, that the decision wasn't theirs, but that of the child—the person—in question. Charles "Brown" Heist had his provenance to make this indisputable. He could quote their own principles back to the Rabbits. He was also the product of them.

All this I had to drag from Heist, the proverbial pulling teeth. He wouldn't talk of what life among the Bears had been like for him, at nine or ten, or later. He was ashamed of having been groomed into this yin-yang halfling. It was both the mystery of his Bear self and his shame at it that drew me to him. I wanted him then again, with a tiny seizure of desire that startled me, that didn't seem fit for daylight or our mission into the sands. I was getting overly identified with my cage, the Jeep, as if by driving it, Heist drove me too. I wanted to cover the dog's eyes and do something to Heist while he shifted gears. I also felt jealous.

"Did you ever have a girlfriend?"

"Depends what you mean."

"Did you do—Bear things?"

"I'm not sure what you mean."

"After the Rabbits, they just lived without women? I find that hard to believe, Charles."

"There are always women. The desert's more full of people than you'd think. The Bears had a lot of groupies in the trailer population. As I said, they ranged wide."

That word, *groupies*, blew an ugly little fuse in my imagination's engine. I thought of Arabella, of all I wished to be true for her about how the world was changing, and how it wasn't, really. "You were a teenage boy."

He said nothing.

"I get it," I said. "It's a Bears, Bears, Bears world, but it wouldn't be nothin' without a woman or a girl."

"Phoebe."

"Never mind, don't tell me. I don't need it in my head." The Bears might be no more than a rustic enactment of Donald Trump and Anthony Weiner and Bill Cosby, the usual shitty reality I'd fled but that no one left behind on any road, on any inhabited planet.

We were quiet for some time after that. Heist hung a right at a dirt road leading off toward the distant topography, then stopped the Jeep after putting the last of the paved roadway a few hundred yards behind us. He and the dog jumped out, Jessie for a pee against a rusted steel post, Heist to fiddle with the wheels. At first I thought he was checking the pressure, but he held the tool too long against one hissing tire, meanwhile squinting into the long-shadowed hills.

"What's wrong?"

"Nothing. I'm letting some air out." Now he circled the Jeep, venting from each tire in turn.

"What's the big idea?"

"Soft tires grapple better. We're going to do some rock hopping."

The next hours were spent climbing on the softened tires out of the flats, into the articulated rockscape, using creek beds of tumbled boulders as our street. The Jeep lumbered side to side like a searching spider, needing every inch of its clearance to keep the chassis from ruin on the points of the rock. Then, abruptly, the clearance wasn't enough. We'd crunch sickeningly into place, settling backward in a granite crevasse.

Each time I imagined the Jeep was wrecked, speared like a crab on an impassable stone. But Heist never flinched. He'd get out to puzzle an approach. Usually he backed us off the obstacle, then wrenched the wheels to some implausible steering radius to scale it from another angle. Other times he'd shift a few stones beneath the tires, giving us something to climb. At these delays, Jessie leaped out to study the stones with Heist, while I sat in the shade of some rock or a twisted tree or cactus, trying, frankly, not to whine. Then Heist would beckon me back into the car. Revving like the engine might explode, he'd thrust us up and over some boulder, the mushy rubber squealing along some diagonal wall, the chassis shrieking clear of its prison. More than once I praised my nonexistent Lord for the roll bars, so certain was I that we'd vaulted sideways to ruin.

We lurched this way at speeds maybe totaling five miles an hour, maybe fewer, but soon enough it felt unimaginable that there had been a road, that anyone could follow or could want to even try to follow where we'd gotten. We shared water, the three of us. The desert smelled of seeping heat, which the sun had trapped in the rocks cumulatively, over eons. The wide vistas disappeared. We were always at the bottom of some arroyo or maze of stone, never at the top, where the views presumably were. This actually eased my sky anxiety. The Jeep was stuck time and again in a rut inside a rut inside a rut. Our sole object the next few yards in front of us.

My mind was like that as well. Life narrows at transition points, the wardrobe between England and Narnia, the cloistered space capsule launching to another world. I began to try to assist Heist in shifting rocks to put under our wheels, so I wouldn't feel useless. He accepted my help uncritically, but ungratefully too. We were in whatever we were in together, and since we barely knew each other, we were alone too. Yet the Jeep needed to get out of the next trap, and the next—there was work to do.

Be vewwy vewwy quiet, I told myself. *We'we hunting wabbits.*

26

THE FIRST RABBIT ENCAMPMENT WASN'T MUCH MORE IMPRESSIVE THAN
what I'd seen on entering the San Antonio Wash, when the giant Laird had emerged from his hidey-hole in the rain. Like that
site, this was a refugee village, made of salvage, with buckets
set out for rainwater, ringed by abject evidence of homestead-
ing projects taken up and abandoned. There weren't teepees but
two low adobe huts, roofed with sheet metal. The first Rabbit
popped out of one of these and stood before us warily. The sun
made her an outline, a flat silhouette, and I couldn't read her
expression, or tell if she recognized Heist. The scene was like
that in the Wash, but it was different too, because of the price
of distance we'd paid to enter it. The barefoot woman who stood
before us, now putting out a hand to let Jessie sniff and lick it,
represented the first encounter of two humans on the surface of
a distant planet, or the moon at least. Her presence was improbable as that.

We'd driven free of the last of the rocky traps, off-roading
through pylons of tangled Joshua limbs, to a high point now
behind us. There Heist had surveyed the landscape, located some
clue I couldn't discern, and the three of us had set out on foot.
We left the Jeep and its contents—including our spare water—
high on the rise as we scrambled down along a grade. If my
purse hadn't contained my phone I'd have left it behind too. I

was grateful it stayed looped around my shoulder, as I felt the likelihood I'd land on my hands at any instant.

In fact, I might have been more comfortable on all fours. I felt I'd entered a hallucinatory compact with Heist and the dog, to find a place to shed our clothes, and then our human skins. After Heist's story, I was ready to crawl into some shady dell, there to suck rocks for moisture. It was then, before I lost my mind, that we came into the Rabbit compound.

"I'm Charles Heist," the Feral Detective said now. Jessie nosed past the woman, into the hut. The woman didn't try to stop him, or turn from us at all. My eyes began to adjust to the contrast that had first made her look like a flat cutout against the glare. She might have been twenty or twenty-five—younger than me. But she seemed to gaze out of a WPA photograph, shorn of any vestige of the present, her gray dress practically sackcloth, her hands twisted together at her waist. I wondered if I showed her my iPhone whether she'd worship or bite it.

"I'm looking for Anita," Heist said, as gently as if talking to a child or an animal. "She can tell you who I am."

"I know who you are," said the woman. "I know all about you." She spoke in a dead monotone, giving nothing away. Her eyes were dry as the landscape.

Heist nodded at me, as if inviting her to examine me for restraints or fresh bruises. "I'm not a Bear." I chose not to point out that he'd just spent the past hour explaining to me that he was one, at least in part. Instead I nodded encouragement, raised my hand to show I wasn't sporting rope burns. She just stared.

"Can you tell us your name?" Heist said to her.

"Sure, man. I'm Spark."

First Sage, now Spark; probably Sunrise and Saffron were out there somewhere if we persisted. I checked the urge to introduce myself as Sluice or Snivel. But I was baffled by Heist's eggshell-tiptoe approach. Was this part of his feminist super-

man act? It was at that instant I saw the gunmetal glint in her
hands, which weren't being wrung together in the manner of a
stereotypical ninny, as I'd imagined. Rather, her fingers steadied, and slightly twitched, around a pistol she trained on us from
the center of her body.

The opening in the barrel formed a tiny black eye, like the
pupil of an animal. I'd never stood at the point of a gun before,
never known how it could shrink a whole universe, or seem to
swallow my sight. The Bears had had to dig a giant catastrophic
mud-and-blood pit on a snowy mountaintop to achieve the same
vertiginous result in my mind that this woman had gained with
one casual glance of the gun's eye. Score one for the Rabbits.

"This is Phoebe," Heist said. I suspected he'd spoken my
name as much to steady me as anything else. "She's looking for
her friend. Do you have a way to contact Anita? Do you have a
walkie-talkie?"

"I don't know where Anita is right now. Neither do you."

"Of course that's true."

"Anita says she doesn't have time to fuck around anymore."
The woman with the gun spoke to Heist but stared at me.

"If you'd tell her I was here, she could decide. We're old
friends."

"Yeah, but you and I aren't. And here is where you are right
now, not with blah blah blah Anita."

"Why blah blah blah?" said Heist.

"I might know as many things as Anita. I might know more
things."

"Would you tell them to me?"

"Why would I do that?"

"Okay," said Heist. "Listen, you could put the gun down."

"No, I can't," said Spark. "It's my job." I'd read the situation
inside out. It wasn't just the gun. Spark was a sentry, not a scat-
terling. Her mud hut a well-placed post, a kind of border crossing.

Or she was a semi-outcast, like Heist had been. The two weren't exclusive. She might be one of those you pushed to the periphery to face their violence outward, where it served purposes.

"You did your job already," Heist suggested to her. "You can see us for what we are."

"Nothing's that easy."

"Okay," said Heist.

"Take your dog," said Spark. "I don't care where you go now."

Heist gave a low whistle, something I'd not heard before. Jessie returned from the hut, to our feet. With that, we took Spark's go-ahead and set off around her, to the right. The pistol stared us over the ridge as we went.

27

I HAVE SOME KIND OF ONLY-CHILD-OF-CRAZY-THERAPISTS CHATTER switch that flips on under certain circumstances. It did now, as if the whole desert were one of those rooms drained of oxygen by my parents' fighting, and which I tried to reanimate by sheer childish will. I began monologuing, telling Heist about Renee Lambert, with whom I'd shared a triple at Thayer Hall, right in the middle of the Yard, freshman year.

Renee wowed us with her astounding indifference to her studies right off the bat, and with her feats of insomniac partying, punctuated by equally awesome bouts of daysleeping. We'd find her in the common area, still up, clinging upright on a couch, when we woke for breakfast—she'd need to be told to go to bed, like she'd forgotten how it worked. In contrast to Arabella at Reed, Renee had lasted through her first semester—somehow. When we both returned to New York for winter break I found myself invited to a New Year's party with Renee's Dalton friends, but I lost track of her at the party until I went into the back bedroom for my coat at two or three in the morning. There, I'd found Renee sitting amid the coats and handbags. She stared, with a cross-eyed cosmic expression I couldn't parse, until I focused on her hands, which held a hypodermic needle. It had waited, like Spark's gun, right below my line of sight.

It was just this echo, the startling rupture of my unworld-liness, that had brought Renee to mind. Yet actually, oddly, once I'd made the connection, Spark so strongly recalled Renee Lambert that I wondered for a minute—and aloud to Heist—whether they might be the same person. Maybe after dropping out, she'd come west? But no, that wasn't right, Renee would be older by now. My age, and I was old.

Heist humored me. In this fashion, in a tizzy of my own chatter, I was able to carry on, to progress beyond the sight of the gun and, perhaps even more objectionable, beyond the fact that we strode into the desert with no supplies, and farther from the Jeep. Well, if we needed we could drink the sky, and nibble my unleavened naiveté for a cracker. I seemed to have held on to a stash of it.

I felt closer than ever to Heist. As my manic comparison trailed off, he didn't speak, but then he'd given me so much in the Jeep. We had different styles. I made myself candid in fickle bursts, he reciprocated with marathon ruminations or silence. He'd led me into his desert. I took his arm. He let me.

28

THE LARGER COMPOUND SNUCK UP ON ME COMPLETELY. I SHOULD HAVE noticed Jessie take off ahead of us. One instant we trudged pathless sands. The next, around a rise, we'd entered a maze of human signs. Small habitations littered a span of landscape: huts like the two we'd passed, a few teepees, yes, and also half-submerged, tin-roofed pit dwellings.

Heist steered through the smaller huts, and I followed. He found his way to a muddy well, a broad, unsheltered excavation with scraped-rock steps leading down to a place where mud and water pooled in tepid shade. The well looked as though it had been in use a long time. I supposed the gathering of structures had grown up around it.

Two people stood at the lowest step, submerged in shade. A woman and a scrawny, Christ-bearded man, both dressed in soft, dun-colored clothes. Heist went halfway down and spoke with them. This wasn't a nervy encounter like that with Spark. Heist was known to them, or spoke the Rabbit language in a way that took them off their guard, or they weren't on guard to begin with. Spark might be the exception. Waiting at the top step, I caught a first glimpse of one of the children, a barefoot longhair, gender impossible to verify. It crouched like a cave dweller in the mouth of a hut, then made a face at me and rolled into a ball and tumbled comically backward, out of sight.

Afterward, Heist took me to the largest building, a small cabin. There we met Anita. She wore the white robe I'd soon learn was for approaching her hives. Heist introduced me, and Anita gave us water and set out a bowl for Jessie, who lapped appreciatively. Then Heist went right to the point, asking about a girl who might be called Arabella or Phoebe, apparently trusting Anita not to be confused by the overlapping names. Anita gave me a bright, skeptical look-see, but smiled too. I was relieved to like her when she opened her mouth, even if she seemed ready, even eager, to squash our hopes.

"Sorry, Charles. Your girl was never with us."

"But you know who I'm talking about?"

"Not by either of those names. Or any name. We've had rumors and sightings. The Bears' priorities are changing again. There was talk of a girl, among other things. But then there always is."

While she spoke, Anita knelt disinterestedly at what appeared to be a small heap of stones in the center of the floor. When she nudged one with a forked stick I saw a spray of sparks, and a glow from beneath. Jessie leaped backward, then nosed back. It was some kind of banked fire, not that we were particularly cold at mid-morning, even in out of the sun. We took seats beside her. My eyes adjusted to the cabin's gloom.

"What about the mountain?" Heist's question was noncommittal, it seemed to me. It didn't reveal what we'd seen on Baldy. Yet his tone cast Anita as his willing partner in broad speculation. She seemed to take the bait.

"Oh god, the mountain. I've heard the usual Bear stuff, about a coming flood, but with a stupid new emphasis on some crafty deal they'd struck up on Baldy. I got the feeling they'd been fleeced by someone or something."

"I thought they were going to stick to their carnival and stay out of trouble," said Heist.

"Since when have you known the Bears to stay out of trouble?"

"Aren't they getting too old for this?"

"Like all of us, Charles. But they have a young new king. The worst yet, which is saying something."

"Do I know him?"

Anita nudged the stones again, and then I saw they weren't all stones. Some were stone-like shapes in blackened foil. Using her prong, she teased these onto the floor, then vented the foil to release trapped steam, some savory essence out of nowhere. I was struck dumb with hunger.

"I don't think anybody knows him, really. The only name he goes by is, get ready for this, Solitary Love."

"Ex-con?"

The references in their talk whizzed over my head. Heist and Anita seemed to speak in some ancient code. But I didn't feel jealous. Instead, I felt party to the investigation at last. Enveloped in the conspiracy, whether I understood every detail or not.

"Love claims to be an Enduring Storm vet," she said. "But I doubt he got the tattoos or that nickname in Iraq. If you squint, he looks almost human. Our plan is to set him on fire next time he comes near enough."

Heist raised his palms in a gesture of surrender. "I saw that movie. One time was enough for me."

Anita had clocked my interest in what she'd plucked from the coals. Now she used the forked stick to shove one of whatever it was my way across the floor. I juggled it up for a look. The food within was some kind of cornmeal pouch around a chunk of green. "Go ahead," she said, and when I paused, she added, "Cactus tamale." She shoved another steaming packet in front of Heist, and one for Jessie too.

"Thank you." I slurped in a bite too hot to swallow.

I was more than Heist's sidekick now, I was the new girl-friend being shown off, and welcomed by—what? His ex? His mom? Distinctions didn't so much matter; I was under her wing, in the family. The tamale was delicious, stingingly spicy and hot. Looking back, it was obvious I was coming down off a jag, a combination of hunger and pistol derangement. At the speed I decelerated now, if I wasn't careful I'd curl up and pass out on the floor.

"Looks like I need to go and see this new young king," said Heist. He spoke as if to no one, as if to the ragged horizon that bound this hut on all sides.

"Never forget," said Anita.

"Never forget what?" he asked.

"All this could have been yours."

29

WHAT HAPPENED NEXT HAPPENED FAST. HEIST STALKED FROM ANITA'S cabin, leaving his tamale half-eaten on the floor. Jessie went too. Anita smiled at me again, as if it were natural I should be left flat-footed on her sandy floor. The way of the world. I gobbled the last of my food and grabbed my purse and bolted outside, to follow.

I had to run to catch up. When I did, my reward was to have him turn and say, "Better you stay."

"You're kidding me."

"I'll be back in a few hours." He never broke stride, gaze locked to destination as firmly as if he drove. It was the Jeep he moved toward, of course. We went past the two huts where Spark had stood and confronted us with the gun, though I saw no sign of her there now.

"No fucking way," I said. "I'm coming with you."

"I should do this alone."

The language between us grew rudimentary, then, and circular. I kept telling him the search belonged to me, that he didn't even know Arabella, and that I'd followed him this far for a reason, not to be sloughed off at the threshold—deposited like a spare Rabbit at the hutch. He kept, well, sloughing me off. Soon Heist was silent while I railed at him, amid empty hills born to swallow human language, carved by time to make my protests small. I'm sure I was screaming by the time we reached the steep crag that had kept us from driving right into the Rabbit town. The Jeep was visible up above. I recall the phrase *fucking macho bullshit* with no particular pride.

Heist opened the driver-side door, and Jessie leaped inside. I entered the passenger side. There, I found myself temporarily quieted. Sitting in the Jeep again, I remembered our long drive, the tenderness with which Heist had allowed me to sleep off my fear, his hand on the crown of my head. Besides, maybe simply by following him to the vehicle I'd won, and he'd take off to confront the Bear King with me aboard. At least he hadn't physically booted me from the passenger seat.

But Heist wasn't going anywhere. Typically passive, he sat, the key in his hand resting ready on his knee, and let his insistence saturate me wordlessly. When I spoke again my tone was seething but quiet, and I heard my own defeat in it.

"Are you and I even on the same *planet*?" I said.

"There's only one planet."

"Thank you, Mr. Spock. You know, I figured you out now. You may look like a wolverine, but you're the opposite. You're one of those Leonard Nimoy types, a total Asperger's robot. Human beings are just puzzling animals to you, worth saving for the sport of it, no better than stray dogs. There's only one planet, sure—but you're studying it from the wrong end of the telescope." I knew this was nonsense, really, yet I wanted to claw at the door behind which Heist had sealed his infinite sadness. The vanity with which he concealed it from me was suddenly repulsive.

Heist didn't reply, but Jessie did, by thrusting up to lick my face, making me aware of the tears I'd uncorked. Heist only closed his eyes and stretched back, making a physical sigh without accompanying sounds.

"It's like I'm watching you reel back into these ancient tribal grievances," I told him. "It makes me furious, because I dragged you into this to find a real lost living girl, a young woman." I didn't mean myself. But I left Arabella unnamed, to permit the implication. "It makes me sad too, in like a hundred different ways. If you say it's a sad planet you're going to make me puke." I wanted to unentrench Heist from the past, into the present life—that one in which he and I were at least tenuously lovers.

"It's not about any of what you say. It's about not showing up with another ready-made hostage."

"You're as much a ready-made hostage as me."

"That isn't how they'd look at it."

"Great. Excellent. Let's examine everything from the Bear perspective. It trumps anything I could possibly say. I hate how that word is ruined, among so many other ruined things."

"What word?"

"Never mind. I know current events aren't your bag. When you've got a minute go ask the Owl, or the wise old Badger, they'll explain." Jessie licked my gluey nostrils. I smooched with him a bit, my booby prize, just to show Heist what he was missing. "Fine, go do your man shit. Jessie and I will be waiting in the menstrual lounge area."

"I need Jessie with me," said Heist. "I need a tracker."

"Oh, that's right, Jessie's got a penis. My bad."

"You know how to get back?" Heist only had to tip his chin. The Jeep looked out toward the way we'd come, the rise behind which the Rabbits did their Rabbit things.

I told him I knew the way back. Then I said, "Did I break through to you in any way? Because you broke through to me. I saw you howl, Charles."

All day I'd been wanting to remind him how we'd been in the Airstream, that we'd unpeeled one another there, that we'd each come. But that was common, really. I'd had that with plenty of fools from whom I'd parted—easily, absently, gratefully. It was what had happened on the mountain that bound us, or I believed it did. *Trauma makes you a family,* I thought absurdly. I'd believed Heist and I had been wrecked together, but maybe we'd only been wrecked at the same time, in two different ways. I didn't know what the mountain meant to him, after all.

"I remember." That was all he said, but he turned toward me then, and his eyes softened inside the worn mask of his features.

I wasn't letting him off so easy, not this time. "You remember what? That you got to come in my mouth?" I needed Heist not to turn out to be some top-level Western-style pickup artist, one so strung out on his internal event horizon that he couldn't even be bothered to properly neg me.

"That's not what I meant."

"Feel free to elaborate."

"I . . . I see you, Phoebe Siegler."

My whole name: I was in *his* mouth now. It moved me, but I pretended it didn't. "You see a lot of things," I pressed. "I don't come from nowhere, you realize. I've seen some things of my own, some things that would freak you out as bad as that mountain, maybe worse." I couldn't think of what these exactly were, at the moment. But never mind.

"I don't doubt it."

"I'm not some stray in a drawer. I'm not a Rabbit either."

"No," he agreed. "You're a woman, a different kind."

"What kind?"

"I don't know yet."

The *yet* I liked. Heist might have been bargaining, to be rid of me. I didn't care.

Then we were kissing, for a while. Jessie tried to join us, confused by my encouragement a moment earlier, but we shoved him off into the back seat, where he quieted down. Good dog. The way Heist and I kissed didn't translate into more than it was—neither of us persuaded the other of anything, and we weren't about to strip off our clothes right there either. I had the distinct impression that I was kissing a sculpture, an odd and interesting statue, the interior of which was solid to the core, and inaccessible. I felt us as two topographies, abutting, yet lonely inside. But for all that, hey, it wasn't bad.

I remained terrified, at how Heist had instilled in me a fear of abandonment I'd never previously tasted. If my illusions were like exes, I felt I'd been dumped eight or ten times in the past week. Yet at least I could feel, just for an instant, how my fears were themselves rooted in a stark appetite for something unnameable but real. Under everything that had been taken from me, I did observe myself rustling around. Maybe Heist was the same as a desert: a void encounter, one putting me in a heightened relation to a certain Phoebe Siegler.

He was more than that. He was a figure about to go howling again, off into his own wild. He might also be Arabella Swados's best hope. I didn't ask him again to take me along.

"Be careful, Charles."

I hated his guts, and feared for them too.

30

WHEN I PASSED IT AGAIN, I LINGERED FOR A MOMENT AT SPARK'S HUT, the dark entrance she'd popped from. She wasn't there, but I felt her presence. I was being watched. I moved off to the ridge behind which lay the well and Anita's cabin, the small Rabbit civilization. Then I looked up and found Spark there, silently keeping pace with me on a rise to the right. The pistol was hung on a rope around her waist; I had no difficulty spotting it this time. That was one way I was changing.

31

NOW, TWO HOURS LATER, RETURNING FROM FETCHING STICKS WITH LORRIE, as I walked with Anita toward Neptune Lodge in the flattening golden light and chafing wind, I sensed her again. Spark. A special nerve in me was attuned to the girl with the pistol, and now it reawoke. I turned and searched the hills and sure enough, there she was, scrambling along a distance from us.

"Anita?"

"Yes?"

"We're being followed by that young woman from the outpost. Spark, I think she's called."

"Yes, I noticed that too."

"I think she's following me specifically."

"I'm sure you're right. Apparently, you interest her."

"Am I that interesting?"

"To Spark you are."

"*Bada bing, bada boom.*"

But Anita charged on ahead, Red Queen to my Alice, forcing me to follow, oblivious to my wit. Her dickishness made me want to take her at her word and be grateful I had at least Spark for an admirer. My charms seemed lost on Rabbits on the whole. I wondered whether it was optional or mandatory: my visit to their sick captive Bear, this deepening involvement in Anita's skewed, dusty kingdom. During my interlude gathering sticks, I'd begun looking forward to the fire. I could feel the allure of a bite of charred food and the cover of night—a place beneath the stars and a certain distance from the madness of these women. It might be the next best thing to a hot shower and a Wi-Fi signal.

In this mood, Neptune Lodge came as a little bit of a shock. I'd been in the Mojave less than twenty-four hours, but the large satellite dish, which loomed up as we came around a rocky out-cropping, appeared like some clarion of modernity, an Eiffel or Empire State. The building's wide, low roof sported solar panels too. The structure nestled in a cradle of rock, sheltered from wind. We approached it from above, on steps notched in the stones. Here were glass windows as well. Maybe a hot shower wasn't out of the question. I recalled that tantalizing prospect Anita had held out: a room with a door that closed.

The so-called lodge wasn't larger than a suburban ranch house, really, but I'd had my expectations shrunk to the local scale. Did Heist know about this place? I couldn't imagine, but then again my confidence at any guesswork concerning Heist's hopes, dreams, motives, turn-ons, or any other of the contents of his skull was in an all-time ditch, along with my wish to con-tinue giving a shit.

"Is this a Rabbit place?" I asked Anita.

"It belongs to an ally."

"Why wouldn't you just all live like this?"

"A question smothered in money."

"You're squatters," I blurted. "The owners aren't here."

"The only squatters are your norms. They're squatting in your mind. I don't have time right now to chase them out."

"Yes, I've been hearing how busy you are. I'll wait."

The lodge was laid out like a split-level family home, with an open-plan kitchen featuring a refrigerator and stove, though the spaces were mostly bare and the rooms dark, no evidence of electric light despite the solar panels. There I met a black woman Anita's age, in the ordinary Rabbit-Bedouin gear, named Donna, and another white girl approximately my age, who wore a plastic windbreaker and sunglasses indoors. She struck me as a slumming debutante, perhaps the Edie Sedgwick of the group. Maybe the lodge belonged to her parents, even. When we were introduced, she mumbled her name, which sounded like Glinda or Glimmer, and made a special effort to buffalo me with shrugs and eye rolling. I wondered if all the norms squatting in *her* mind had been chased out, or if that effort was still pending. I'd lost sight of Spark as Anita and I had come down the hill, and now I wondered if she ever came indoors, to a place like this—I didn't think so. My study of Rabbits was a fledgling thing, but I was beginning to make out a few different subspecies.

32

DONNA LED ME IN, WITH ANITA, WHILE GLINDA OR GLIMMER HUNG BACK. The large high-ceilinged room was at the end of a corridor at the back of Neptune Lodge—the master bedroom, I'd have said, but I didn't think they'd care for that name, under the circumstances. The windows there were shadowed by overhanging stone, and as the sun dimmed I felt ushered into an underground cavern. At first I thought the room was empty, and that I was being shown my quarters, which were ample but spooky—but no. The downer Bear lay across the bed, his body a still lonely mountain beneath a light sheet, his Mennonite beard and heavily inked arms tucked out over the top of it. Then I saw that a shackle and chain ran from his arm to an exposed pipe in the far corner of the room. It didn't look uncomfortable—he had worse problems—but it didn't look friendly.

The Bear's mouth hung wide, the sound of his breathing so ragged I felt certain he was asleep. Then we moved nearer and I saw his eyes not only were open, but charted our presence in his sickroom. They appeared to be the only living thing in the vast choleric pudding of his face. His lips never rippled to produce the sound, the wake-snoring or undeath rattle that filled the room—instead it seemed piped in, as if a speaker had been secreted in his beard. His earlobes showed signs of lapsed tribal-style piercings, but only loose flesh remained. The metal had all been removed from his body, perhaps by the Rabbits, as if to free him of his chosen toxins.

The room's scent was earthy and saline, like fresh deep sand dug from a hole at the beach.

"Shockley, I brought a visitor." Donna spoke in a low murmur and nodded at me.

"I told you I want my *sister*." The Bear talked around the guttural, corroded breaths, but they didn't abate just because he spoke.

"Your sister can't come. This is Phoebe. She's from New York City." Donna turned to me. "Shockley used to ride a motorcycle, and he likes to talk about places he's been. Don't you, Shockley?"

"I been to New York City, shit," said Shockley. His eyes found me. It took a surprising effort for me to choose to step up nearer to his bed.

"What did you do there, in New York City?" asked Donna.

"Shiiiiiiiiit." Beyond this, Shockley only breathed, and we all listened. Goya could have painted the scene. I tried not to be ashamed for either of them: the ancient whalelike body, scarred by fantasies of criminal glory, now imprisoned in patronizing solicitude, or Donna, the only black person in the entire Mojave Desert (so far as I'd seen) behaving like his nurse. This wasn't for me to point out.

Donna spoke again. "Shockley had a good day today, but he gets tired around evening time."

"No, I want to talk to Phoebe, man. I *like* Phoebe."

I was having trouble finding my voice. "I like you too, Shockley." Why did he make me want to cry? Because he reminded me of Heist, goddamn it.

"You know who Andy *War*-hole is?"

"Sure."

"Well, I don't look like much now, but when I got to New York City in 1967 goddamn if Andy *War*-hole didn't want to take my picture." His rasping groan seemed to warm to the tale, growing more expressive, even when he had to pause for breath.

"Did he give you a copy?"

"Sweetheart, I never thought to ask." He managed a hoarse cackle.

"Would have been a valuable keepsake."

"Awwwww, I'd have lost it by now anyway, or rolled some drugs up in it and smoked the thing. Best speed I ever tasted, up in that Factory joint."

"That must have been nice for you."

"Got my ashes hauled by a lady who wasn't a lady too."

"I hope that was also nice."

"Gotta try *everything* at least once. Well, let's say twice." He attempted a smile, just legible in the gasping mouth and the heavy beard. "Now you tell me one."

"My stories aren't very interesting."

"Hell, everybody's got a story. It's what makes us human. I just want to hear you talk, Phoebe from New York. Tell these Bunnies I need some goddamn privacy here." He startled me by lifting his hand, the one without the chain, to flick a finger at the door. The effort seemed to cost him, and when the hand fell again the fat hairy fingers twitched slightly, as if palsied.

Donna looked at me, and Anita.

"It's okay," I said. "Leave me alone with him."

"I'm going to make some coffee," said Donna. "You want some?"

"Yes, please," I told her, and she and Anita left the room. Against a few of my better instincts, I got up and shut the door behind them.

33

"LISTEN, MR. SHOCKLEY. WE PROBABLY DON'T HAVE LONG."

"Sweetheart, that's real touching, but I don't know if I'm capable at the moment."

"No, just listen." I'd had my big idea. The effect of being so far off the grid wasn't so different, I'd now understood, from the result of being too much on it. Self-invention prevailed. If these people had crept out of the cities, out of late capitalism, to become Rabbits and Bears—if Renee Lambert might as well be Spark—then what kept me from being the Feral Detective? In the Mojave, no one knows you're not a dog. "Mr. Shockley, I'm not who you think I am."

"Who do I think you are?" The Bear's eyeballs moved in a not-quite-panicked way, or so it seemed to me. It might actually be the case that you couldn't read eyeballs in an absence of other body language. Well, I'd see if I could panic him a little.

"I'm not a Rabbit."

"No Rabbit," he echoed, as if it wasn't real unless he chewed it in his beard a little.

"Nor am I Rabbit-affiliated, despite any impression I may have given just now. Those women have no idea, but I'm working undercover here in advance of an all-out paramilitary raid. My people sent me in to get a certain young woman out before the shooting starts."

"*Shooting?* Shooting *who?*"

"The agency I work for, Mr. Shockley, necessarily nameless at this point, is a pretty blunt instrument. They're not too interested in distinctions between different species. I wouldn't want to be out here on the dunes when the helicopters show up."

"Helicopters?"

"Black ones."

"Fuuuuuuuuuuuck."

"That's about the size of it. But I've been authorized to offer you amnesty in return for a modicum of cooperation." Yes, folks, she could do the police in different voices. I was the apotheosis of a latchkey child addicted to *Law & Order*.

"You're going to get me out of this room?"

"Maybe not instantly, but yes. I could also try to contact your sister or get you into some other kind of safe house." I felt this was when I crossed into the territory of what could fairly be called malicious: Shockley was going to die in this room, in my estimation.

"Shit, let's get to cooperating."

"It feels like we're off to a good start."

"To me too, honeybunch."

"So, lead me to my missing person. She calls herself Arabella, or Phoebe. I assumed her name, in order to confuse the Rabbits."

"I got nothing. Who's the target of this big raid, anyhow? Don't tell me they're sending black ops after some lost girl."

"My agency is pursuing a number of targets, including a certain Mr. Love, Solitary Love. I believe you know him?"

"Crazy-ass Love'll never be brought down alive, and to kill him outright might require a bazooka."

"I'll take that as confirmation. Do you also know Charles Heist?"

"That's the great white hope you're talking about." Shockley's breathing deepened, and quickened. "Flesh of my flesh, blood of my blood, fur of my fur." His free hand flickered to life again, beckoning to his distant tribe. I thought of old ladies I'd seen on Madison Avenue, in mink, barely able to hail a cab. "The boy broke my heart but I could never do anything but forgive him."

"He's been sighted in the vicinity and he's wanted for questioning as well."

"He's back because they *called* him back, man." His voice grew introspective, and his eyes rolled back. "It fucking *worked*, I knew it would. They laid a trail and he came in from the cold."

"You're saying what? That the Bears called Heist back here?" I leaned in close enough now that I smelled him, the must of his body under the sheet, the tang that wafted from his mouth.

"Sure enough. His destiny's calling, really. We're just the telephone." The Bear reached for his spooky voice. He had a knack for whispering in capital letters.

"How'd you place the call? With contrails?"

"A sign was left on the mountain."

"I was afraid you'd say that." Now I was free to hate the man in the bed. It didn't conclude my fascination with him but gave it a new flavor. I wasn't through with my questions either, if only the Rabbits would stay put on the far side of the door. I had to hope it took a good long time and lots of collective manual labor to crank out a cup of coffee around here.

"So, what's his destiny?"

"If anyone can make it right, it's old Charlie-boy. Wish I could be there to see it."

"How make it right?"

"They're going to have a Bear fight. By the end of it we'll have a true king."

"Who'll fight? Solitary Love and Charles Heist?"

He cackled, in the affirmative. "Somebody's going to die." This came as barely a whisper. The Bear was fading again, the thrill of our private encounter no longer enough to kindle him through the evening hours.

"Why is that necessary, that someone should die?"

"Freedom, girl. Death's its bedfellow."

"Maybe. Maybe I'm a little less impressed with freedom than you are."

"Spoiled bitch."

"God, I wish. I remember what it felt like. I hope somebody spoils me again at some point."

"Liar."

"How about you talk about Arabella now?"

"In hell."

"Oh, are we playing the word association game? I'm good at that one. I played it on long car trips with my parents. And here I was, thinking you wanted to get *out* of here."

"Pussy."

"There you go. The word of the year. It's number one with a bullet." I doubted my gambit had any further juice in it. The man was dying, but he was dying to me even faster. He wasn't a man anymore, but an oracle trapped in diseased flesh. Now the oracle was out of answers.

I turned to discover the door open behind me, Donna and Anita standing there. For how long I didn't know.

34

THE COFFEE CAME OFF THE STOVETOP IN AN OPEN POT. THERE WERE eggshells in it, to leach the acids, and the coffee was very good. The shells were from some bird smaller than a chicken—or from a very small chicken. I just hoped they weren't rattlesnake eggs. But the electric coil on the stove had worked, by some measure or another. While we sat in the kitchen, Anita and myself on hard wooden chairs, Donna perched on the sill of a window opened wide to the gathering dusk, I watched the coil cooling from orange to black again. Whether it was generated by the solar panels or not, Neptune Lodge featured electricity.

If the satellite dish was also in order, there might be some kind of signal. I doubted I could keep my promise to the prisoner Bear to call in a flotilla of black helicopters, but I might be able to let some authority know where I was, or to bask in the latest Twitter outrage. I filed the thought away. I didn't want to take my phone out in front of Donna and Anita because I didn't want them to confiscate it. Our klatch seemed friendly enough, but I wasn't sure of my standing with the High Rabbits after whatever they might have heard. I preferred not to end up shackled by my wrist to their other guest in some sort of cute Hitchcockian nightmare.

"I'll show you your room, when you're ready," said Anita.

"Is there a continental breakfast?" I joked. "Does my door

lock from the inside or the outside?" They ignored me, Heist-style.

"I smell rain," said Donna.

"Does that mean tonight's fire ceremony is canceled? I was looking forward to that. I brought a *lot* of sticks."

"We'll start a fire," said Anita.

"I could sleep in the Jeep," I said. "If you show me how to get back there."

They ignored this too.

"Why did you bring me here?" I felt feisty enough to lay my cards on the table, if it meant I got to see a few of theirs.

"We thought you should see what the Bears consisted of," said Anita. "Conrad Shockley got you up to speed. He's the short course."

"Yeah, so what's the deal with all the bikers and ex-cons? I was expecting brocaded vests and drum circles." I didn't want to say how disappointing I found the Rabbits as well. I'd been waiting to see womb-based architecture, wax-dripping ceremonies, harmonium-flavored incantation. Instead everything was flayed and stark, life barely clinging to an exhausted surface. They were survivors of the catastrophe that hadn't happened yet, which was maybe the point. They were readier than I was.

"Listen in the night," said Anita. "You'll hear the drums."

"I thought the colony was founded by a lot of idealistic hippies." I found I couldn't quit needling them. "Or was that just the women? You couldn't find better boyfriends?"

"The Bears all started as hippies," said Anita. "But then, everyone does. Humans are born polymorphous and free."

"Not me. I was born in a short black skirt. But go on."

"The challenge is to stay what you call a hippie, isn't it?" said Donna. "They failed." She spoke while gazing off, into the rain she smelled and I couldn't yet see. I didn't doubt her. We'd come to Neptune Lodge for coffee and philosophy and a roof.

"The desert wore them down," I said. "Not like you guys."

"Not in the same way."

"Maybe they just got old. Though that doesn't explain the young ones."

"Men are stuck in the past," said Donna. "Really, you could say men *are* the past of the human species. They need a lot of help from us with that."

"What kind of help would you say you're giving Shockley in there?"

"Shockley's beyond any help besides listening," she admitted. "But the listening's worthwhile on both sides, I think. A lot comes out of them at the end, when their souls are separating from their bodies. I wouldn't call it wisdom exactly, but *meaning*. I like to try to take the meaning in with my highest loving attention."

"I think you're flattering yourselves, but never mind. What are you going to do about Heist? They've got more than drums in mind for tonight. Heist came in right on schedule."

"We can't do anything about that."

"You like it," I said, realizing it with the words.

"Let me show you your room," said Anita. It was an Igor line, if you could imagine Jane Fonda getting cast in the Igor role.

35

BUT THERE WERE NO BARS ON THE WINDOWS, NO LOCK ON THE DOOR. THEY
didn't care about me. Or, just one of them did. She came after
nightfall, while Anita and some others were out building the fire
on the ridge. They were preparing something special, a bonfire,
whether for me or as their counterpart to the drums, a signal to
beam across the dark in the direction of the Bears.

Spark came to the open window. I got the distinct impression that this one entered right-angled buildings only through
windows, when she entered right-angled buildings at all. I didn't
see her gun, which was fine with me.

"Hello," I said.

Spark blinked at me, once. She didn't blink often.

"Is there something you want to tell me?"

"I've seen your friend." She said it as though Arabella had
come to her in a dream, but I didn't doubt it. Everything might
be like a dream to her. Anyway, I couldn't afford to doubt.

"Is she okay?"

Spark nodded.

"That's the best thing you could have told me, then. Thank
you."

"I'll see her tonight."

"How?"

"I'm going to watch the Bears. She'll be there."

"Watch the fight for a new king, you mean?"

She nodded again, again unblinkingly.

"Can you take me there?"

"It's a long walk in the sand at night. It's going to be beauti-ful, but I don't know if you can do it."

"I'd like to try."

She seemed to be thinking. "There's going to be a lot of light from the stars, but the ground isn't flat."

"I brought comfortable shoes," I said. I grabbed my purse, then climbed out the window, not because I thought the other Rabbits would have stopped me—they were all out by the fire—but to show Spark that I could.

PART IV

NIGHT AND MORNING

36

AT FIRST I MISSED THE ARENA. I WAS SO MESMERIZED BY THE SKY. MY feet had made their sanction in the crisp ground, and I'd been gazing upward, after the first few hundred yards and further reassurance from Spark about the hibernation of rattlesnakes. I'd had no particular difficulty with the walk. People from other parts of the country always underestimate how comfortable New Yorkers are with distance walking. In rhythm behind her along the soft contour, the easy way around the pilings and arroyos, I began to feel like Spark's shadow, a function of her animal prowling, even if she was the one doing all the navigational work. We'd left the glow of the Rabbits' bonfire, though not before I'd caught a reflected glint of the gunmetal on Spark's rope belt.

Now, perhaps half a mile beyond, I'd finally understood what city dwellers meant by *light pollution*. The dark opened my eyes. The sky flooded in, without boundary. It was sick with stars, a hundred for every one I felt ought to exist. I had to keep an eye on them all at once, in case they began to fall. I dreaded the unveiling of the moon, a prospect as unbearable as I'd once thought only the sun could be. But the moon, if it was really there, appeared snarled in low clouds as brackish as mud. I couldn't foresee it making any progress.

So I was like a toddler, spinning in place, making herself drunk on vertigo, when the arena, a kind of natural outdoor amphitheater, opened before and below us. I'd have been likelier to see it if they'd lit the torches, but they hadn't. The torches waited instead, scattered amid other upright shadows on the desert floor, the Joshua trees, the tilted stones. This was it, what my altered attention had learned to tabulate: tilted stones and their shadows. There were no buildings here, no skyscrapers or sheds, no busy lanes of traffic or jets queued for takeoff to resort destinations, no crappy chain stores or alluring hipster boutiques. No person pulled another an espresso shot. I couldn't scroll up or down or swipe left or right. Only stones and shadows of stones, Joshua trees, unlit torches, and, as my eye accustomed to the scene, a scattering of human creatures out under the bowl of night. These negligible few resided on perches above the crater floor, like fleas on a punctured soufflé of salt and waste, inferior to the star-stuff that illuminated and scorned them. These were Bears, I supposed.

Well, I was here for human creatures. For Arabella, I kept reminding myself. Never mind Bears, or firstborn absconded Bear-kings-elect. Find Arabella, and get out.

Spark navigated us along the upper rim, avoiding contact with the clustered spectators. The nearest few looked, predictably, like Santa Claus, their body type not even gussied up with a Harley motorbike and a Germanic helmet. Others, trickier to pick out of the landscape, more resembled ambulatory cacti, or twists of barbed wire, men like residue of the desert floor, in blackened jeans and thin wifebeaters. Here and there, cigarette or joint tips flared orange. The breeze through the arena carried faint sulfurous and meaty odors, and grim snorting laughter. Some of the smell persisted when the wind died. That was me, suffused with dog hair and woodsmoke from the Baldy cabin, growing rank in clothes two days old, in underwear I'd saturated a couple of times necking with Heist.

I followed Spark along the periphery, not yet descending,

though there looked to be plenty of room to navigate a nearer view. I unslung my purse and dug to confirm the obvious—no signal. Seeing the battery nearly dead, I powered it down. My fingers found a lipstick tube. I impulsively drew it out and applied, puckering coverage to the edges. Spark stared.

"My lips are wrecked," I said, not mentioning I'd been routinely abrading them against a steel wool man-mask. "Unless you're sporting some kind of goat milk balm, this is all I've got." In fact, I'd acted on a vestigial *threshold-of-the-party* impulse, as if stepping from an elevator in a Chinatown loft space.

I was smarter than to think I could arrest Heist's notice with Red Amour Crème Smooth by Laura Mercier. Wasn't I?

"You want some?"

She shook her head.

"How's my teeth? Never mind. Take me to my friend now."

"She's not here yet."

"How do you know that?"

"She's part of the ceremony. That's what I heard."

"Even better, then. Let's go kidnap her from the green room."

Spark turned her head three-quarters, as if perusing modern art. "You're funny, Manhattan."

"How do you know to call me Manhattan? You been going through my wallet?"

"You talk a lot, that's all. Come on, we're meeting up with a guy I know." She sounded like a teenager. "You'll like him. He talks a lot too."

"A Bear?"

"They aren't all Bears, despite what you might have heard."

"Heard from Anita, you mean?"

"Yeah. Her and Donna."

"Oh." I was trying to talk less, so I left it at that. We crept over the ridge, going to see a guy Spark knew. My new life was rich and full.

THE KID SPARK LIKED—I SAW THAT IMMEDIATELY, THAT HE WAS A KID, and how much she liked him—could talk, all right. He was lodged up in a little triangle of rock, perhaps something someone had once arranged at great effort, with an excellent view of the surround and the pit below.

He was tall and beautiful with Jesus-y hair and the kind of beard that's adolescent in its parameters—still not filled in everywhere along his jaw, or very high on the cheeks, but splendidly unkempt where it grew. His eyes were pale blue even in the dark, and there was something knowing and beatific in them. He recognized Spark and accepted my presence too, and handed us a thermos to drink from. I took it, expecting water. It wasn't water but some kind of hard desert cider, perhaps fermented agave nectar. I knew it was silly for me to trust it and unhelpful in the best scenario even as I took a couple of hearty slugs.

"A night like this is a test of one's concentration," this angelic youth said, by way of welcome. He imparted real warmth in the remark.

"How so?" I asked.

"We're embedded in the dream, but it doesn't actually care about us. It's very harsh to consider, really. I feel a weight on my chest like the embodiment of a large animal, but it probably isn't trying to comfort me. There's a taste in my mouth like burnt flowers. I haven't smoked anything, but I did eat some seeds."

I didn't know how far I should try to follow him. "I'm Phoebe," I said. "What's your name?"

"I'm not entertaining a name at present."

"Fair enough. I'm trying to keep things simple, myself. I'm trying to find my lost friend, before someone gets hurt."

"Simple is good! Just don't take anything personally. When the big storm hits, they'll be staging their drama underwater."

"You mean the Bear battle?" I glanced at the arena below. Shapes stirred in the gloom, preparations perhaps, though the torches remained unlit. A soundtrack had begun to float over the night. Someone, then three or four someones, beating on what sounded like plastic tubs. The tonality was too ticky-tacky and hollow to meet the old *Iron John* standard.

"Yes," the beautiful boy said. "It seems important to us because we're human animals, so we can't help but think the story matters. But this whole silly game could be washed out."

"Like a rain delay, you mean?"

He didn't blink. "I played ball in college, second base. One day at the plate, I took a line drive to the temple. Telling the coach I wasn't coming back was one of the hardest days of my life. I dropped out of anthropology too. I'd been living as a vegan, but even that couldn't get me close to the things I really wanted to know about."

"So you came to see the Bears."

"People worry too much about particular animal embodiments," he said. "It's good just to recognize we're large mammals, and how odd that is. What I like about the desert people is that it's the only place you can have an honest conversation about the apocalypse. That's as true of the guy at the gas station on Twentynine Palms as any of us way out here."

"What seeds did you eat?" said Spark. She'd moved into the

shelter of his stone triangle. She was drawn, as I couldn't help but be myself, to his extraordinary sweet limbs, his fulsome reeling brain. His beauty made me feel differently about the desert, about the Bears. It made me feel differently about Spark too. Before, she'd had starvation. I could envy her cheekbones, but not much else. Seeing her crouched beside him, I understood she had starvation and wild youthful fucking, likely on a regular basis.

"Dry autumn seeds," he told her. "Datura. It's a pretty strong trip. I vomited and urinated a chalk-white stream. The two of you, for example, are embodied as canine right now. Before you came along, I was enjoying a discussion with a being made of cornhusk and cinder. I grew up near a cornfield, but that doesn't mean it belonged to me."

I didn't recognize the drug he'd named, but I grasped the principle. I'd been around tripping persons before. "The people talking about the apocalypse aren't always disinterested parties," I suggested. "Some of them might be trying to bring it about."

"We all did it," he said. "We ruined the earth."

If you were in the market for a *Men of Global Warming* calendar, the boy made an ideal Mr. January. But I felt a rage flare in me, that he'd rolled us into an absolving ball of confusion with the toxic villains in suits, the grabbers and falsifiers, the Machiavellian extractors and disruptors and enclosers, the Electoral College. Perhaps all of them were large mammals, sure, but not all possessing human souls.

"Not all of us," I said. "Some of us, a handful, stuck it to the rest." What had the boy in the hole on the mountain been, most likely, but a rhapsodic truant like this one, before donning those furs? "You need to leave here," I said, feeling suddenly parental. "Someone might kill you early. What a shame it would be, to miss your apocalypse."

"It's impossible to miss. We're inside it constantly."

Maybe I'd tasted some datura seed residue from the lip of the thermos we'd been sharing, but his words made just enough sense to me. Here in the desert we were enclosed in an unboundaried thing that *apocalypse* might be the word for. Somewhere, I could smell kerosene ignition, a flavor more evil, I suspected, than the kid's apparition of cornhusk and cinder.

It was an out-of-fashion word, *evil*. But I'd gotten more friendly with it in the past few months. It did some heavy lifting that I liked.

"They're capable of anything," I said, to remind myself.

"I'm free of expectations."

"That's fine, but they're not as free as you. They're into death, only not their own. What did you think you came here to see?"

"Hollow and circular rituals are really great. It's a way of humbling yourself to the chimerical dream of civilization."

This was all very interesting, but as I girded myself for a descent, I decided I had to get free of this kid. I'd need Spark with me still, to function as my surrogate Rabbit eyes, to recognize familiar and dangerous players in this game. Perhaps also for the gun strung at her waist. But her boyfriend was excess baggage, not only because he was unmistakably incapable of stealth. So long as he was nearby, I'd be increasingly prone to contact-tripping—the infectious risk of his seed-born philosophy.

"Just remember that a man is meant to try to kill a man," I said. I took Spark by the hand, and she followed.

"They'll look tiny from up here," the boy said.

"Yeah, well, I'll still be rooting for a rainout."

38

THE SIZE OF THE ARENA WASN'T PLAIN UNTIL THE TORCHES WERE LIT.
Their light pollution and plumes of soot blotted the interstellar
vastness that crowned the desert. But in its place the breadth and
depth of the pit we'd entered was illuminated, partly by their
inadequacy to do more than pierce its darkness with islands of
light. As Spark and I crept downward along the stadium's face,
the distance to the bottom became more evident. Pockets of
dark remained, and we stuck to those. The night was growing
cold, the stars clouding over, and I envied the spectators' little
fires. I missed Jessie. Spark didn't look much like a cuddler.

I spotted Anita and Donna, with a couple of other senior
Rabbits, in their own high perch on the crater, the equivalent of
a box at the opera. I shouldn't have been surprised, I suppose. It
was Friday night, if I'd kept count, and this was the only show
in town. My disenchantment felt familiar, like learning that
Chuck Schumer was gym buddies with Jeff Sessions, that all the
top dogs gathered in tuxedos to drink martinis when partisan
Kabuki was done for the day. Other women were visible in the
stands as well, not looking so much like Rabbits. They were desert dwellers of another stripe, perhaps the Bear-groupies Heist
had mentioned.

I once rode a crowded 4 train, the Lexington line, in a car
cowed by the presence of a newly released Rikers inmate. The

status was unmistakable for the terrifying, grenade-pin paranoia seething in his eyes. He'd been too long away from anything like a packed subway car, where bodies weren't encroaching on his in some meaningful jockeying for power but only helplessly, trying to get to work. Each time anyone came too near or made the mistake of meeting his glance, he nearly uncorked from his own skin in their direction. It was also unmistakable for the man's obscene slab musculature, the kind otherwise seen only on top international leading men, those who've compensated for the lizard terror they inspire in other humans with soft, puppyish eyes and sheepish grins, to remind you that shows of force are accompanied by lives of prissy luxury, by big hearts and steroidally shrunken and harmless genitalia.

Not Solitary Love. The king of the Bears, like the man on the train, embraced his terror, and that of his witnesses. He wore a bearskin costume that flapped around his shoulders, bound with straps across his chest, and nothing underneath. His shadowy junk swung heavily, as if he were never less than slightly aroused. Even from where I perched, when he stepped near the torches, I could see his eyes were too wide open, and inside his beard his mouth was a terrible wreck. I remembered that from the train too. There were barbells in prisons, not so much dentistry. You had to remember to floss.

But it was a mistake to lean too heavily on my involuntary association, that of Solitary Love with the parolee on the Lex. I was consoling myself, thinking that way. I wasn't in New York anymore. The man on the train had been probably half an hour from his next encounter with law enforcement, perhaps a day or two away from re-arrest or death by baton chokehold. We might have feared him on the train, but it was our train, not his. Solitary Love was a true distillation of this desert, and we were at his mercy. Spark's nameless tripping boyfriend was right. Solitary Love's look and manner were a correction to what the nameless boy had called the chimerical dream of civilization. Seeing the Bear King stride into the flickering stony rink, it wasn't even so much that all human charity and feeling, all taste and order and sense had been dispatched, rendered null—well, it was that, but it was more, too. Seeing him, you kind of wished it to be. Bring the flood.

It was at this moment I did the math and realized that we were some number of hours into the new world. Barack Obama was no longer president.

Other figures scurried along the edges of the arena where Solitary Love waited, but it was easy enough, next, to spot Heist. He was the other guy in a bearskin, head bent low, seated on a rock. Beneath the costume he wore his red leathers and dirty jeans, the usual costume that caused my heart to lurch. He was alone.

A pulse began to beat in me to match the drums. "We have to get closer," I said to Spark.

39

THE FIRST RAINDROPS BEGAN TO PELT OUR UNCOVERED ARMS AND DOT the dry rocks. The two bodies rose and moved nearer to each other in the arena, a space now described by a closing noose of bodies. Outside this ring, four women wearing beaded shawls covering bikinis or less than bikinis danced in and out of a low, flickering fire, but when they were near enough to be outlined I saw they were shorter and thicker than Arabella, who anyhow had taken a lot of African dance classes at Saint Ann's and was unlikely to move her arms in such hackneyed ways. (Then again, the quality of drumming here was ruinously low.) The spectators were otherwise men—Bears, I had to suppose. I didn't know how much farther into their company we were likely to be able to pass, though Spark remained intrepid. I had to salute her for that. We scrambled from shadow to shadow, the breadth of the bowl still opening before us, the rim, its stars now completely darked over with thunderhead, threateningly far.

The two bodies collided at the same moment the sky opened like a door. Needling rain instantly ran in the dust at our feet like electric current working its way through circuitry. The water hit the kerosene lamps, which didn't douse but threw up replying gouts of malodorous steam. The drumming didn't quit— the signature of drumming, I guess. But it had begun to be subsumed in human voices, screams and bellowing, dark jeers.

Through curtains of rain and belching steam, with intensifying cacophony bouncing off the shattered walls of the pit, it wasn't difficult for Spark and me to descend into the spectacle. Then came a frenzied time.

Solitary Love had broken Heist's nose, possibly with a first blow. Heist circled with his head low, crouching beneath his opponent's eyeline, but I still made out the purple gnarl of injury between his brows, the course of red-bright seepage on his chin and neck and jacket. From that moment I was screaming. I learned something about a fight crowd then, entering one for the first time, a place I'd never wanted or expected to be. If you cared in any way for one of the combatants, you weren't separate from them, but inside the fight with them, and time slowed. The rain came in cascades, a metronome, but all else went still and deaf, then stuttered again into demented blurting action. Heist hatcheted at his opponent's ribs with his hands clasped into a single fist, then slipped back, feet careening in the mud. I was side by side with others, inciting and admonishing the fighters who inflamed and disappointed us. Who knew what anyone wanted? We might all be screaming for Heist, or for Solitary Love. We might each have a separate fight and a separate fighter whose pain was our own, yet this incoherence made us one thing together. It might not be too late to go home and read Joyce Carol Oates after all, if the rains didn't, as prophesied, fill up the bowl of stone and drown us. Heist, in the mud, clutched at one of Solitary Love's legs, rolling to avoid the other. I screamed and screamed and screamed.

Arabella was screaming too, when I spotted her at last. She'd been suddenly pushed to the front of the throng, nearly into the warfare between the Bear kings. The private-school New York kid I recalled taking to see *The Grand Budapest Hotel* wasn't *embodied* as a Rabbit, nor as a she-Bear. Instead, she'd been granted some species of her own, a falcon or desert crow. They'd put her in a feather crown, peacock plumes now sopping, with a necklace of claws across her breasts. The ornaments were maybe nothing more than chicken feet salvaged from a barbecue picnic, but the effect was ominous as shit.

She stood otherwise naked in the downpour, tall and stunningly pale, making no attempt to cover herself. Like all millennials, apparently, Arabella shaved her bush—all I could think was how cold she must be. She hadn't cast herself as the abductee here, though, no matter if the whole picture screamed Stockholm syndrome. She wasn't apart from the frenzy that wreaked us, she was within it too, barking at the fighters, convulsing herself in pornographic rage, as much a figure of chaos as anyone present, including Heist and Solitary Love. I don't know if this qualified as a ceremony, but whatever it was, she was part of it, all right. I was too. My relief at seeing her alive stood in a kind of suspension, as though my emotions were as much prisoner of this ritual as she was.

I believe Arabella was shouting at Heist to die, though I'd never ask her later if this was so. She hadn't seen Heist before, after all. She probably couldn't imagine a rescuer who'd come in such a form, if she'd imagined rescue from Solitary Love's kingdom at all, as opposed to escape or submission or ruling it herself. Anyway, he wasn't her rescuer, I was.

Solitary Love's foot found purchase in Heist's armpit. After slipping off too many times to count, it didn't slip, but crunched downward. I heard it, and Heist's broken grunting exhalation, even over the drums and the rain and my own screaming. It was then that I couldn't be held at the edge of the circle but had gone inside myself. My hand went into my purse, not to replenish the lipstick I'd surely chewed off and let be rinsed down my throat by the rain but for the klaxon, that tiny rape horn I'd tried and failed to explain to Heist back in the Airstream. I found it and moved in sheer animal frenzy. Even amid the torrents of rain and diesel steam and human noise, the hate-music I blasted in Solitary Love's ear—I shoved the aerosol horn in as far as it could go, *I sound-fucked him brutally in his side-brain*—stood out like nothing else in that glistening stone arena. His murder-sized forearm detonated outward to wallop me free of him, bruising my shoulders and jaw and brain all at once and instantly. I was caught before I fell. It was Spark, behind me.

But I'd placed the prison-built giant under arrest, in the original sense of the word: he was *stopped*. All else stopped too, for one shocked instant, apart from the rain and smoke. That instant was all Charles Heist needed. A torn mammal, parts of him not working, he rose without standing. Instead, Heist appeared to climb Solitary Love's body like a ladder, hell-bent for the soft parts at the top. Heist's head turned sideways, and his teeth went into Love's neck. I viewed the act with admiration, even if I'd never have attempted it myself, but it was the behavior of Heist's left hand that made something plummet to the floor of me.

The hand had come up holding a stone, and with it smashed at Love's eye of its own volition until the socket collapsed. The stone was tossed aside. Heist's fingers went around what remained of Love's eyeball, deeper than I wanted to know about, making a fist inside Love's face. By this time the great body had toppled. Heist crouched over it, blood on his mouth and chin. His hand wrenched in and meddled. I turned away before I couldn't.

We'd had the same instinct, to assault the behemoth's head. The rest of Love was too much, but stuck on top was still a human face with flesh openings, parts that couldn't be beefed in a prison gym. Even if Heist's approach made my little horn look pretty gentle, I felt I shouldn't judge. Such idiot thoughts danced in my own brain, but it was really my body that judged. All the animal fear that had attached to Solitary Love now flowed to Heist instead, and I was poisoned. I'd been wrong, before. Solitary Love had nothing on his opponent, appearance aside. Heist had raged for his life like a creature not even a prison-monstered man could contend with. He should have been called the Atavistic Detective.

The rain fell like hammers. My body went on making decisions. Exploiting the embrace of my rescuer, I'd gotten my two hands around the butt of the pistol at Spark's hip. It shocked me to remove it, like I'd separated a part of her wiry little body, a thing made of bone. But again, my brain was only catching up, or failing to. Someone had once told me you never know who you'll be in an emergency. I discovered that apparently my response was to try to make myself into the whole emergency. I pointed the gun at Heist, who lay groaning in the mud with Love's head-insides in his hand, and I pointed it at Love's twitching dying body, which sported a bowed erection, a fountain of blood and the reeking contents of evacuated bowels, all at once, a thing I wouldn't have otherwise known was possible— *Oh, the Places You'll Go!*

I pointed it at anyone near to Arabella. She stood frozen, the entranced feather-creature, maybe beginning to recognize that I'd come for her but also that doing so had driven me insane. I pointed the gun at everyone simultaneously, a frantic wheeling action. The rain was like a medium we should breathe in, if only we could grow gills. Meanwhile my voice made words out of my screaming.

"STOP STOP STOP YOU FUCKERS YOU GOD-DAMN INSANE BASTARDS! LOOK WHAT JUST HAPPENED TO THEM!" The words strung from me like banners across open sky. "WHY DO YOU THINK YOU CAN DO THIS SHIT?" No one answered my question, though I believe to this day it was a valid one. "DO YOU EVEN KNOW WHAT'S GOING ON, YOU STUPID FUCKING ASSHOLES? DID YOU FUCKERS EVEN *VOTE*?"

In the awed silence, I stepped up and wrenched a shawl from one of the zaftig dancers. It was soaked, but I thrust it at Arabella. "Put it on." I pointed with the gun, not intending to threaten harm, but because it had become my voice, my directing body. It struck me that people with guns often felt this way. Awesome epiphany! "Take her," I said to Spark. I meant for them to climb the crater. Spark took Arabella and they began to go.

Now, with no cessation in the rain, the tableau began to unfreeze. The magic spell of my klaxon and insanity and Spark's pistol began to wear off, it seemed. The Bears resumed movement through the steam, like the gorillas in the Museum of Natural History, the stuffed ones in the foreground, but also those painted on the distant mountains, all coming to sluggish life. There was no pane of glass between me and them. I stepped backward, fearing them more than I did Heist's broken form or Love's corpse behind me.

"Get back!" I screamed, but my voice, like my mojo, had begun to fail me. Nobody was cowed except the dancer whose shawl I'd stolen.

Several of the Bears appeared with an old wooden door held aloft. They moved toward me. I wondered if it were meant to be used as a shield, to plant between themselves and my gun. But they ignored me. The door was a shield not for battle, but for bearing up their wounded firstborn. Rather tenderly they lowered it and knelt and edged the moaning Heist onto the surface of crackled paint, the old bronze-plate address for some house that had fallen and vanished in the desert, leaving only the door.

I think I stood dumbfounded, my gun hand wavering, lost in seeing Heist's beautiful strange body, the violence in it now expunged, reduced to this wrecked totem. I didn't know how many reversals I could suffer, but I'd suffered one more—I pined for him. Then Anita and Donna took me, each at one elbow. They turned me from the scene, to start together up the near path, now coursing with mud, to follow where Spark and Arabella had gone.

"No!" I pulled free. "Let go of him!" To Anita I said, "We have to take Charles."

She shook her head. "They won't let you. He's their king."

"A crippled king," I said.

"A crippled king is good for all concerned. It's what we like."

"He needs us."

"They'll care for him. Your friend needs you. Come."

In my rage I pointed the gun at her. "Fuck you, I'll do it alone."

Anita smiled at me. "Everybody knows Spark's gun has no bullets."

Even through the blaze of my fever, this explained a few things.

40

OUT OF THAT CAULDRON I BEGAN TO RETURN TO MYSELF. A DUNE BUGGY
had parked itself as near to the lip as possible. At the wheel,
Donna. Spark had helped Arabella into the back seat, where
they huddled beneath a ragged black umbrella. Anita guided
me lightly, her hand on the small of my back, like a lover's. The
dune buggy's engine idled, the headlamps beaming through the
rain. It was like the stove, another one of the Rabbits' working
machines.

I handed Spark her pistol. She took it, saying nothing but
gesturing for me to join them in the vehicle's back seat. I couldn't
imagine how to speak to Arabella, toward whom my fear and
love had turned temporarily to rage. I felt for her as one might for
a teenager who'd been discovered to be self-harming—cutting,
say, or bulimic. Yet as with such a teenager, it was enough, for
the moment, that her body was rescued, that her body was still
alive. Words and emotions could wait.

I scanned the horizon. Something drew my attention. On
the far side of the arena, the Bears marched with torches alongside the stretcher-door on which Heist rested, making it unmistakable in the night. I stood a minute watching it go, and no one
hurried me. Then I got into the dune buggy.

41

DRIVING BACK, HUDDLED UNDER SPARK'S UMBRELLA, I WAS SURE I WAS
meant to be holding Arabella, speaking reassuring words as I
ushered her back to civilization. In fact, we clung together. Her
lips were bluish. I couldn't speak. My body shook, and I'd peed
myself at some point, though nobody but me would know in
this rain. The convulsions gripping me seemed to align me to the
body I'd helped kill. Solitary Love had had to die to be proven
human. I had no more to offer Arabella than she did me, at that
moment. Maybe less. Anyhow, who knew if anyone was usher-
ing anyone to civilization? We could have been pointed anywhere, to the next arena.

Yet as we came out of the realm of smoke and drumming
and my own blood-rage, I reattuned to the earworm of my own
thinking—the hum of self-adjusting, like a pop song never silenced in my skull, to which I only intermittently attended. One
part of my brain was still busy composing the red-state tell-all
op-ed, the career I'd salvage from the ruins, my triumphant return to New York with surefire viral content. Only now it had
expanded, an epic including Heist and the battle in the desert
pit, my own complicity, the things I had to teach you. Probably
the *Sunday Magazine* was a better destination, or *Harper's*—it
could even be a Folio. Out of that, needless to say, would come a
book deal. This disassociation from what I'd just seen and done

wasn't subsequent, but something that had been writing itself continuously, even while I'd clung to Love's shoulder, even while I'd held the gun.

There's more. On another mental track, one completely unreconciled to my dream of fame and the reclaiming of my cosmopolitan life, was its opposite: I was a Rabbit now. I finally understood something that I believed Anita and Donna, my guides piloting the buggy, had been trying to let me know. It was the message they'd intended by showing me their downer, Shockley: that to be a Rabbit was to kill a Bear, or be willing to. To be a Rabbit was to take some of a Bear inside you, by force, and therefore to be both things—that was what made Rabbits bigger than Bears, who were actually to be pitied. These thoughts were, I'll agree, insane. But they only furthered themselves, against my will. If I was part Rabbit and part Bear, I wasn't unlike Heist, was I? He and I belonged together—I'd been right before, only not known in the least why. Now I knew.

These incommensurable trains of thought would cohabit in my skull through the rest of that night and long through the morning, until Arabella and I cut loose of the Mojave, or were set free. They made little sense together—no Rabbit would dream of viral fame—yet they nested easily. The first just entailed that I pretended to myself that I was only pretending the latter. Either involved pretending I was not essentially in ruins.

42

THERE WAS FIRE AGAIN, OR STILL, DESPITE THE RAIN. I FELT ABSURDLY proud of the flame's persistence, as if my little stick-gathering session was at its heart. Maybe it was. The rain had tapered. The wind that brought it had died altogether. The little accommodations, the lean-tos and parasols, the half-covered teepee structures that ringed the fire pit, these were enough for us all to shelter there. Neptune Lodge was in sight; a desk lamp even showed through an unshaded window, proving the existence of electricity, but it didn't call us away from the fire. My bed, the room with the closing door, didn't tempt me. I had work to do at the fire circle, though I couldn't say what it was.

More Rabbits were here than could have been hidden in the dark pockets of the arena, surely. Nevertheless, this gathering had the air of a vigil or witnessing council in the aftermath of that other scene, as though the fire had been built in its anticipation. Those Bearish energies needed a decanting to the desert sky, in the form of Rabbit smoke and murmuring. Someone played a soft guitar, open circular chords. I saw Lorrie there, my twig-sister. She smiled when she saw me seeing her. In another place around the circle, I saw Spark, more settled than at any time before. The nameless boy was with her there, seeming to me obviously more Rabbit than Bear now. I felt only love toward all.

I sat with Arabella. Anita had given us dry clothes, thrift store sweatpants and T-shirts, pulled from a green plastic trash bag. We changed in the open, like women in a locker room. My pants said *Juicy* across the ass. Then we'd been placed under a triangular canopy and given a little space by the others. We weren't talking yet, but communing on a New York Bear Survivor's solidarity-group wavelength, or so I could allow myself to imagine. Her lips had returned to a normal color. The fire was all we wanted, at first anyway.

But things traveled around the circle, blankets, bongs, substances to drink or eat. A younger Rabbit, one beaming a terrifying surplus of warmth and acceptance, put wooden bowls in our hands. There was a hot and sweet mash inside. She explained it was made of desert stuff, piñon and chia, cactus, mesquite pods. Aromatic with juniper, it seemed a thing you'd serve a child on Christmas morning, and we scooped it to our mouths with our fingers, gratefully. Before she passed, the Rabbit said, "It's so nice to see you again, Phoebe," but she said it directly to Arabella. Besides, I didn't know her.

"Were you using my name?" I said to Arabella when the Rabbit was gone. I'd forgotten.

Arabella nodded, facing the fire. Her hands were in the muff pocket of a large shapeless hoodie, punching it down over her knees. She could have been twelve, on a beach at Truro.

"It's okay," I said, not wanting her to feel censured. This desert, I now understood, was a place where things came to be unaffixed from old purposes. So my name had voyaged ahead of me, to taste lives I couldn't imagine, perhaps to do some work in protecting Arabella. I didn't own it.

But I couldn't keep from wanting to know whether I'd rescued her, and what from. Heist was gone, with parts of me along. Residual purposes were all I had. There weren't words for the unreal loss I'd suffered, so I fell to my mission statement—my quote-unquote core values.

"I promised Roslyn I'd find you," I said. I called her Roslyn instead of *your mother* to say I knew we were all just people now.

"Okay." She continued to stare at the fire-impervious-to-rain. It was easy to be transfixed by it.

"Are you sad?"

"I don't know."

"Did you have a . . . Bearfriend?" I knew she'd understand this conflation.

"I guess I had a couple, yes."

"You don't want to go back, do you?"

"No. Those people are pretty boring."

It wouldn't have been my word, but I was relieved.

"Was Solitary Love your Bearfriend?"

She shook her head. "He was strange. He called me his eventual queen. It was all kind of *Game of Thrones*, actually."

"Were you scared?"

Arabella only shrugged. I didn't want to raise the question of whether she'd seen the bodies on Mount Baldy, of what forms of violence she'd had to absorb and make regular within herself. I couldn't make these things regular for either of us, so I preferred that she seemed not totally disarranged. I could imagine she'd endured nothing, though I knew she'd at least had a front row seat for the duel of kings and for my own performance there. That, and been naked in feathers and a necklace of claws. But if she was fated to disintegrate, let it wait until Brooklyn and Roslyn.

"The other man," I said. "The one who killed him—"

"I know who he is, Phoebe. Charlie-boy. Baby. The First-born."

"Charles Heist, yes."

"Was he *your* Bearfriend?" Now it was her turn to look at me, and mine to look into the fire.

"I think maybe."

"They told me all about your man," she said.

"Oh, did they?"

She actually had a glint in her eye, one I liked to see. Mocking the wretchedness of my dating life had been one of her teenage sports. "Yup," she said. "He's the super-boring Bear who doesn't want to be one, who keeps rescuing the Bear and Rabbit kids, even when they don't want to be rescued." That she was capable of goosing me this way was hopeful, the sort of signal I wished I could beam directly to Roslyn. The precocious girl was in there.

"Yes, well, you know that's how I like them—ambivalent. Crazy and mixed up." *Plus, Arabella, I am the super-boring Rabbit who is rescuing you whether you like it or not.* But I didn't say this.

"He sounds like your typical lame Phoebe boyfriend. I'm lucky I didn't catch your taste in men. He's going to make a lame king too."

"If he lives."

"He's got a better chance than Solitary Love." She actually sounded bitter, but I tried not to take it personally. Around this time, as my adrenaline surge receded, the Nancy Drew instinct returned, and I considered how, for all I'd witnessed tonight, Solitary Love didn't remotely fit the description Sage had given, of the older man, friend of monks, who'd led her and Arabella down from the mountain. Was I pursuing a phantom? I'd need to ask Arabella if such a person existed. But first I had to get her fully back on my side. As it stood, the war in the pit still raged inside us.

"Even if we have different favorite Bears, we can still be friends, can't we?" I tried to locate the proper joshing tone.

It might have worked.

"It's okay," she said wistfully. "I don't really have any favorite Bears." This sounded like permission to do what I'd done—come and find her, I mean, not help murder a man. I wasn't seeking permission for that.

The fire and the aimless strumming guitar, plus the bellyful of hot piñon and chia, was having an effect, not only on us but on others in the circle. It was almost as though the bowls held some dose of soporific enchantment. By the time we'd finished licking our fingers, Arabella and I were settling ourselves on the ground, curling together like Heist's dogs for a snooze. My purse was dry enough to put beneath my head for a pillow. Anita came to put a blanket over us, and we left the party for a while. In this, we had company.

43

A BIT LATER WE WERE AWAKE AGAIN. THE TEMPERATURE HAD DROPPED. Someone had built up the fire. It still rained lightly but the clouds now showed gaps where the stars raged through. Spark and her nameless Jesus crawled within our shelter. We four shared a joint and listened for a while as he talked about the coming flood, the places in the desert that would soon be beachfront, the drowned cemeteries and malls. The boy had a lot of facts about water. He also told us nuclear war was a metaphor.

I broke into his monologue. "It's not a metaphor."

"I know why you would say that!" His tone was very understanding. "But think about this for a minute. The things we're taking out of the ground and roasting into the atmosphere, they're made of atoms, right? The word 'nuclear' comes from 'nuclei.'"

"I know that."

"The stratum of particulate matter that's shrouding the sun and boiling the dolphins in the sea, it's basically nuclear winter in slow motion. Did you ever see that movie where Inspector Clouseau is a German scientist in a wheelchair who wants to take all the beautiful women down into an underground fallout shelter?"

"Sure," volunteered Arabella. "My dad made me watch that movie, like, a dozen times before I was twelve."

"That's not surprising. It means a lot to people of a certain age. They talk about the Cold War like it's something that they survived, or averted. Actually, it's a record of something that's still happening, and we're trapped inside it. The bombs already fell. But they're also still falling. The bombs are named Ford and CIA and Google. When I was at Davos, I realized these people are basically just Inspector Clouseau, rich people planning a really sexy bomb shelter for when the dark falls on the rest of us."

"Wait, you were at Davos?" I said.

"Once, yeah. My parents go every year. It only took me one visit to understand, though. Sometimes it's easiest to hide the truth in plain sight."

"What truth is that?" I said.

"They're not going underground. That would be stupid! The water flows downward, remember? They're going to the mountaintops. That's what Davos *is*!"

"Okay, well first of all, I think you mean Dr. Strangelove, not Inspector Clouseau. Second, I don't think the two things are the same." In truth, I wasn't even sure what two things I meant weren't the same, only that elements had drifted together that would have to be put apart in order to think about them straight. It was possible that what I meant was my life. I was in the desert, drinking something from a communal bowl that I'd been told was called Mormon tea. The sun was coming up and Donald Trump had been president for a whole day. Not only was I not writing an op-ed or *Harper's* Folio, I was debating Peter Sellers and Davos with a trust fund Jesus tripping on datura seeds. I might even lose the debate.

Then Arabella looked at me and said, "Too much Bear-splaining," and we both began shrieking.

"What?" said the nameless boy, alarmed.

"Bearsplaining," said Arabella, through laughter. "The world is ending, okay, we get it."

"I'm not a Bear." He came off a little sulky.

"Whatever. Just *splaining,* then."

"Sing," I commanded, or maybe pleaded. "Show him."

Splain/rain was a joke Arabella and I had originated months before, in Roslyn's backyard on Cheever Place. The canopy of trees, the narrow, high-fenced yard, Roslyn's tulips and plate of tea sandwiches. Even before we could go there in an airplane, the joke brought us back there. It was something I needed, as badly as I'd ever needed anything.

"*I can't stand the splain, against my window . . .*" Arabella had a beautiful voice, a trained voice. She'd fronted a band a few times, at Saint Ann's parties, three punk boys not worthy of backing her.

"Do 'Splainy Night in Georgia.'"

"I don't know that one."

"I played it for you! I'm disappointed. What about 'It's Splainin' Men'?"

"No, remember this one? *Splaindrops keep falling on my head—*"

I joined her, though I wasn't any kind of singer. Miraculously, across the fire, the Rabbit guitar was picked up and strummed in accompaniment, the right chords so far as my limited ear could tell.

Now Arabella and I were up at the fire, dancing as she sang. The sky blazed with dawn shards, the storm bearing the night off with it. We swayed at the rim of cinders, she in her blue camouflage hoodie, me in my Juicy Couture. I heard a waking Rabbit groan, "What's going on?"

"The two Phoebes are dancing," another told her. "It's a happy thing."

The guitarist, a droll, gap-toothed woman with a head the shape of a pomegranate, rose and danced with us, still rollicking on her instrument. Arabella improvised from the melody and lyrics, loading it up with copious *American Idol* melisma: "*Splainy splaindrops, splainy sidewalks, because we're freaks, nothing's worrying meeeeee*—" She could have been a queen of anything she wished, certainly something more than Rabbits or Rabbit-Bears; in her youth's splendor, she could have conquered cities. This thought revealed my lingering bias against the desert people, even though I'd arguably become one. Perhaps in my inevitable new postelection lesbian phase I'd fall in love not with my friend but with her daughter, if that wasn't a monstrous thought—it probably was. But I was free and dancing alongside my monstrous thoughts now.

I screamed, "*It WON'T be long till HAPPiness steps UP to GREET me*," and it sounded fine, it sounded terrific.

The sun came up. The rain stopped. We still danced. Arabella switched the song. "*I can see clearly now, the SPLAIN is gone*," she sang, and we dancing Rabbits, five or six now, screamed it with her, while the others watched and clapped. The guitarist knew this song too. Donna came up the hill then and took me by the sleeve. She wanted to lead me back to Neptune Lodge, where she and Anita had disappeared for a while without my paying attention, and why should I have? The reason she'd sought me out wasn't clear. Was it something about Heist, some news? No.

"There's something you'll want to see, I think."

The downer, Shockley—was he dying now? Had we sung him to his finish line?

They led me inside to a small television on the kitchen counter. The satellite dish worked. The station was CNN. The images, of the cities in the East, Boston, New York, Washington, streets flooding with bodies and signs, with jubilant pink. The march. I'd been tracking the burgeoning scheme in my feed for weeks, but like everything in the desert except for the desert, it had become unreal to me. Now it was a grainy feed that was also like a pure injection of who I'd been into whatever it was I'd become. My people were there, revealed in their secret mighty number. Tears belched from me to see them in exultant riot, in knit uterine hats, blaring their raw oceanic refusal into the face of the monster—he who you couldn't help guessing looked on, raging like a pitiable infant. But my people were also on this side of the screen. That they'd wanted to lure me in to see, that it mattered to them at all, caused me to see the march as a Rabbit event, a fulfillment and reply to what we'd endured in the night. Later that day, arrived with Arabella at the Ontario, California, airport, I'd find an outlet for my charger and my reawakened phone would flood with the images, the texts and selfies, but for now there was only this, the satellite's feed, enough. We watched awhile and then I went back to the daylight fire and beautiful singing Arabella. *"I can see all obstacles in my way—"* It was a much better song than the earlier one, really. The word *splain* had fallen away, done its work. *"Here is that rainbow I've been praying for—"* The morning sky, short of the rainbow, lived up to the song.

I took the lipstick from my purse a second time. This time Spark allowed me to apply it to her. She leaned in, closed her eyes. Arabella shared it too, and others as it was passed like a joint around the circle. *"I think I can make it now, the pain is gone—"* While we danced and Arabella sang, the Rabbits pointed to the far hill—again they wanted my attention. I turned to see a non-human living thing, a line segment streaming in our direction, a sidewinder? My trite brain still drew imaginary snakes. But no. It was Jessie, wagging his tail. He coursed into the Rabbit circle and into my arms. I had all I needed.

PART V

COBBLE HILL

44

WE REENTERED THE BROKEN WORLD. TO RETRIEVE ARABELLA TO ROSLYN'S doorstep, to the brownstone peace of Cheever Place, the old refuge—these past eight days, out in the Great Nowhere, in Upland and on the mountain and in the wastes, this had been my compass, my beacon. But Arabella had clammed up on the plane, when she wasn't sleeping. By the time we stepped through the dystopian construction-zone labyrinth of LaGuardia, I felt it all going south. Overhead, suspended from the asbestos ceilings, each television was tuned to images of the deal-whore as he romanced Congress, informing them that his opponent's popular vote victory had been robbed from him. Then we stepped out to hail a farty cab from a frigid, wind-blasted curb. My return's triumph had already curdled.

Worse, Roslyn couldn't help us. Nine hours earlier I'd texted her from the airport to say I had Arabella safe, that I was bringing her home. I wanted to see Roslyn gather Arabella up and make her right, and I wanted her to do the same for me. Yet, arrived here on Cheever Place, I found I had three cracked women on my hands. Three included myself and two who wouldn't embrace, or meet each other's eyes.

Oh, Roslyn went through the motions, fed us tea and hustled us to hot showers, offering fresh fluffy towels and robes from her vast supply. But she couldn't help because my ordinarily indomitable friend was in trouble, was down for the count. She was distractible and squirrelly, couldn't quit telling us how a new buyer was gutting the upper duplex, destroying her sleep in the process. I have any amount of sympathy for lost sleep, but this wasn't the most relevant stuff. When Arabella trudged downstairs, appearing more like she'd been whipped than welcomed home, Roslyn said, "I can't get on the subway anymore."

"You can't get on the subway?" I obliged her by asking, though as I sat and listened my head was full of the desert.

Despite being needed at NPR's Midtown bureau, Roslyn explained, she couldn't go, couldn't bear the F train tunneling deep to within a mile of Sauron's tower. Everyone was an enemy now and Manhattan was under occupation, by the protesters as much as the Secret Service. When a packed car shuddered to a halt between stations, Roslyn sweated out tremors, a thousand miniature panic attacks. A terror event was a certainty—it was only a question of when.

It got worse when Arabella returned upstairs, her hair in a towel, her presence as shrouded as it had been under that feather headdress. MSNBC wasn't helping. Rachel Maddow didn't seem to have a handle either. I kept snapping the television off and Roslyn kept snapping it back on. She couldn't even organize an order of delivery Thai, and when I did, she ate less than Arabella. Me, I stuffed myself to the brink of nausea.

I had my own interlude under the hot water, in Roslyn's elegantly renovated bathroom. It felt amazing to wash the layers of airport and desert off my body, but when I closed my eyes the falling water made me remember the storm in the pit, so I opened them again. Then I put on my own robe and went upstairs and got the two of them into their separate bedrooms and myself onto the couch.

In truth, if my apartment hadn't been sublet, I might not have stayed in Roslyn's. Though the subway hardly beckoned to me either. But I had an app for that, and for anything else. I could Uber again. My phone and my brain were each flooded with activity, each lit like a pinball machine. I'd returned to what Stephanie, in Culver City, had called the *caffeinated neurotic atmosphere*. The city still buzzed with the devious crush of possibility, of millions of young bodies just on the other side of the wall. In a flush of avidity I spent a few minutes in the dark on Roslyn's couch browsing Tinder, then passed out.

45

I WOKE IN DAYLIGHT TO FIND ARABELLA IN THE KITCHEN, CLEANING. SHE didn't see me at first. Roslyn had been upstairs at the hour of the wolf, drinking white wine—I'd just registered it through my slumber on the couch. Now Arabella rinsed the glass and set it upside down on a cloth, as she'd been taught. She rinsed the bottle too, and placed it in the recycling bin, gently, not wanting to wake either of us.

She was dressed in her old clothes, her high school uniform, which was to say a shirt filched from Roslyn's collection of threadbare concert tees—Zappa at the Fillmore East, in this instance—and a skirt, over leggings and a halter top, with laced-up boots. Like the early rising and the kitchen cleanup, it seemed chosen as a mild rebuke, as if to say to Roslyn, *Which of us is really the bad girl here?* Arabella might have reverted to a Saint Ann's senior, headed up to smoke clove cigarettes on the Promenade.

Instead of that, I enacted a ritual of ours together, mine and Roslyn's, but also mine and Arabella's, from the days before, when I used to spend the night on this couch with regularity. I dressed in the clothes Roslyn had laid out for me, another New York costume, and though it was drizzling it wasn't cold, and we walked all the way up across Atlantic Avenue together, to Iris Café. Our favorite fussy breakfast joint, one where we didn't have to glance at the menu to know we wanted the paprika-salted poached eggs and avocado toast, and where we had once had all our best talks—mine and Roslyn's, but also mine and Arabella's, though never, never the three of us together.

Of course, the atmosphere was gutted. This was the new world, still just two days old. Nevertheless, for me it was like traveling back in time, into the city I'd quit and lost and been fired from, no telling which anymore. It was still here, at least in its basic lineaments and rites, but I wasn't, even if at the moment I happened to be.

Arabella waited until after the lattes appeared. "Last night while you were downstairs in the shower, she told me she'd made an appointment for me with her doctor and her shrink."

"What did you say to that?"

"I said I'd see her shrink if she came to the session with me. She wants him to ask me questions but she's afraid of hearing the answers."

"I'm a little afraid of hearing them too."

"No, you're not. You know the same things I know."

"What things are those?"

"You know she went to the Poconos to canvass for Hillary? That's where she went every summer, the same place, to make out with her cousins and pity the locals on their porches and feel superior about being a New Yorker. And it's where she got raped, which she never talks about. Well, I *don't* feel superior because I'm a New Yorker."

Though I had some knowledge of the facts she cited, Arabella wasn't making full sense. Yet the language she spoke reached into me, it rhymed with my own incoherence.

"Are you capable of being kind to her?"

"Sure. I'm just talking this way to you, blowing off steam."

I looked around the café. A middle-aged Heights couple studied Section A together, as if somewhere in its columns lay a description of the hour and manner of their death. They should have bought two copies. No one was going to have time for The Arts or Science Tuesday again anytime soon.

"Did anyone rape you?" I asked her.

Arabella shook her head.

"No one even *tried*?"

"Solitary Love picked me out. He had a sense of . . . ritual."

Inside the shame at hearing that name, I felt a sudden fury at her stupidity. "Do you realize how lucky you are?"

"Yes."

"If I ever find out you're relying on a sense of ritual or any other mystical horseshit to protect you from men like that, I'm going to find you and strangle you myself, you understand?"

"Yes."

"Were you on Baldy when the kids were killed?" The Nancy Drew part of me needed to see if she understood the question. The big-sister part no longer cared to protect her from the fact of what I'd seen.

"No, but I heard about it."

"There was a girl named Sage with you," I suggested.

"Yes, I remember her."

"Was she a friend of the kids on the mountain? The ones who died?" I only looked like what I'd been, a single neurotic with a favorite café. My real self hovered indefinitely over scenes of madness. My civilian body was secretly a drone-operator's station, housing for a remote eyeball crawling over terrain, pits of slag, stone arroyos, high-altitude clearings amid pine.

"Sage was like me," Arabella said. "She was new. We had just met the desert people."

"The two who died weren't new?" I wasn't sure I understood.

"They'd already been to the desert. I guess your friend Heist helped them escape."

"They didn't want to be Rabbits or Bears?"

She shook her head.

"Well, too bad, since they died as them." I spoke with cruelty, as though the cruelty I'd seen was inside me now and had to come out.

Arabella flinched, though she didn't cry. But I believed her then, that she hadn't been at the scene. It might only have been rumor to her. I let her sit with confirmation of the rumor for a long moment before I continued.

"What do the Bears want on the mountain?"

Even as I posed the question, I knew. The answer had been buried in Spark's boyfriend's datura monologues, his Bearsplanation. He'd even said it was hidden in plain sight, but I hadn't seen it, not until now. The Bears didn't want something on the mountain, they wanted the mountain itself. It was high and defensible ground, their Davos redoubt.

"They talked like they're employed up there," said Arabella, shrugging again. "Like, providing security, I guess, for the Koreans." She was telling me what she knew, but I knew more now. The compound's owners had struck a fatal bargain on Baldy, maybe something like the error the Rolling Stones had made in hiring the Hells Angels to provide security at Altamont. Invited in, the Bears had seen something they'd wanted, something they were convinced they needed in the coming flood. Years of dreaming about the end of the world had met the paranoia of the Korean survivalists and taken it as urgent dispatch, a call to action. Only the urgency was exaggerated. The Bears were dying hippies, like the downer Shockley, convinced the world was dying with them.

"What are you going to do?" I asked.

"Stay with her until it's okay for me to leave."

Maybe there was datura seed extract in the lattes at Iris Café, or maybe I was just synaptically yawned open now, prone to revelation. Caffeine was a good enough drug. I thought I'd gone to Upland to rescue Arabella, but I had it backward. I'd fetched Arabella in order to place Roslyn in her care, not the other way. The thought reminded me of the theory, circulating lately, that early humans hadn't so much domesticated wild dogs as been domesticated by them.

"Go where?" I asked her. "Back to the Rabbits?"

"I doubt it. I might go to Canada. There's somebody I met who split and went to Halifax. They have good music there."

"I still love your singing."

"Or a Greek island, I haven't decided."

"Leonard Cohen, huh?"

She shrugged.

"I don't care if you call yourself Phoebe."

"It's not, like, the weirdest thing I ever did."

"I didn't say it was." I was distracted by something outside the window, in the sky: a jet contrail. How many messages unfurled over New York each hour, unread?

"What are you going to do about Charles?" said Arabella.

She'd surprised me. It wasn't that I'd emptied myself of intentions. I just didn't think they were written all over my face. Maybe Arabella had read it in a passing contrail.

"Go back and find him, of course," I said.

PART VI

MOUNTAIN, WASH, DESERT

46

WHEN NOLAN HANDED ME THE KEYS AND TOLD ME THE CAR HADN'T MOVED, I asked if he was sure—had he been watching it the whole time? He didn't seem to get the joke. Maybe he had been watching it the whole time, neglecting his flagstone sweeping. Anyway, my suitcase was where I'd left it, in the trunk. I tried not to consider the late fees I was racking up on the rental.

The souped-up green Econoline was back, parked at the far side of the lot from my car. I almost asked Nolan about it, but thought better of it. It wasn't his—on my earlier visit to the Zendo I'd observed it missing, while he'd stayed put.

"You mind if I change?" I asked him.

"Change is the only certainty."

"Now you're making fun of me, Nolan."

Seeing my open suitcase in the open trunk, he widened his hands and smiled, to say *feel free.*

"I mean inside, not out here. I'm a shy girl."

"Mi Zendo es su Zendo."

I went inside and traded Roslyn's Eileen Fisher slacks for jeans and a hooded sweatshirt, anything to make myself more typical where I was going. Then I thanked Nolan and returned to the lot.

The van's rear doors were open to the woods behind the fence.

47

THE VAN LOOKED DIFFERENT TO ME, NOT BECAUSE IT HAD CHANGED, BUT because I saw it with new eyes. The large tires, the high clearance on the suspension: a desert vehicle, a rock climber. Its panels wore a layer of fine yellow dust, nothing to do with the mountain.

The figure sitting cross-legged in the shade of the van's rear was cherubically rotund, in loose garb that could pass for robes. In silhouette, which was all I could make out through the tinted glass of the door's square window, I might have taken it for a gigantic sculpture of the Buddha, something being shifted from one of the Zendo's porches or gazebos. But between the doors, along the top of the wooden bumper, I saw a hairy fat Caucasian ankle taper into a running shoe. Neither ankle nor running shoe belonged to the Buddha.

Did the figure's head turn my way?

I'd failed to press Arabella on the topic of the older man whom the daft girl Sage had mentioned, the possible procurer of young bodies up and down this mountain. Was I seeing him now?

I memorized the plate, then got into the rental and drove down the hill to the Mount Baldy Lodge to call the police.

48

I'D ALREADY BEEN PLANNING THE CALL. IT WAS ONE OF THE ONLY MOVES I arrived certain of, after scheming my way through two airports. I wanted to discharge my obligation to the bodies in the pit, to put their lonely deaths on the road to discovery by grieving parents, inflicting the horror I'd feared bringing home to Roslyn. It wasn't better than anything but the alternative: that no one would find them for so long that no one still searched, or worse, so long that no one could recognize what they'd found.

But I wanted to do it without enmeshing myself. The lodge still kept a pay phone, to oblige day visitors whose cells didn't work. I didn't know if the Upland police were so vigilant or competent they'd trace the call, but I figured it was best if it came from the mountain. I had to wait awhile for a table near the phone to clear out. Meanwhile, I found a spot from which I could watch the roadway, in case the van appeared. There might be a back door off the mountain, but this was the popular route.

It took a couple of false starts before I was on the phone with anyone really focused, but I eventually got their attention by saying I needed to report a double homicide. The cop asked my name and I refused. "I live on Baldy. I don't want any trouble. I'm just a regular hiker who found something."

I explained that the trail was fenced and posted; they'd need a warrant, unless they wanted to send someone up quietly, to confirm what I'd seen. "The owners are absentees. It's a survival-ist compound, if you ask around you'll hear. Everyone around here goes up there anyway." I thought of frozen prints and re-minded myself to trash the boots I'd worn on the hike.

Then I gave them the van's license plate, and described it as a green Econoline with wooden bumpers. I didn't mention the yellow dust. The cop fished for more but I said I was done. I could have pointed them to the desert, of course, to the trail that connected the runaways and rescuees of the Viscera Springs tribes to Upland and Baldy, but I needed to stay a step ahead. Let them have the mountain and the van for now. I needed the desert to myself, to get Heist out. Any killers among the Bears had waited long enough for punishment; they could wait a bit longer. That was, besides the punishment the Bears inflicted on themselves, or that which the Rabbits sporadically meted out, as in the case of Shockley.

49

TWO DAYS BEFORE, THE DAY OF THE RABBITS' DANCE FOR PEACE AND Justice, Donna and Anita had driven me and Arabella across the hills in the dune buggy. We still reeked of bonfire, of the juniper and mania proudly seething through our pores. They took us not to Heist's Jeep—pointless, when no one had the key—but to a site called Giant Rock where they said there'd be enough traffic for us to hitch a ride. I still had my purse, but my phone's battery had gone dead from chasing signal where there was none.

From among the day-trippers visiting Giant Rock we'd cadged a ride to the Twentynine Palms Highway, as the Rabbit matriarchs had predicted. In Joshua Tree, I found an ATM. From there, a local cab was willing to run us to the airport in Ontario, more than an hour away. The cabbie didn't stop talking, which didn't stop us leaning into each other and sleeping, which didn't end his talk. Arabella and I woke groggy and startled at the terminal curb, our mouths glued like morning-after drunks.

Jessie had stayed behind. Spark took him.

Charles Heist and I had left dogs and vehicles scattered everywhere in our spree. Now, on my return to the scene, it was cleanup time. While waiting for my luggage at the carousel I'd already called the rental place in Montclair, scheduling an exchange of the car for a desert-ready Jeep. I tried to keep myself on an efficiency basis, my actions clean and unsentimental, so I didn't dwell on Heist, on fantasies of rescue, more than was useful. I didn't have to—I was headed straight for him, even if I hadn't a clue how.

50

THERE WASN'T ANY SIGN OF LIFE AT HEIST'S OFFICE AT THE BUILDING ON Foothill, but when I steered the Jeep through the maze of mobile homes to the Airstream at the back ridge of nowhere, I found her inside, as some part of me had been certain I would. She wasn't as filthy-looking as the first time I'd seen her, not quite. Her hair was pulled back from her face and she wore an oversize L.A. Clippers T-shirt over her leggings, but her eyes were just as furtive, her movements still darting, sidelong, like when she'd startled me emerging from a cabinet. The furry girl, Melinda.

I'd had to work to retrieve her name, behind those of the many Rabbits in whose company I'd been marooned in the days preceding—Lorrie, Anita, and the rest. It was reasonable to guess she'd been raised by Rabbits, but Melinda didn't feel like one to me. The Rabbits, young or old, whether I'd liked or distrusted them, seemed to float in the weightlessness of their collective proposition—even an outrider like Spark. Melinda, by contrast, was like a coal that had fallen from the sky, completely singular, still burning. She wasn't pretending to be the feral thing she was—she had no choice. She was like Heist himself, or anyway that's how she struck me now, in his Airstream with the two remaining dogs. It was incredible that such broken things would presume to care for one another, yet it was also the way of the world. And now here I'd appeared, to add myself to the collection.

I said her name, and she allowed me to come in. It helped, I think, that Miller and Vacuum were so glad to see me. Their back halves blurred, working like outboard motors. I glanced away from the bed, not wanting to remember. Instead I snogged awhile with the dogs on the Airstream's tiny floor. Melinda stood to one side, nearly in the shower, watching me. Then she said, "Where is he?"

"I don't know exactly. The Bears took him away."

"Why are you here?"

"I want company," I said flatly. "I have a Jeep. I'm going in to find him if I can. The dogs can help me."

She didn't speak, just glared.

"You're welcome to come along." She surely knew the lay of the land better than I did, if she was capable of sharing what she knew. But I wouldn't presume. Heist's camper was like a larger version of the cabinet in which she'd been hiding when I first visited his office—a nook of consolation for what she suffered: autism, agoraphobia, or simply a righteous certainty that the world was fucked. I could relate to practically any of it.

"They need food," she replied, ignoring my invitation.

"I'll get them some."

"I do too."

"He didn't leave you food money?"

"The money's gone."

"That's not a problem," I told her. "We can eat now, before we go."

It wasn't so long before dark, in the diminished January light. I didn't want to wait overnight. The police were in motion now, thanks to me. Not so long ago their missing persons division had directed me to the social worker Jane Toth, who'd sent me to Heist, and it wasn't too hard to imagine this sequence could work in reverse, culminating here at the Airstream. Meanwhile, for Heist, every minute might count. Who knew what next ceremonies awaited him? I imagined driving by night to the desert's edge, the girl and the dogs asleep in the rear seat. If I appeared at Viscera Springs at dawn, I might gain some advantage of surprise.

My own need for sleep I pushed off the table. I'd slept a bit on the red-eye, and there was always coffee or Mormon tea brewing somewhere. Really, I was full of bluff, but I needed to be.

"What do you want?"

"The dogs like In-N-Out burgers." She didn't mention her own preferences. Still, I felt the dawning of her willingness to be beguiled into my vehicle. The prospect seemed marvelous and improbable. I'd begun to fix on the magical notion that by a law of similarities, Melinda could function as a dowsing rod to locate Charles Heist.

"Great," I said, swiftly finding the nearest In-N-Out on my phone. It was just a half mile down Foothill. "We'll drive through."

"Okay, but it has to be animal style."

"What's animal style?"

"You'll see."

Fifteen minutes later we gorged in the In-N-Out lot, the dogs in the back seat, Melinda in the passenger spot, all snarfing up massive, sopping burgers. Animal style turned out to be an order from the restaurant's so-called secret menu, consisting of patties drenched in pickles, mustard, and Thousand Island dressing. I got through half of mine and then passed it back to the dogs. It wasn't that I didn't enjoy the thing, but I needed to stay awake on the highway—I wasn't betting on Melinda for a conversationalist.

"How'd the dogs develop this taste for In-N-Out?" I asked her, after gathering up the slimy wrappers and cardboard trays.

It was plain I'd be sacrificing the cleaning deposit on the rental Jeep.

She made a shrugging face without moving her body. "We walked down here. When the money ran out, we could find plenty to eat in the trash."

"I guess you would in a place like this. You could even hold out for animal style, I bet."

She didn't respond.

"You ready for this drive?" I asked her. "You need a . . . potty break?"

"I'm fine." Then the girl surprised me. "The desert is big."

"Yes, I know."

"Things move around there," she said.

"Things?"

"The Bears hide." She was thinking about my plan, or lack thereof.

"I'll find them somehow." I didn't want to tell her she'd become the better part of my plan, if not the whole of it—that her capacity for dwelling at peripheries and moving at odd angles made me believe she could command the secret landscape. She was just a kid.

"Somehow how?"

"I know where there's a Bear. Can you get me to Neptune Lodge?"

"Sure. Neptune Lodge is easy. It doesn't move around like everything else."

"Then we'll go there and take their Bear. If we have him, he'll lead us to the others." Would I be able to get Shockley into the Jeep? Or did I mean I'd be wheeling his hospice bed across the dunes? These problems I'd solve when I came to them.

"We should do something else." She spoke so laconically it took me a moment to understand I should ask.

"What do you mean?"

"There's a Bear right here. He's not really one anymore."

"Where?"

"He lives in the Wash."

Again, I knew without realizing I knew. "Is he called Laird?"

"Yeah. Laird'll help us. He loves Charlie."

These words opened a little sore place in my chest that I didn't want to attend to just then. The name, Charlie, shorn of Shockley's insinuating *boy*, suddenly sounded real to me. Maybe I'd call him that someday.

"Should we go talk to him?" The uptorn fence, entrance to the Wash, was close. We might have an hour of daylight still. L.A.'s subliminal winter had shifted again, from an afternoon sun that had me sweating in my winter coat to a bone-dry chill, sun bowing toward the rumored ocean, breeze whistling to magic-hour hills in the direction we'd be going.

She nodded, then surveyed the Jeep's interior as if measuring it. "I can sit in the back with the dogs."

51

HE'D ALREADY BUILT HIMSELF AN EVENING FIRE. THERE HE SAT, ELBOWS on knees, still barefoot, in sweatpants that reached mid-calf now, and with a large woolen poncho covering his distracting upper body. His skull glowed in the fire, and the scene brought out his resemblance to the people I'd come to know in the Mojave, the watchers in the pit, the gleaners at the Rabbit circle. He was reading a Tom Clancy novel, a stout paperback that resembled a pack of cigarettes in his clubby fingers. He greeted Melinda without rising, seemingly unsurprised. The dogs danced in to join him at the fire, one on each side, as if daring him to meet their animation. This dare he ignored, preferring to go on scowling at his pages. There wasn't a puppy in his camp this time. Perhaps the puppy I'd seen earlier had reached a size enough to be worth eating.

"Hey, Mary Poppins," he said when I got close. "Where's your umbrella?"

"I loaned it to the Penguin," I said.

"Mistake," said Laird, not missing a beat. "You'll never get it back."

"That's okay," I said. "I'm learning to live without excess baggage." I wasn't sure what I meant by it. There was something about Laird's size and stillness and wooly poncho that made me feel silly.

Melinda sat right beside him. "We have to go get Charlie," she said.

"How's that?"

"He got tooken by the elders."

"I think he can handle himself."

"Not at the moment," I said. I hadn't told Melinda about the fight. I invented a version to tell them both now, one that included Heist's injuries but left out the murder I'd abetted. "The Bears took them both away," I lied. I left out the words *Solitary Love* too, not wanting to hear myself speak them. Like other names I censored lately, this was a vote against invoking monsters, against etching their reality into the air.

"Come with us," said Melinda.

"Maybe after I finish my book. I'm on the last hundred pages."

I studied Laird. It seemed to me now that he split the difference between Solitary Love and Bartleby the Scrivener. I should feel rotten to be pulling the gentler giant back into what he'd fled, but I did it for Heist.

"Read it in the Jeep," I said. It sounded like *read it and weep*. "We're leaving for the desert tonight." I couldn't keep from feeling that my run was a race, even if I couldn't see my opponent.

"Nah, that always makes me want to puke." Laird stuck the book in the waistband at the back of his pants. He shook himself loose in a plume of smoke, as if he'd been sitting in the same position for a long time. He stuck his feet into a pair of blackened Adidas, the laces already tied.

"C'mon," said Melinda. She took him by the hand. Resembling a shot from *The Princess Bride,* they padded toward the ascent from the Wash to Foothill, where the Jeep waited. I followed, while Miller and Vacuum streamed past to forge the trail. Melinda, like the dogs, had become my agent, my deputy. Now Laird too. I felt better about the dogs, since I hadn't managed to find a way to lie to them.

52

WE DROVE FROM THE LAST OF THE SUN. AS DARK GREW ON THE ROAD before us, the dogs and Melinda curled to sleep in the back. I kept wishing my Golden Girl would reappear—the woman on the motorcycle, my emissary into the desert the first time I'd come here, with Heist. Seeing her again, I'd feel my aim was true. But no.

The only voice in the Jeep was Laird's. He sat in his poncho, staring out ahead, intoning like some blunt irritable GPS: *"No, this way,"* or *"You want to gas up here, it's the last chance,"* or *"I told you, just keep going."*

Under his navigation, we'd gone off the major route sooner than I'd expected, veering north through sprawls bearing the names Hesperia and Victorville, then east, onto two lanes of asphalt called Old Woman Springs Road. From there, into the scruff and crunch, the places the Jeep was for. The sun at our backs painted a distant rime of orange as we reached the limit of roads with names and began to jostle across rivulets of sand and gravel.

"Should we deflate the tires?" I asked Laird.

I was proud to brandish the lore, but he brushed it off without interest: "We're not climbing anything yet." So we fell into silence again, our headlamps illuminating a tunnel through yellow dusk, our treads crossing and recrossing palimpsests of the vehicles that had gone this way, whether an hour or a month before I couldn't tell. If Laird had that tracker's gift, he wasn't saying.

I felt emptied out and complete. My giddy nonjoke about excess baggage lingered in the air—for me, I mean. From outward appearances, Laird hadn't viewed his life in terms of baggage in a long while, if he ever had. That made him, with his Thoreau-of-the-vacant-lot aura, his salvage Adidas and spinner-rack paperback, a suitable companion for my current mood. The Girl Who Quit had only been testing her cage; now I was The Girl Who Divested.

Old fears had flown the coop without my noticing and been replaced: I was positively aching to abscond into the Mojave again, the fewer road signs the better. No cities for me now, or families or tribes. This skeleton crew—Melinda, the dogs, and Laird—was the utmost human arrangement I could ratify or sustain. I wanted to call Arabella and apologize for hustling her out of this wonderland of vacuity, out from under this sky. Except I didn't, because I didn't want to call anyone. I'd stopped looking at my phone. The Jeep was my true body.

In November the previous year, when the mask had been peeled off, when the worm had reached the bud, I remembered my eyes lighting on a magazine cover at my bedside. It featured a comic illustration, showing the man I now had to call president sawing an elephant in half, like a stage magician. The elephant was the Republican Party. How we wanted him to do it! Our confidence was sickening—it was the disease itself. That morning I'd thrown the magazine in the trash, feeling a savage distaste for artifacts from the old knowingness. Then for weeks I'd gone every day onto the Internet in search of a new and better knowingness to fill me up again. The disease still inside me, even if reversed into trauma.

Maybe I'd now moved through the void encounter Stephanie had predicted for me that evening in Culver City. (Had Stephanie ever really had one herself, like I had? It didn't seem likely!) In any case, I'd found my purpose, not in Cobble Hill, trying to settle Arabella back into that old world, but in making my own contrail back to find Heist.

He was the thing I'd seize for myself, in this new world. An untamed creature of the middle spaces, a resister stranded from all camps, tending to decline needless battle, infinitely kind toward the weak, yet capable of killing if cornered. I'd be Heist's other, he'd be mine. I understood him now, his appetite for distance, his noble disaffiliation—I'd show him we shared this, and then he could affiliate to *me*.

Further, I should cease taking lustful glances at Laird's veiny forearms, since he was something akin to my adoptive teenage son. Like a lot of overgrown teenage boys, he'd help his mom with a task, reaching a jar from a high pantry shelf, say, and unscrewing its tight lid—the equivalent to his effort in this rescue mission. Like a lot of overgrown teenage boys, he was on the endearingly sullen side. And Melinda could be Laird's little sister, in our feral family. Heist and I, once I'd rescued him, would care for these two, along with our beautiful dogs. That such thinking was fucking insane didn't make it less consoling. We lived in a fucking insane world. Such thinking might be the right gear for my expedition through it.

Needless to say, all these epiphanies and delusions were native to the condition of steering a powerful vehicle through silent dark. The difficulty would be to sustain them when the night ride was over, when I found the Bears and whatever remained of Heist—assuming Laird had what it took to accomplish that, and that I could control him (my fantasy adoptive son).

Maybe I was the one sawed in half.

53

OUT UNDER THE DARK, WE CONTINUED NORTH, AT LAIRD'S DIRECTION. What had been a road was now a rut, an established track in the cracked lake bed the land had become. We were hardly the first to go here, though the marks on this Etch A Sketch surface grew directionless and baroque. The joyriding treads inscribed grooves on the planet, suggesting the possibility of a tire-based language for communication with drones or satellites above, for beaming meaning back at passing contrails.

Laird pointed again. I found what he wanted me to see. It appeared as a white blot on the dark horizon. It resolved as I approached in a wide arc: a string of mobile homes, their white broadsides strung in a circle, like a wagon train. One link in the chain wasn't a mobile home, but a long trailer, with a ramp tilted off the back to release whatever it had released into the desert, a monster truck or military-surplus tank. The ring of vehicles made a flotilla in the desert's dark sea, one lit by strings of bulbs like Christmas lights, and also by a pit fire at its center. Even as I curled toward it, adding my own track to the compilation, I made out another similar flotilla, burning white, far off and to the left of the one we approached.

"Stop the Jeep," said Laird.

"What's this place?" I said to him. I whispered now, not for fear of waking Melinda, more in a spirit of stealth. It was a foolish compensation on my part, since Laird jumped out even before I'd killed the engine. I pocketed the key and hurried after him, but left the headlights on to see by. The surface underfoot wasn't sandy, more a layer of powder riding a floor of baked clay.

"Hammertown," he said.

I'd stopped fifty yards or so from the encampment, near enough now to see by their light. We charged in its direction, Laird heedless of any type of caution or consultation. My eyes adjusted to the starry show blanketing the antediluvian lake bed. I thought I could make out other constellations of mobile homes on the distant flats.

"Okay, what's Hammertown?"

"It's where they crown the King of the Hammers."

"A Bear thing?"

"It's a race."

"A race? Like *another* desert tribe, you mean?" I tasted adrenaline laced with possibility. I got ready to meet the Hammerhead Frogs now, or Armadillos, or whatever.

"No, a motor race, like bozos in Evel Knievel suits tearing up rocks in Ultra4 vehicles. It's quiet now. In a month there'll be a million day-trippers out here. These RVs and toy haulers are just holding down the playa in the meantime."

Melinda and the dogs came up to join us from behind as we approached the Hammertown encampment. No, we wouldn't escape anyone's notice. Melinda fell into step, groggy and uncomplaining.

"You're looking for the carnival, ain't you?" she said to Laird.

"It's a place to start," he said.

Carnival. It was the second time I'd heard that word. The first time I'd taken it as metaphorical, the same mistake I'd made with *rabbits* and *bears*. If there was one thing I should have learned this past year, it was to take my fellow Americans literally.

So I asked. "What's the carnival?" I was willing to play the dopey mom, the one needing all the latest slang terms explained.

"I wouldn't get your hopes up," said Laird sardonically. "It's just a few Tilt-A-Whirls on flatbeds, and a Ferris wheel with the buckets held on by duct tape. Oh yeah, plus a bouncy house, if you like that kind of thing. The Bears once had the idea of using it as a walk-in bong, which I have to admit was actually pretty cool."

"The Bears have a Ferris wheel? Uh, could we slow down, actually?" Laird's long strides would have us charging in between the mobile homes and into the midst of the Hammerkings, or whoever they were, in no time.

Laird obliged me, barely. "They're not Rabbits, Mary Poppins. They don't know how to make cactus pie or tell time by the dewdrops. They need U.S. currency for beer and dope and frijoles. Some of the elders make bank driving their sad rides around and parking at campsites where even sadder people pay to put their kids on a rusted carousel in the noon sun, or into a bouncy bag full of diesel exhaust from a fifty-year-old compressor."

"Okay," I said placatingly. I'd begun to grasp the necessity behind the Diogenes routine. Laird had copious rage. I'd hope to tap it usefully when the time came, or at least point it away from myself.

"These people give the Bears handouts, like at Jellystone Park. They let them park their stuff here sometimes. Not likely now, because the race is coming. But they might know where they're at. They won't hurt you, Mary Poppins."

"Okay," I said feebly. "I didn't mean to upset you."

"I'm not upset. I'm just not digging saying so many words."

"I'll save my questions."

"I could be reading my book."

"I appreciate that."

"Anyone wants to wait in the Jeep, that's cool too." Even as

Laird said this, Miller and Vacuum had wagged their way into the center of the ring of mobile homes, toward the fire. Melinda ran after them.

"I want to hear what they say," I said. We'd gotten close enough now that I could hear the music, something recorded, metalish or countryish, metal-countryish, if that existed. I felt responsible for Melinda. Now that I'd roused him, Laird stalked the planet like an indomitable ghost, unwary of what might see or touch him. But I'd lured the furry girl onto this quest without telling her she sought one of the Bear King's murderers, and accompanied the other.

54

THEY WEREN'T ONLY MEN, BUT MOSTLY MEN, AND THE WOMEN HUNG back. And they weren't all white guys with beards, only mostly so—some were Latino guys with beards, and some had no beards at all. There were trucker hats and bandannas, fancy sideburns, beer cozies. Maybe twenty or twenty-five people, and nothing to distinguish the scene, really. It could have easily been a tailgate party in a stadium lot, or a gathering at the far side of an outdoor concert, where the stage was so distant, it wasn't worth your attention. Except it was a gathering in the dark at the end of the world, a ring of RVs and trailers shored against the sand and wind of an apocalyptic vacancy, and the whole thing scared me shitless.

Ordinary people might be the most terrifying thing on earth. Or ordinary Americans, I should say. For months now, I'd studied them in the backdrops of the ceaseless televised rallies, stacked in those vertical arenas revering the back of a blue suit and a red hat, trying to fathom what it was they saw in him, and wondering where they went to, after. Here was one place, anyway. Apparently they carved up immaculate desert in their off-highway vehicles, things somewhere between a monster Jeep and a tricycle, two of which came barreling back from the rim of darkness just after we'd entered the camp. The headlamps made two columns of riotous dust flare before them, the stuff they'd been out kicking up with their treads—I guess we were breathing it. All shouted huzzahs at the vehicles' return, and the riders were quickly enfolded into that mellow, aimless atmosphere that I could interpret only as one of utter seething menace.

Was I unfair? Probably. True, there was the one guy who made it his business to corner me and Melinda away from the fire long enough to ask if we liked to party, but you could meet that anywhere. (It was when five or six asked the question as one that you'd worry.) We'd created a little hubbub, coming in unknown from the wild, but maybe less than I would have predicted, to be honest. They were nice to the dogs, fed them sausages, which they offered us as well. Some paid us no attention at all. But I was helpless not to consider them in light of the Bears. They made a tableau of both what I feared finding—the citadel of Monster Men—and, at the same time, its banal opposite. I suspected many of these guys could likely pack up and stow these vehicles behind suburban homes, even if in some cases the homes would be those of their parents. A few of the older ones surely had wives, or divorces, and underwater mortgages. They hadn't journeyed to this apocalyptic frontier honestly, weren't fugitives from Vietnam conscription or SDS or LSD or of a Janov scream that never ended, like the Bears. They'd watched a movie, perhaps starring Mel Gibson, or a YouTube clip, and geared up. I saw guns—a rifle rack in a pickup's cab, and two handguns inside open jackets—but they were slickly holstered, locked away, probably with their safeties on. I'd have bet they had paperwork.

Laird loomed in among them, searching for someone in particular. I don't think he found the person, but he mingled easily, despite his height and strange garb. I suppose he'd been acting as the checkpoint between the People of the Wash and the outside world. Who knew what earlier experiences with the social services bureaucracy, or with desert people, lay in his arsenal. I shouldn't underestimate his versatility just because he didn't care to use my real name. There were others with shaved heads at that circle, and I'm sure his muscles impressed everyone else as much as they did me. The men here appeared to find him a kick in the pants.

Contrary to what I'd said, I didn't stick near enough to listen. I stayed with Melinda instead, helping her to keep tabs on the dogs—I had a guilty wish for leashes, but it would have felt betraying to Heist—and held to the edge of the gathering, rather than on its inside, and accepted the hospitality of a Dr Pepper instead of a Pabst Blue Ribbon. By the time I figured out that Laird had been right, that they weren't going to hurt us, I was almost disappointed.

It occurred to me that these were the people who could afford to pity the Bears, my sacred enemies—to throw them a little charity, to treat them as harmless talismans, as "desert rats." It made me hate them even more than my enemies. In my new incoherence, I'd become affiliated. The people at the campfire seemed contemptible to me not because they provided a glimpse of the ethical and aesthetic mysteries of the Other America, but because in their jolly way they condescended to the Viscera Springs tribes, to Melinda and Laird, to Heist, to me.

55

BACK AT THE JEEP, LAIRD ASKED ME FOR THE KEY. HE WANTED TO BE THE driver. Melinda was just now in front of the vehicle, in the aura of its headlights, soothing Vacuum through a gastric episode. Someone in the fire circle had found it amusing to feed him a long sequence of ungrilled frankfurters, as if in some Coney Island contest, and they were coming back out.

A wind was rising.

"It's rented in my name," I said.

"I won't fink," Laird said. "It's easier me driving than telling you where to go in the dark."

"Involves too many words, huh?"

"That's a thing, yeah. Maybe Mr. Heist mentioned to you, I have a few extra voices in my head."

"I might have overheard something about that." He'd done well enough mingling voices with the men at the off-highway campsite, but maybe those were nearer to the variety he heard in his head. I wasn't going to quibble. I handed him the keys. With this wind picking up, I wanted to be inside the Jeep. "Do you have a license?"

He gave me a look I suppose I deserved. "You know there's no police out here, right, Mary Poppins?"

"I know."

"We're going to drive into the Twentynine Palms base. Marine land, where they train for all their desert shit. If the MPs spot us inside their perimeter, they aren't going to be worrying about our driver's licenses. Apart from that it's no-man's-land."

"I'm just thinking about the insurance."

"Close your eyes and drive in any direction, you'd go an hour before you hit anything. That's exactly what these people are doing out here."

"Aren't we likely to be rock climbing at some point?"

"The Bears you want pretty much swore off rock climbing when they got old. It's a lot of work welding car parts back together. They're more in the market for things like lumbar support. We'll find them on the flats."

"So you learned something back there?"

"Let's say I eliminated some variables."

"They know where the elders are?"

"It's more about knowing where the marines are conducting their fake-Fallujah deal these days. Where they aren't, that's where we'll go. I have an idea or two."

"Let's go, then."

"Uh-uh. I don't know what you might have heard, but I'm not a nocturnal animal."

"Meaning?"

"Meaning I know a place we can shelter for the night, a natural windbreak, not far. You don't want to drive in the dark if you're concerned about the insurance, anyway. And there's the kid." He turned his head to indicate Melinda, still ministering to the dogs, out of earshot.

"I thought you could drive with your eyes closed."

"Maybe I overstated. There's abandoned mines, you'd hate to run into one in the dark. Plus, once we're on military acreage, you could blunder up on unexploded ordnance."

"I want the cover of night."

My stubbornness had an undertow of despair. Our approach to the encircled RVs had already trashed my expectations, which were based on the earlier Jeep jaunt with Heist, searching for Rabbits. I'd wanted to engage with the Bears on intricate terrain, where they might not see me coming, where Spark-style stealth and swiftness could win the day. The Bears disappointed me in having abandoned the hills. It seemed sad. It also left me without even a *pretend* plan. To brazenly waltz in across the playa in the company of a schizoid Marfan-syndrome case wasn't appealing; now Laird suggested we'd do so in broad daylight.

"This actually isn't a discussion," he said. "Because I need to sleep. Unless you want to slip me one of whatever mother's little helper's keeping you jacked up all night."

"I'm not jacked up on anything."

"Well, maybe not something you can share. Too bad, I'd love a taste. I'd like to slow you down, or speed me up. Either way you'd come out less annoying."

"I'm just a New Yorker," I said.

"You're a lady on a mission, that's for sure."

"So, we ride at dawn?"

"We ride at dawn, Mary Poppins."

56

LAIRD SKIRTED US PAST A FEW MORE OF THE RV ENCAMPMENTS, EIGHT OR ten miles into the night. I tried, semi-surreptitiously, to track the mileage, though with no road markers of any kind it wasn't as if I could have retraced the route. Laird's destination, his windbreak, was a convenient arroyo notched between two spills of boulders, a Jeep's-width rut below the horizon. Tread marks said others had employed it not long before.

Laird killed the lights, and the sky filled in. Melinda and the dogs were already slumberish in the rear. I didn't know what Laird had in mind but he took himself out and made a dugout in the sand beneath the Jeep's chassis, ceding me the front seats. Not that stretching out across the gearshift was a temptation. I cracked the window—the surplus of bodies generated a lot of steam and stink, even minus the giant—and tried to close my eyes.

I might not be on any mother's little helpers, but I couldn't deny I was wired. I wished I hadn't surrendered half my In-N-Out burger to Vacuum, or that I'd said yes to a pulled pork sandwich at the RV encampment. Well, a Trump November and a Heist January had been good for my thighs, at least.

I rolled up the window when I realized I could hear Laird snoring from underneath the Jeep, even over the steady squalling wind.

57

MY FATHER HATED WESTERNS, BUT THERE WAS ONE HE LIKED. HE WATCHED it every few years. It was in color, and starred a strange and embarrassing mixture of aging movie stars and '60s television celebrities. At one point, they all sang together, in a jail. My father would have said he liked the film because of its director, but I think he liked it because the characters, a bunch of misfits, came together to form a kind of family, a better family than we had. As if to underline this, my mother would always storm from the room when the Western was on. I remember her calling it "unspeakably dumb."

Maybe my mother had made the mistake of identifying with the movie's female lead, unable to execute the reversal that Arabella had performed on Leonard Cohen's "Chelsea Hotel #2." The female lead spent a lot of the movie stuck in an upstairs room, in a corset. She made a small contribution, if I recalled right, by dropping a flowerpot from her second-story window, onto the head of one of the bad guys. But she wasn't involved in the finish, in which the motley family of men destroyed the villains using rifles and sticks of dynamite. Along with a pulled pork sandwich, I could wish I'd liberated something from a gun rack in one of those pickup trucks, back at the RV compound. My feral family was all I had. It wouldn't be much, if my sense of chaos failed to rise to the coming occasion.

58

LAIRD KEPT HIS PROMISE. IT WAS DAWN WHEN HE CLIMBED BACK IN AND started the Jeep. Melinda and the dogs and I crawled out for a pee, then hurried back inside, while he kept the motor running. The sun was just up but the wind hadn't slacked off, and it was colder than it had been at any time during the night, it seemed to me. The windshield wore a thin yellow layer of the finest desert grit, the same stuff that had trailed the off-highway vehicles into the RV camp. I would have spritzed the windshield and run the wipers—I would have tried the radio too—but it wasn't me at the wheel. Melinda and I shared a water bottle with the dogs, nearly the last. Laird just drove.

Despite Laird's suggestion that they represented the elders' livelihood, the carnival items looked shored in ruin, conveying a definite "Ozymandias" vibe. *Look On My Works, Ye, and Despair.* The bouncy house was folded in on itself, half covered with a green tarp pinned in eight or ten places with desert rocks yet flapping madly in the wind. The rest was still, seeming long abandoned. The Tilt-A-Whirl devices resembled hermit crabs retracted into their shells, their limbs drawn down to endure the wind's assault. Two of the chipped and rusted single-seater spaceships in which a child would ride had been unbolted from their mounts. They sat half-dug in sand, akimbo and forlorn, as if awaiting a wave that would never come to set them bobbing away. Two of the flatbed trucks that might have moved the stuff were parked to one side, looking as inert and distressed as the rocket ships.

The Ferris wheel, at least, stood at a right angle to the earth. It was a little farther off, uphill, beside a windowless storage shed. Like the rest, it appeared abandoned, but in contrast to the rest, it towered over the scene, conveyed a certain weary grandeur. Maybe the wheel was the last moneymaker in the Bears' arsenal, though it was hard to imagine making adequate return on the gasoline for towing it back and forth through the wastes.

We'd arrived after maybe half an hour's driving, along what just barely resembled an established trail, scantly littered with human signs—tipped road markers, a rusted gas canister, a cold fire pit ringed with beer cans. The carnival materials sat at the mouth of a ledge of tumbled rocks, beyond which lay an ancient roadbed: asphalt split by time and weeds and gated with a scribble of barbed wire and a POSTED sign. The road vanished off among irregular boulders and out of sight. It was the most variegated landscape for miles. A puff of gray rose from beyond the outcroppings, maybe half a mile off. It looked like steady exhalation from a chimney, or at least a morning fire.

Laird halted the Jeep at the barbed wire gate. I read the fine print on the posting. It was a mining claim. Then Laird began to crank the steering wheel, to move us beyond the wire.

"Could we stop and talk a minute?" I asked.

"What now?"

"Let's stretch our legs."

Taking a cue, Melinda climbed out and wandered off with the dogs. Laird switched off the engine. The tank was half-full, but I felt further along than that. *It's too late to stop now.* The air was suddenly full of insects, a weird cloud that surrounded us but didn't sting. I slapped them away anyhow.

"Flying ants," said Laird. "They don't usually look for a new home in the winter." It was another reminder that everyone knew this desert better than I did. "Must have been flooded out."

"Floods seem to follow you around."

He glared. I flicked an ant off my cheek.

"So, what's up ahead?" I nodded at the entrance to the boulders.

"Mining camp. Old wrecked shacks, a couple of them. It's a pretty good bet they've got Charles in there, especially if he's hurt like you say. I'm also hoping they've got breakfast. I can't subsist on pure anxiety, like you."

"I don't want to go straight in like that."

"Unless you mean to fly over with your umbrella, straight in's the only way."

"I just can't."

"Maybe you should tell me what you're not telling me."

"Do you know the name Solitary Love?"

"New king, right? Scary dude? I never met him. Guess this is my chance."

I shook my head. "He got killed. I'm involved. The Bears only saw me at night, but . . ."

"Well, hell, Mary Poppins." He turned his head to several points on the compass, like a big bald owl. "You were, what, just thinking of *trading* me for Charles? Like one big ugly problem is as good as the next?"

"I never thought that."

"Right, now say what you did think."

"They're paranoid, right?"

"In what sense?"

"They believe in contrails, black helicopters, I don't know what else—you tell me."

"I'm paranoid too."

"We can use that against them," I said, desperately trying to ignore his remark. "I just have to figure out how."

"You can bring black helicopters? Are you a police person, Mary Poppins?"

"No."

"Did you *call* the police?"

"Only a little. Not to the desert. I sent them to the mountain."

"You're making me confused. I'm going to go in and see if Charles needs my help, okay? You can wait here if you want."

I looked for Melinda. I couldn't see her. Miller and Vacuum trotted uphill, toward the Ferris wheel. The new sun glinted violently through the wheel's spokes and struts, nearly blinding me. I looked straight up instead, into the sky, searching for a sign, for a contrail I could use to intimidate a nest of Bears, claiming some high power of interpretation. The sky was empty. Wind and shame chafed my face. Here I'd be again, as with Heist. The woman sidelined, waiting for results while a man plunged into action on my behalf. I might as well be in a corset, looking for a chance to drop a flowerpot.

"You'll come back?"

"There's no other way out. I won't ding up your ride."

"Ding it all you want. Just—bring Charles out."

"If he's even in there."

"If he's even in there."

"Anyhow, maybe I'll bring back some breakfast."

Laird gunned the Jeep back into life, then curved it around the ineffectual wire barrier. I watched him go. Before he rose up and into the confluence of boulders he was shrouded in a flume of the yellow dust.

59

I WANTED TO FIND MELINDA. I CIRCLED BACK TO THE FLATBEDS AND THE hibernating Tilt-A-Whirls and the flapping decompressed bouncy house, but she wasn't there. The dogs were the clue. I should follow them. I looked uphill again, at the Ferris wheel. A residual image of its form was still blazed onto my retina from my earlier glance, and it printed false wheels on the screen of the blue sky. I wanted to be where that sun was. It was too cold down in this rocky hollow full of moribund rusted machines. Laird's departure was still traced in a funnel of silt, and the wind wouldn't quit blowing it back in my teeth.

As I climbed the hill, I caught a better angle. They made a silhouette scene in the glare: Melinda stood with the dogs at the base of the Ferris wheel, talking to a fat man in a chair.

60

IT SEEMED TO TAKE FOREVER, CLIMBING THAT HILL. THE BEATING OF blood in my ears and behind my eyes made the sun seem to pulse between the wheel's spokes. The ride was bigger than I'd realized, once I was under it. The whole thing was made of rusted steel, the armature raw, the gondolas painted in chipped pink, yellow, purple, and pea green. The entire device was portable, with eight double sets of wheels attached to a truck-bed frame, but it also featured eight stabilizing feet, extended on all sides to find spiderlike purchase on the desert hill. I supposed at an actual carnival the truck bed and the feet would be concealed with colorful panels, bunting, sideshow advertisements for the Two-Headed Baby or the Moon Girl. Nevertheless, unlike the disabled Tilt-A-Whirls, the wheel was set up and ready to go.

The man was up out of his chair by the time I reached them there. He'd unlatched the metal grate door of the two-seater cage that dangled nearest the ground, swinging squeakily on its ancient axle. Melinda climbed in.

"Wait—" I panted.

"You too?" In contrast to the wheel, the man wasn't so much bigger up close, or taller standing than he'd been sitting. He wasn't a giant of a Bear, if he was one. Not built on the scale of Solitary Love, not close, even if he'd been decades younger. Nor a Shockley looming monstrous on his deathbed. Instead, he had a droll nimble quality, for a fat man. He made me think of Nolan, which should have told me something, but didn't quite. His smile was disarmingly warm. In short, a *Yogi* Bear.

"Melinda—" I began. I instantly regretted supplying the man with her name. "Honey, we don't have a ticket—"

"Gratis, today," said the man. He exuded mildness and tolerance to a nearly embarrassing degree. "You can even ride in your own cab, if you prefer. She's a big girl, doesn't seem scared in the least."

"No." I moved toward Melinda, who'd situated herself at one corner of the love seat and begun to buckle in.

"I want a ride," said Melinda.

Was it so much to ask? For a feral girl, a Ferris ride? Between her glum wish and the grinning man, I felt bewildered into compliance. I'd still had no coffee. The rented Jeep that had departed with Laird had borne off with it the better part of my sense and intention. The wind continued to bruise us, though it carried less of the earth with it. But its voice, a steady low whine, made it difficult to think. I went in reaching for Melinda's seat belt, even as I felt only half-decided that I'd forbid her the Bear's likely harmless offer. I had to sit to get hold of her safety buckle. The man latched the cage door shut behind me and moved to the wheel's operating lever. I leaped up and tried to budge the grate that had closed over us. I couldn't.

"Why is this locked?"

"Standard specs," the man said. His voice shed its tone of curdled ingratiation. "Liability concerns, litigious American society, you know the score. Take a seat now." He squeezed the handle and wrenched the lever backward. A grinding, whirring, wheezing sound emerged, as if the gigantic device was seizing, inoperative. There was no masking backdrop of calliope music, just the whistling wind, seeming to originate with the sun itself, and my screaming at the man to switch it off, which he ignored. I couldn't imagine the wheel turning. It turned. I grabbed Melinda's hand and we rode it up backward, in our swinging cell, to the top of the arc. Then he jammed the lever forward. The machine grumbled to a halt and we dangled like a teardrop, at perihelion.

THE WIND, swinging our cage. Miller and Vacuum, snouts up, barking like machines, like angry tape loops.

THE CREAKING of our cage on its grease-black hinge.

VISIBLE NOW THROUGH THE GRID OF SHADOW: THE SUN-BRIGHT CORRU-gated tin roof of the storage shed and, behind it, a drab green Econoline van with swollen tires and wooden bumpers. Beside it, Heist's Jeep, the first, which we'd abandoned to hike into the Rabbit camp. The vehicles were tucked in a hollow, deliberately hidden from the trail by which we'd approached. The Jeep felt like a piece of my body that had been stolen. The souped-up van looked like a black sun, a piece of darkness blazing with the same fever as the white sun now fully cut loose from the horizon.

64

I SCREAMED DOWN AT HIS TURNED BACK AS LONG AS THE WHEEL CRANKED, until I felt I might vomit, then we were at the top of the sky and I saw the van and I shut up. All I'd accomplished was riling the dogs.

"You okay?" Melinda asked.

"I'm fine." My voice was shredded.

"I'm sorry."

"You didn't do anything wrong."

He stood below, staring straight up, shielding his eyes with one hand. Now that I'd grown quiet, it seemed to make him curious. He put his hands out, unafraid, to crown each of the dogs, settle them down. The gesture couldn't help but remind me of Heist. Soon Miller and Vacuum quit barking, though they ducked from under his hands and circled, whining, seeking a better sight line to us, or a staircase into the sky, one that didn't exist.

"Have you ever seen him before, sweetie?" I kept my voice small for a few reasons. "In the Wash, maybe?"

"I don't go to the Wash a lot." She sounded defensive.

"That's fine. I didn't mean anything by it."

"I just brought you since I knew the Bear was there."

"You mean Laird?" Had Melinda, in her fear, forgotten his name? I suppose she might not be strong with names. She might have lost track of mine too. It might be enough that she had any language at all.

"Yeah. The one who drove with us. I wish he was here right now."

"Me too, darling." I couldn't keep from calling her *darling* and *sweetie*. Under mortal stress, I was apparently transformed into my mother.

"Are you comfortable?" shouted the man below. The wind had eased, and our cab's squeaking rotations had stilled. The mob of flying ants had risen to find us, and I heard the whirring of their wings, occasionally a *tap-tap* as their bodies bounced off the grate. Miller and Vacuum were settled into a low keening, deep in their throats. The man's voice reached me surprisingly easily.

"No!" I shouted back.

"Normally it goes around and around!" he called out. Even shouting, his voice had a grin in it. "I wish I could show you! It makes a better illustration of the Three Turnings of the Wheel of Dharma!"

"I know how a Ferris wheel works, thanks," I shouted back. "I'm not in the mood right now. Let us down."

"I can't do that, sorry!"

"I'm calling the police." My phone had no signal, of course. My attempts were draining the battery, so I'd switched it off.

"Go ahead, but I don't think they have any influence on the *dharmachakra*!"

"I'm not talking to you anymore."

"That's okay, we'll talk later!"

The sun crept upward. We were still higher. Nothing was visible past the boulders where Laird and the Jeep had gone. Our creaking grew slighter until we came to a dead stop. Motionless, I felt our jeopardy reconfigured into one of pure height. The wheel's larger structure, its prospect as a form of vehicle, evaporated; instead, I felt we teetered top-heavy at the summit of a giant flagpole, our swaying more ominous for being nearly subliminal. Below, our captor puttered, the dogs danced and yipped, the dust rippled slightly. It nauseated me to look downward, but I couldn't quit.

"Who is he?" Melinda whispered. She'd curled onto me, astonishingly small. She carried a warm-bready smell, albeit sourdough.

"I don't know." I couldn't whisper, not with what I'd done to my throat. But I murmured, a voice just for her. "I'm pretty sure I saw him on the mountain. I saw his van. I think he picks up runaways and strays around the Zen Center, and maybe in the Wash." I didn't want to tell her he sometimes might also slit their throats. "It's good you never met him."

"Why doesn't he let us down?"

"He uses the wheel as a jail." I hadn't accepted the whole fact into my body until the word escaped my mouth.

"I'd like to go down and bust his head."

"Me too, honey." My insipid condescension was really pointed at a child in myself, in panic at being caged in the sky. Was it possible to trigger agoraphobia and claustrophobia simultaneously? I'd feared the mountain and how it touched into the blue, two abhorrent vacancies. Now I was the mountain. It sucked to be the mountain. There was nothing to do up here but fear the sun. Everything sickened me, the vertigo, my own helplessness.

"I called a SWAT team," I yelled at the man on the ground. "They're right over that hill." Gazing over the wastes, where my empty threat wasn't about to materialize, I found myself recollecting my twig-sister, Lorrie.

"*Instant karma's gonna get you!*" I screamed, covering Melinda's ear with my palm.

His only reply was "Interesting!"

"Aren't you worried?"

"Funny thing about me! I only worry about what's right in front of my face!"

"We need a bathroom break."

"It falls right through! Here, I'll fix it so you don't shit on the gears! Go ahead, I won't watch!" He restarted the Ferris wheel's motor and pushed the lever the opposite way, so we jerked backward. I screamed. The dogs shrieked. We descended a quarter turn, then stopped. Though he'd halved our distance to the ground, we dangled now over thin air and a rocky arroyo.

We'd lost our view of the vehicles behind the shed and the sheltering shade of one of the wheel's giant struts, so our cab was further bared to the sun—not a win.

"What about water and food?" He'd put us in better range of a normal speaking voice, once he killed the *put-put-put* of the motor.

"Later," he said distractedly.

The quarter-rotation seemed to agitate Miller and Vacuum. Though we'd gotten nearer, they acted as though something precious to them was getting farther away, on the far side. Perhaps it was. Were there prisoners besides us? I squinted through the sun-slashed armature to see whether other inmates languished in their gondolas. Perhaps at night they communed by a special language of Morse hinge squeaks. Maybe I could foment a riot. But there wasn't any way to see into the distant cabs—or, for that matter, the closer ones.

Now that we were nearer to the fat man, Melinda squirmed from my lap and unbuckled from the bench to press against the far side of the cab. Something rose from her throat, a gargling, yowling sound unresolving into either a sob or scream. Before I noticed, she began to climb the front grate. She moved in a state of panic, I thought at first. I was afraid to touch her, to drag her back to safety—I might be trapped on the wrong side of the zoo bars, with a creature who couldn't fathom captivity. (I'd at least grown up in a New York apartment.)

But no. Melinda spider-monkeyed to the wide seam at the grate's top. Was it possible she'd crawl through? Having felt the narrowness of her silverfish body in my lap, I bet the only limit was her hat size. Her reward would be to cling to the outside of a dangling metal basket, a possibility that merely terrified me.

The action set our cab swinging again, reviving the squeaking, which made a call-and-response to the whining dogs. Our jailer looked up. Melinda froze, like an insect playing dead.

65

TIME STOPPED, LIKE THE WIND. HE SQUINTED UP. BUT YOGI WAS NO BETTER at staring into the sun than I was. He missed the wiry shadow clinging to the interior grate.

When he glanced off again, Melinda wormed through. Her weight on the roof of our cab caused a mere squeak, then she'd clambered from it, onto the rigid frame. I held my breath. She didn't fall. She began a climb—not downward, but across the struts, to the wheel's far side.

A single flying ant had squeezed through, as if in exchange, and now crawled on my forearm. I let it crawl.

66

FOR AS LONG AS SHE JOURNEYED SIDEWAYS, CLAMPING HERSELF TO THE Ferris wheel's rusty framework, exposed and also disguised in the glare, inching farther from our cab, I underwent a bizarre hallucination, a kind of synesthesia: I was as much out there with her as I was in here with myself.

But no, that wasn't quite it. It was more as though I'd *become* the wheel, and it was my large body along which Melinda's tiny one inched. In marsupial species the newborn grub has a first task no one can help it with, to voyage through its mother's fur, from womb to pouch—that was how it felt. I felt her, like a tragic, hopeless itch I couldn't reach.

The sensation was that of an immensity of physical sorrow, like the night of the election, or that moment when I'd stood with Roslyn while Reed College security used their master key to let us into Arabella's abandoned, squalid dorm room. All the mothers, powerless to help daughters jaunting or plummeting into the bleak unknown. Yet as usual I was really only daughter, or mother, to myself.

67

THREATENING HIM WITH POLICE HAD BEEN DUMB. OUT HERE, POLICE WERE
as theoretical an influence as contrails. My captor was a member of the Viscera Springs confuckancy—if I meant to distract him while Melinda crawled, I had to keep that in mind. However much he came on with the Zen-cosmopolitan flippancy, his worldview arose from inside a Bear's fear and desire. I should speak to him in Bearish.

"When I said SWAT team I meant a *Rabbit* SWAT team. They're coming with a message." My voice was a croak, a sexy one, I hoped.

"Eh?"

When I had a better look, he'd shed his Buddha nature. His slablike cheeks were etched with fine lines, corroded by sun and wind. His broad glinting smile was made of crap dentures, swimming unmoored in blistered lips.

I tried not to glance at Melinda. If she fell, I'd know.

"It's not a message in words," I called out. "It's a reply to the sign you laid out on the mountain." Pushing my face to the cage, I made a cutting pantomime across my throat, bulged my eyes. "I was there."

He looked at me differently then. "That wasn't aimed at Rabbits."

"Too bad. Heist and Anita called a counsel. There's a Rabbit army in the hills."

"I doubt that. They don't get along. Heist's been civilizing their offspring for years now."

"I thought you wanted him back as your king."

"In the Yahoo tribe, the king is blinded and kept in a cave. In times of war, he's strapped on a horse and is the first to die."

He'd seemed to journey a distance inside himself to dredge the little parable from his inventory. I'd say or do anything to get into that place and wreck it. "Charles Heist was your last chance," I hissed, feeling savage. "You didn't know what you had."

"Possible."

"Laird's going to pull Charles out, then give the signal."

"Laird's another disappointment." The fat man's face clouded and seethed, like a pan of gravy on the verge of boiling. "But he won't find Charles there."

"Even better. The raid can begin immediately."

"What's the signal?"

"The sound of one hand clapping. I think I hear it now!" If only I'd kept my little horn, but no. I'd spent it in the dead king's ear. Nevertheless, I felt that same madness summoned in me. It was what I had, and enough. While Melinda moved on the wheel, I'd use the madness to enthrall him. "The Rabbits want your mountaintop!" I'd speak past his provocations to stream anxiety into his animal core. "They're in talks with the Koreans. They're cleverer than you, and aging better, and taking younger boyfriends and hipper drugs."

"Not the Rabbits I know."

"Seen Neptune Lodge lately? They've got drones and surveillance tech. They've got an espresso machine that makes ayahuasca lattes. They put Shockley in the witness protection program. The Wheel of Dharma has *four* turnings!" I began taking off my pants. "Come closer, I'll pee on your face." (I did this

once—long story.) I suppose it was my equivalent of a flowerpot to drop on his head, from the window of my captivity. Yet
it was too much to hope he'd center below me, since he'd risk
tumbling into the arroyo. "You know you want it!" Meanwhile
I'd palmed the pepper spray from inside my purse, just on the
chance I'd get close enough.

The sound that stopped us both was a familiar one. The latch
sliding open on the outside of a cab, the same as it had sounded
clanking shut. We both turned. Melinda wasn't hidden. She
wrested open the grate of a cab at the far side from me, the
one that had consumed the attention of Miller and Vacuum.
The man below turned and sprinted for the controls. If only the
dogs would suddenly bite him to death, or at least bite his hands
off. Instead they darted and cringed, seeming almost to be in a
state of worshiping the wheel. Just as my pants were around my
knees, the gears ground to life, and the cab lurched into motion
again, jostling me into the seat. I sank, and they rose. Melinda,
and the arms that emerged to draw her inside the opposite cab.
They were Heist's arms. I'd have recognized his stained crooked
knuckles even if they hadn't stretched out from the red leather
cuffs of his motorcycle jacket.

I pulled up my jeans and covered my flowerpot.

68

THE MAN AT THE BOTTOM HAD A PROBLEM. HE COULD TRY KEEPING ME down low, and Heist at the top. Melinda hadn't unlocked my cab. She'd feared the noise, or not thought of doing it before she started for Heist's cell. But when the man halted the wheel Heist began his own journey out. Even injured—and he looked still badly injured—Heist was stronger than Melinda, and he wasn't trying to hide. He scaled on the limbs of the wheel like it was a thing he'd been training to do. The man at the bottom restarted the wheel and we grunted into motion again. I aimed the pepper spray.

The renewed motion of the wheel froze Heist for a moment, but only a moment. Then he began crawling from the center to the periphery. If the man kept the wheel moving Heist would soon enough be at the bottom of one of the turnings. The man saw this and stopped the wheel again. We were all silent, watching, watching one another, except for the madness of the dogs, their murderous music that was incessant and substituted for any thought beyond simply watching. Heist resumed descending the ladder of the wheel, his limbs acting like those of a panther, or some diligent automaton. The man jerked the wheel to life for an instant, then stopped it short, trying to toss Heist free. Heist clung.

I saw the man below slapping at his face, which was shiny

with sweat now. The flying ants had come to drink. They were like the pepper spray I'd had no chance to use, probably better. He waved angrily at the whirring cloud, then set the wheel in motion again, at top speed. This only slowed Heist for an instant. He was nearly at a point where any of us could imagine him jumping free. The man at the bottom left the controls then, and darted with his abhorrent grace for the shack, and behind, into the hollow where the vehicles waited. The Econoline with the giant tires and the wooden bumpers stuttered into life.

I dipped low and lost sight of the van, then found it again, rushing from the hollow, toward the entrance to the boulders, to skirt the gate of wire, even as I watched Heist find his limit and allow himself to drop to the wheel's boarding platform, inert. I whirled round and round, watching. It was as the van veered and accelerated beyond the wire that the Jeep came roaring up the other way, out of the trap of boulders. Laird jerked the wheel to skid the Jeep sideways in a spume of yellow dust, to collide its rear driver's-side portion like a sledge against the van's front. The impact was abrupt, shriekless, the treads unable to grip on the surface, the brakes of no use. The van sat sprung unnaturally high on its tires, and it lost the battle with the sturdy, low-centered Jeep. The dogs were silenced, nuzzling their master. I heard the flying ants buzzing everywhere, their numbers still massing around us. No one had stopped the wheel, not yet. The fat man had come halfway through the windshield and lodged there, and his hands momentarily flapped on the hood, until they quit flapping. My finger jerked spasmodically on the pepper spray nozzle and the wind blew the little toot of pepper back into my face and I instantly vomited through the grate.

It takes a village.

PART VII

DESERT HOT SPRINGS

69

I'D WOKEN HIM IN THE PARKING LOT OF THE WALGREENS, AFTER I'D GONE in and found him a pack of clean white undershirts to wear beneath his leather jacket. He'd obliged me by putting one on, but when I pulled up to the gate at Two Bunch Palms, he was asleep again in the passenger seat, my little bundle of joy. The strapping young man at the front gate confirmed my name on a clipboard checklist and when he saw my sleeper, I put a finger to my lips and smiled. The gate man smiled back and pointed me to registration. He was a welcoming person working at a welcoming place, and once my name was on the list he didn't see anything suspicious in a mid-afternoon nap. They probably got a lot of tired people here.

Then, as I began to roll through, the gate man noticed the state of the Jeep's rear wheel well and bumper. It drove fine, but it didn't look great.

"I hit an animal," I said.

"What kind of animal?"

"An animal driving a van," I said, and left him that to think about.

In the palm-shady parking lot I listened again to the message from Jane Toth, the social worker who'd first given me Heist's name and phone number after the police had sloughed off my first inquiries. "I thought you should know that Charles

Heist is missing . . . the police have been to his mobile home and office . . ."

There were only so many ways I could read between the scant lines Jane Toth had offered. Mostly, I tried to read her tone. Was she warning me to protect myself? Was Heist a suspect in an investigation, one I'd triggered?

But analyzing her motives for the call was pointless. What mattered was what I made of the fact of it. I couldn't drive Heist home, which is what he'd asked me to do. I'd be driving him into a trap. I put my phone away and chanced leaving him sleeping in the Jeep again, in the resort's parking lot, while I went in and got a key card for the room and brochures about the massage and the mud baths and the qigong classes. We were going to hole up here awhile, and we might as well know about the amenities. If Heist didn't die on my watch, we might even make use of a few.

70

ANYONE MIND IF I SKIP THE CHASE SCENE? IT WASN'T MUCH. *EXIT, PURSUED by invisible Bears.* Laird, somehow so thorny and so copacetic at all times, hadn't riled them at the mining camp. (This was by his own account, which was all I had to go on.) When he'd gathered the lay of the land—that Heist had been abandoned into the care of Yogi, whose real name, I'd learn, was Paul Apollo—he'd done as he'd predicted: accepted some breakfast. Made small talk of the ex-Bear-but-no-hard-feelings variety. He hadn't mentioned my presence, or Melinda's—for this reason, he had to apologize for not bringing any food or coffee out for me. Then he'd driven my rental Jeep with aimless calm back out of their camp, only breaknecking it back in our direction once he'd been sure he was beyond range of their hearing and sight.

Did they follow? We didn't wait to see. Melinda pulled the lever that stopped the Ferris wheel at a level where I could be freed from my cage. Heist had gotten himself upright, sitting in the shade at the base of the wheel. He was dehydrated but alive. His beard had filled in the gaps between his sideburns, making his face a crazy quilt of lengths. Shirtless, he wore beneath his red leather jacket a kind of heavy poultice, bound by cloth to his damaged ribs and shoulder. It had a rank yeasty smell, but I left it alone. Laird and I helped him into the front seat of my rental, after I'd proven it was aligned enough to drive and moved it nearer to where Heist sat. I gave him water.

Then we went around the shack, and there quickly found Heist's keys, unconcealed in his Jeep's cup holder. Laird started the car, and we watched the needle bob up: half a tank. Laird drove it from the hollow, and Melinda and the dogs joined in it, as if by some previous arrangement. Then Laird piloted us, making a comet of dust, on a run from whomever was or wasn't compelled to try and stop us.

Heist went into a daze, his eyes half shut when they weren't all the way shut. Laird didn't stop our little train of Jeeps until we'd come out of the unmarked wastes, to park in the front lot of a drab little liquor and dry goods store in a town, or the idea of a town, called Landers. I picked up another bottle of water from the desert hippie inside. Laird went around the back with the Joshua trees to pee and brood. He had one bright red slash on the bare skull over his left ear, where the Jeep had touched him in the collision. Though I suspected his entire left side might be purple with bruises tomorrow, he claimed to be otherwise uninjured.

I conferred with Melinda by the side of the road.

"Laird wants to go see Anita," she told me. "We gotta find Jessie too. The dogs belong together."

I nodded, but I wasn't clear on just what she proposed. Melinda made it clear.

"Take him away from here."

"Okay," I said.

When a pickup truck passed by, we both started, but it was only a pickup truck. The driver could have been a stray Bear, or just an old white guy with a beard. It had begun to seem possible that it didn't matter. The man with the Ferris wheel was killed, or close to killed; we hadn't examined him closely. There wasn't a storm or a flood, not at the moment, and this wasn't a pit in the night. It was a dusty two-lane road, and a pickup could roll by without it meaning so much, even if it had a bad bumper sticker or two on it. In the absence of the fever to anoint a king, Bears might merely be old white guys with beards.

"Take care of him," she said.

"I will."

"He'll be worried about me and the dogs."

"I'll tell him you're with Laird."

She almost laughed.

71

THE TWO JEEPS PARTED THEN, MELINDA AND LAIRD GOING NORTH FROM
Landers, up in a direction I could now begin to chart, toward
Giant Rock, there to turn eastward off the two-lanes, seeking
into the hills to find the Rabbits. They'd shuttled back into their
own old worlds, really, the Viscera Springs lineage that wasn't so
simple to depart or be rescued from. To be feral wasn't merely to
be a wild child, but to be one cut loose, or run loose, from some
point of origin. I fooled around with the allegorical implications
a little, as if I were still the person who'd try to pitch an op-ed or
a *Sunday Magazine* piece, then I dropped them, because I wasn't.
My task was simpler. I was in Heist's role now. I had simply to
extricate a person from the perversities of Viscera Springs, to let
them breathe free, set them on their feet. I'd do it for Heist as
he'd done it for others, whether it was destined to stick or not.

I'd been headed west, back to Upland. He'd waved off the
suggestion of a hospital, twice, so I left it alone. It freed my
fantasies: we'd go back to his Airstream. I had him to myself, to
soothe and rehabilitate. He might not require a hospital for his
ribs, but he and I both needed a place of recovery, a circle drawn
around us within which we could determine what we'd be to
each other in the wake of our bold, strange conspiracy in desert
murders and absconded kings.

I almost couldn't believe it had gotten so simple. Then it

turned out it hadn't. On the Twentynine Palms Highway I pulled in to gas up the Jeep and checked my phone. We were back on the grid. My newly loathsome device, my pocket enemy, suddenly bulged with the contents of the denied world: a few hundred e-mails, Facebook notifications, and tweets, outraged news of appalling executive orders, a couple of late-night texts from aspiring Manhattan booty callers, and the single ominous phone message from Jane Toth. So the Airstream was out.

It was the very nature of my delirium that I was only further exhilarated. I had Heist alone in *my* Jeep now. By magic chance we'd even shaken off his dogs, delightful as they might be. Obligated by our fugitive state, I couldn't deliver him back to his tawdry office, his secret marsupial lounge. Instead we existed in free conceptual space, strung between the Mojave and the suburbs at the base of Baldy, where the fuzz might be prowling. I continued east, into the valley of giant windmills, but before Interstate 10, I hung a left onto a two-lane called Indian Valley Road, heading for the unknown terrain of Desert Hot Springs. That would be our hideout.

A hideout, perhaps a love nest too. I was thinking like a fugitive, maybe like an abductor, and—though it wasn't pretty to admit it—it turned me on.

72

I'D LEARNED ABOUT THE FAMOUS SPA RESORT CALLED TWO BUNCH PALMS
from *Inland Empire* magazine, back in the time of my Doubletree rainstorm occupation, seemingly a million years ago. It was
a place with natural mineral springs and mud baths, a Saratoga
of the West—which meant it also featured a resident shaman,
and Reiki as well as Swedish massage, and a trail called Coyote
Walk. The resort had been used as a set in an important film
by a '70s maverick director, and as the backdrop for an episode
of *The Bachelor*, because of course it had. In the photos in the
magazine's spread, the spa visitors went from their rooms to
the hot springs and massage appointments and even sat in the
plush restaurant in robes and slippers supplied by the resort,
which was useful, since Heist would be arriving without much
to wear besides his mud- and blood-stained jeans and the signature jacket.

I called and got a reservation easily. My credit card, that old
tether to the official reality, cleared without a hitch. When I'd
bought the couple of fresh T-shirts for Heist at the Walgreens, I
also grabbed a loaded travel Dopp kit, with a razor and a tooth-
brush and a mini deodorant, and a black one-piece swimsuit for
myself and some trunks for him, so we could immerse in the
famed healing waters, though I thought first I'd better take a
look under the poultice beneath his shoulder.

He was still out when I pulled around the resort's back edge to park near our room. The cheapest, it was also the farthest from the restaurant and spa and waters, a happy accident. Our view looked out beyond the well-trimmed border cacti and yucca to the hilly scruff beyond. Our room was on no one's route to the tennis courts or morning tai chi circle or anything else. I let him snooze while I moved us in: the assemblage of new-purchased Walgreens crap, a Jeepload of empty water bottles and Kind bar wrappers, and a suitcase it now occurred to me had been thrown together in the Obama era.

Then I went and woke him up. I couldn't have carried him to the room without Laird along to help, and anyhow I was impatient.

God help me, the first thing he did was smile.

"C'mon, cowboy."

"What's this place?"

"It's literally neither here nor there. That's all you need to know for now."

"Palm Springs?"

"Close. Another place with palms in the name. Think of it as where you get to go after you've got nothing left to prove—cloud nine."

The way Heist gazed at me broke me apart. As though even here, being helped from my Jeep, at the furthest limit of his wreckage and rescue, he was still my knight. The gaze said he knew that whatever wacky exhibition I put on was merely a disguise for my troubles, the troubles he'd ease for me if he could manage it. It electrified me, as much as if he'd caressed my nape hair. Fucking men. Of course, the gaze stirred my sensations of being wrecked too.

He didn't ask again where it was I'd taken him—I suppose he knew he'd figure it out from the stationery. Me being me, his abiding silence only unloosed further verbal incontinence. "I'm glad you don't recognize it, since then I'd know you'd brought some other girl here, and I'd be too jealous. I'd have to check us in somewhere else instead, like Four Ripe Avocados or Prune Springs or something. Though probably you've had multiple ladies in all those places." I only wanted my joking to skirt any reference to the Wheel of Dharma and its turnings, or to any animal tribes. We'd keep all allusions vegetal and fruitous for the time being.

He squinted at me in the high sun. "I've never been to Four Ripe Avocados." I'd forgotten his masterly deadpan, which might actually be dead sincerity—it was the uncertainty as to which that kept me so crazy. Maybe I just liked that he listened.

"Heck, I'll take you there tonight, big boy."

Heist steadied himself with one hand on the Jeep's hood, then followed me down the little flagstone path to our door. I swiped the key card and showed him in. The room was nice and clean, stylish, with a big bathroom and a patio area outside sliding doors, with a high fence. Heist halted just through the doorway, seeming not to know where to stand or sit. There weren't so many possibilities.

I gestured him to the bed. He propped himself there on the spread and spent a little while just breathing. I handed him one of the bottles of artisanal water that would surely turn out to be a twelve-buck charge on my card, then carried on my inane nervous chatter, avoiding all radioactive topics. Meanwhile I opened the closet and there they were, just as promised in *Inland Empire* magazine: the white and fluffy robes. I wasn't particular about Heist going in for the full menu of qigong and shiatsu and wheatgrass, but I was damned if, having gotten him this far into my fantasy, I wasn't going to see him, to see both of us, in those robes.

"You rest," I said. "I'm taking the first shower. Then I'm having a look at that shoulder of yours." I said it like I had some kind of Florence Nightingale tendencies to draw on, which I didn't. I just lowered my voice into a Bacall register and hoped it played.

The shower was a walk-in with a smooth-pebbled floor that beveled to the drain. The geyser of hot water and the A-grade freebie soaps and scrubs were a kind of revelation on my tight airplane- and desert-weary skin. Afterward I sashed the robe up high to my neck, playing fair with cleavage for the time being, and woke my poor captive again.

I RECLAIMED HIS NAME, CHARLES, MEASURED IT GENTLY IN MY MOUTH. I still couldn't get to *Charlie* or *Baby,* not quite. I propped him up on the nice pillows and helped him out of his jacket and the T-shirt. The patch extended farther around his back than I'd realized. It was woven with fine grass fibers, through a cement of some kind of herbal gum—aloe maybe, or chewed Joshua branches. Whatever the substance, it had condensed and shrunk during the time he'd baked in his captivity on the wheel. And Heist was a hairy man. Even if I'd trusted that he was intact beneath, it would have been impossible to free him of the stinking thing without waxing a large portion of his chest.

"We'll steam it off."

He blinked his eyes to give consent, like a hostage.

There was a teakwood stool in the shower stall. I cleared it of the bath products it had been holding up, then undressed Heist and placed him sitting on it and got the shower going. While the steam began to relax the poultice back to its mud origins, I took the shower attachment and began gently cleaning him around the patch. My robe sleeves began to get soaked, so I took the robe off and hooked it on the bathroom door. Swirling steam only partly cloaked us from each other. He didn't say anything, but allowed me to begin shampooing his hair. Where the poultice softened at the edges I broke chunks free and let them flow gunkily to the drain, where they dissolved like gray ice cream.

"I can't believe the Wheel Bear spent so much time patching you up," I said. "I guess they wanted you alive."

"His name is Paul Apollo."

"Yeah, well, I think we killed him." I said it just to hear it. I didn't need Heist to explain the parts I didn't know, or to console me for what I'd seen and done. I don't know what I wanted, except to place the knowledge between us.

"Paul Apollo died in a car wreck. Remember that if anyone asks." It was the most he'd said since refusing the emergency room. "And you weren't there to begin with, it was just something you heard about."

I nodded. "He claimed you'd been elected King of the Yahoos. That was a new one on me."

Heist raised his hand to dismiss it, then winced. I put myself behind him to knead foam into his skull. I wondered how long it had been since he'd had a shampoo. Maybe never like this, I thought proudly.

"Why wasn't he the king himself?" I asked.

"Apollo wasn't the type. He had other priorities."

"He was the kidnapper," I said. "The keeper."

Heist only sort of grunted. I worked my fingers beneath the poultice from where it had loosened at his back, and that made him grunt again. "Well, he built you a hell of a bandage, that's one thing."

"It wasn't him," said Heist. "That's Rabbit made."

"You're joking."

"No. I was in a haze, they didn't think I was awake, but I was. I saw her."

"Who?"

"Anita."

I hated her then, a few ways. Not least for touching Heist with her Pilates desert bod. But screw Anita's perfect calves. She had sinew, I had flesh. I let some of it fall on Heist, now that I'd cleared the mud from his steaky lat.

"She knew you were captured."

"She did what she could."

"No, she didn't." I went on talking while I caressed him from behind, letting the foam in his hair and the melting poultice turn to rivers for my hands to ride. "Rabbits are no better than Bears," I said cruelly. "The whole two-party system should be blown up."

I didn't know if I believed what I said. Why shouldn't Anita have salved his wounds, if that was all the king-mad Bears had allowed her to do? I should be more fair. The deep unconscionable complicity between love and hate, between woman and man, or animal and human, predator and prey—this, I could hardly lay at Anita's feet, or at the feet (or paws) of any one species or tribe.

At the rain-and-flame dance to Arabella's song, with the sacrifice of my expensive lipstick, I'd become one with the Rabbits, become one *of* the Rabbits. And I needed there to have been the two Viscera Springs tribes, because it was the conjugation between them that had resulted in Charles Heist. Yet now I wanted it all to go away, much as I pried and kneaded Anita's poultice from his body and rinsed it down the drain. I wanted Heist to myself. I'd draw a circle around us where nothing was left of these brutal oppositions but the enchanted residue between me and Heist, the *vive la différence* part.

The last clumps fell, prodded free of his chest hair by my fingertips. He sighed when I explored the tender part of his ribs, then said, "Careful." I went lower, across his bumpy belly. It might be time for the shutting up on my side of things, I decided.

I thought I had him going—if I had him going half as much as myself, it was a lot, plenty. His hair was still full of shampoo. I took the attachment and rinsed it, petting him downward with the soft jets like an animal whose fur I smoothed. He closed his eyes, but he knew I was near, felt my body dripping on his, sometimes touching him. When I let the attachment drop and hang like an old Manhattan pay-phone receiver, the water coursing against the glass, his breathing said he was ready.

But I wasn't. I opened the glass door and went for the razor and shaving cream. I put some foam on my hands and worked it into his sideburns and the thickened shadow between his sideburns, under his nostrils and into the cleft of his chin, all the sculptural details I wanted to see clear, and to feel with my lips and tongue.

"Don't move," I said, as quietly as I could. While the steam went on filling the space between us, I began to shave him. The steam had softened his whiskers, made them buttery, and the razor was new and good and sharp. The water poured into the drain without touching us, a lascivious waste he didn't protest. I went up under his chin, delicately around his Adam's apple, making my own decisions about where to quit, just short of his clavicle. Then I cleaned the bristles from his cheeks and chin and lips. I didn't cut him once.

Heist scooted the stool to lean back against the tile and let me do it. I took liberties, winnowed the piratical sideburns on all sides. I wished I could flatten them too, and trim his eyebrows, but I didn't have clippers. It was okay. It was enough. I lifted the attachment one more time and sluiced away the foam and hairs, and then I shut it off. I stole a look at the broken part of him then, the shrunken pink and white and purple-blue skin that had been cooking beneath the poultice. I couldn't see anything worse than that, but then I didn't know how a cracked rib or ruptured spleen would look from the outside. His contour was intact, at least. He allowed me to pat him dry with one of the big folded towels, his eyes opening a little now, mostly staying on mine, roaming just enough to my body to make me feel good and shy. I put us both in the robes from the closet. Maybe we wouldn't be in them long, but it was a picture I wanted in my head, along with a few others.

74

AT FIRST HE LAY BACK GINGERLY ON THE BED AND DRANK MORE WATER
and watched me, as if there were other places for this to go, but
there weren't. I opened his robe and I opened mine. You forget,
but your body doesn't.

For the first while I was on top. Then Heist located the
strength with which he'd scaled down the spine of the wheel.
Seeming to galvanize his limbs, he turned me with his arms and
moved over me, climbing me horizontally with that same de-
liberation. Maybe *I* was the true Wheel of Dharma. He slowed
and held his middle stiffly, protecting the damage, but it wasn't
bad that he slowed. It was time for that.

I managed to keep from speaking until what came out
wasn't making any real sense, wasn't mostly words. Like before,
I wept. We didn't let that stop us. Heist had a sound coming
from him too, not sobbing, exactly, but a kind of subvocal baying. The sound reached into me, and I did everything I could
with my hands and my hips to keep it issuing from him.

"We have *this* too," I heard myself saying over and over, an
incantation in breath. "This too, this too."

"Phoebe?" He kissed my eyelids, sipping my tears, seeming
to know what his newly smooth lips and chin were for.

"Nothing. Don't stop."

It was too simple to explain. We fit. I cried then for all the not-fits, the smalls and the bigs as well, exciting as they seemed at the threshold, and for the can't-move-rights, and the can't-move-once-without-comings. I was selfish enough to need this too, and Heist had it for me, all along. The world beyond, the speakable and the unspeakable, closed up shop for a time. The pain went away.

75

TIME SEEPED BACK INTO THE ROOM, BUT NOT TOO OBTRUSIVELY. I'D PAID for this privilege, or anyway I would, when my Discover card hit its limit. Heist and I were still touching in the can't-quit-touching way. Something had to happen, but not yet.

"What's this place called?" he asked.

"Two Bunch Palms." It suddenly sounded very *You Tarzan, me Jane.* "Listen, we can go outside. We're safe here." I imagined he needed open space to feel safe, after being trapped in the cab on the wheel. The way to trick a captive is to give him a yard to wander in. "We don't have to wear anything but the robes. There's a pond." I quoted from the brochure now; I hadn't spotted the water features on our drive along the perimeter of this paradise. "We can sit by the water." I heard myself beginning to chatter and tried to stem it.

"Okay," he said.

"Are you hungry? I'm ravenous, actually." At check-in, they'd told me no reservations were needed at the restaurant, just to wander in.

"Yes. Only not right away."

"Let's walk."

We put on the robes and also the provided slippers and went outside. We found the pond, first thing. That's how paradise works. A pond with two smoothed grassy banks, and empty chairs waiting for us. The pond was full of ducks who weren't afraid of you, and then when you sat awhile you saw it wasn't only ducks. There were turtles inching from the reeds, finding places to rest in the grass a foot or so from the safety of the water. The turtles weren't afraid of the ducks; no one was afraid of anyone. Ducks and turtles, two species on which to found a new civilization.

It was late afternoon now. A few others in white robes browsed the scene, mostly pairs of middle-aged women, but I didn't let it make me feel judgy. Here we all had what we needed, what anyone could need. I hoped Heist could feel the splendor of what I'd brought him to. The desert needn't be only a scene of deprivation. There was something like a feral swankiness here, no need to choose between the flayed landscape of his origins and these enchantments, including me. All it took was a natural bottomless source of water and about ten million dollars' worth of landscaping, plus a resident masseuse and shaman or two.

But I had to go and open my big mouth. I should have stuck to kissing him occasionally, which he'd been tolerating nicely. Instead I began molding his smooth cheekbones and lips and chin with my thumb as if I'd carved them from marble instead of merely with a disposable razor.

"My beautiful fugitive," I whispered. "I should peroxide your hair too."

"I'm not a fugitive."

"Not just you. Us together."

Think of all the runaways we might be! I wanted to say, picturing lovers in a film slipping civilization's snares, into their own territory, whether on horseback or in a Ford Galaxie. After where we'd been and what we'd done, I needed to swell our adventure into a whole world, to replace the one lost. Before this inchoate vision collapsed, I worked to persuade Heist on his own level, to keep it laconic: "You can't go back there. They're looking for you."

"I'm not hiding." He said this resolutely.

I whispered again, as if the landscape might be wired. The ducks didn't look organized enough, but I feared the turtles. "We *murdered* him, Charles. I think we might have murdered them *both*."

Did saying it make it more or less real? It was real enough. Coming to this calm place might be an awful mistake. Terror and fury might still be rising to the surface of me. Possibly I belonged in the whirlwind of sweat and fire, not in a laundered robe. "Tell me you know what I'm talking about," I said, and it came out more like hissing than I'd have preferred.

"If I spoke of it, I wouldn't give it the name you do."

"You're just of the shit-happens-in-the-desert school, then."

"Some people live and die recklessly. You're not responsible."

"Are you?"

"If anyone has to answer, it should be me."

"I don't want any more of your goddamn gallantry, Charles." It was easy to say what I didn't want.

"The second one, Paul Apollo—" he began.

"I'm sure he has a very cute backstory, but I don't want to talk about Paul Apollo either." Even dismissing the subject of the jaded Buddhist kidnapper and his Wheel of Misfortune, I observed that something lay, dire and unmentionable, behind it: Solitary Love, or whatever his real name might have been. A war vet and incarceree, and in the end a giant child of pain. He'd been no match for the Bears who had borne him up as their temporary king, nor for my siren blast and Heist's seized-up stone. My horror flooded back, even as I sat side by side with Heist in reclining deck chairs by the groomed desert pond, in a sea of peace.

The ducks and turtles had no answer for me. My heart

pounded. The space into which Heist and I had fled seemed to be shrinking rapidly.

"I want to help you," I said.

"You did that."

"I mean to get away. Not be part of it anymore."

"I wouldn't know what that means. Your friend is safe now. You took her away. Now you can run. No one has your name. No one will know."

I'd asked for it. The only thing craggier than Heist's silences were his brief, brick-like orations. This one left me stinging, as though the brick had landed on my jaw. Yet how could I dispute Heist's prerogative to shrink into his own distance, that horizon embedded in his glance? It was what he had shown me from the start, the psychic demurral of a man with no good options. I only wanted to be along for the ride.

"Will you send me an invoice?"

"What?"

"Obviously I've forgotten about the fee for your services," I said bitterly.

"We never discussed a fee."

"I just hadn't understood. I'm more than glad to pay for my wilderness adventure, and all the rest." My petulance might blossom into a storm, something roiling off the coast of me, perhaps something global. But global petulance had laid down an awfully good hand just lately, hadn't it? "C'mon, we'll start with dinner. Never let 'em say I didn't wine and dine ya."

THE SKY HAD BARELY BEGUN TO GLOW AS WE WANDERED THE MAZE OF fountains and yucca to find the restaurant. I went a little ahead; Heist followed, in the wake of my little tantrum. We threaded past the Grotto, the hot springs around which the whole resort had grown up. There abundant robes lay flung over chaise lounges while the lumpy bodies they'd concealed stood stranded in waist-deep waters, or immersed lengthwise, eyes squeezed shut, deep in corners shaded by elephant palms. It occurred to me that everyone else venturing from their rooms wore swimsuits beneath the robes, while Heist and I were buck naked. Well, maybe I'd reveal myself before the dessert course.

The resort's restaurant was called Essence, in case you weren't sure you'd attained yours to this point. True to the front desk's promise, they were delighted to seat us in a prime spot along the picture window, over a view of a desert rim that promised subtle astonishments as the light changed. Only a few other tables were occupied. The atmosphere was hushed without seeming too totally precious; the patrons all being in robes undercut any posturing. Maybe the solicitous server and the proximity of actual cooked food stood a chance of reversing my funk.

The only catch was that when my eyes focused on the attractive couple in robes two tables from us, the super-attractive, super-skinny woman revealed herself as my old Facebook friend

Stephanie. She'd spotted me first and been hailing for my attention, though I'd stared right through her, thinking she'd been
beckoning to the waitstaff. Stephanie sat across from a rakish
lanky fellow with a trim black beard and sleeve tattoos poking
from his robe cuffs. This naturally had to be Wild Edge—I'd
never gotten his real name—the installation artist whose exhibition Stephanie's gallery was readying to open, and whose ashes
Stephanie had lately been hauling, to use a phrase of Shockley's
that had stuck in my head.

"Phoebe, my god!"

"Stephanie, holy shit."

We were near enough not to have to wander from our tables
to be joined in conversation. No act of protest short of stalk-
ing from the restaurant, or maybe dropping the robes, was
going to stop this encounter from happening. "I can't believe
you're here," said Stephanie. She introduced him: Kurt. I said
Charles's name, and the men shook hands. I was doubly grateful
I'd shaved him, to thwart the onset of any hipster-beard solidar-
ity. They exchanged the testosterone grunt and settled back into
their seats. "This is Phoebe. I told you all about her," Stephanie
maybe-lied to Wild Edge. "I thought the Inland Empire had
swallowed you whole."

"Like Jonah and the whale," I agreed. "But that's the funny
thing about being swallowed whole. You can always pop back
out, and nobody would ever know the difference."

"Hey, great to meet you finally," said Wild Edge, with disconcerting sincerity. Had Stephanie really been selling me as
her great friend? Maybe she just wanted to retrofit me to her
arsenal, now that I'd turned up at the pricey resort.

Before any chance to protest, our server stepped in to ask:
Did we wish to join tables? Well, fuck it, I thought. I might score
two birds with one stone. I nodded, and the server shifted our

place settings and we moved to the two empty seats at their table. Let Charles Heist have to dabble in my world for a moment or two. It only required that I accept Stephanie's proposition that we were so dear to each other as all that. The last time I'd seen her, in Culver City, she'd played a more hard-ass part. I wondered if poor Stephanie might be flailing, having let herself become the conquest of her gallery's top dog. The art star was so much more valuable to the outfit, after all, than even the most omnicompetent assistant. It probably also didn't hurt that I'd brought along my own tame feral man, as delicious to the eye as hers, however pitiably undertattooed. Beyond merely wanting to spectate, Stephanie might think Heist could set Wild Edge a good example.

"What are you doing here?" she asked me, with the breathlessness that can't wait to be asked the same question.

"What *aren't* we doing here?" I said. "We came for the waters, and unlike in *Casablanca,* we were correctly informed. Except we forgot our suits—go figure!" Nobody laughed but me. I couldn't quit the sarcastic demolition work, even if it was destined to be self-demolition. Somewhere, trapped inside myself, I observed that my tantrum was the opposite of finished. It might be just beginning.

"They must sell suits here," said Stephanie.

"For a pretty penny, I bet. I'd love a piece of this action."

This didn't compute, so she ignored it. "Have you ever been to the Integratron?"

"The *what*? Is that something they feature here?"

"No, no, it's way out in the desert—you tell them, Kurt. I haven't actually been yet."

Wild Edge made a shape with his hands to begin. He was a sculptor, I supposed, and thought in forms. "So, basically the Integratron's an all-wooden structure, a perfect acoustical object.

It was built by this mad-genius aeronautics engineer, he was actually one of the people who worked on Howard Hughes's Spruce Goose, the all-wooden airplane—"

Not one single word of this made the least sense to me. Heist sat, revealing nothing, that default occupation. But his hand was on my forearm. That was nice. Our server brought the coffee we'd managed to order and placed it on the communal table before us, sealing the deal. She also clapped down drinks for Stephanie and Wild Edge: two slim vials of bright green juice, wheatgrass or something even more revitalizing and esoteric.

"—so, you go inside with a group of people and you lie there in a circle and they ring these giant crystal gongs—"

"It's called a sound bath," Stephanie interjected.

"Ah," I said.

Wild Edge seemed a bit leery. He might be a man in a robe, but he wanted to insert a little daylight between himself and *sound baths*. "It's basically a huge machine for inducing collective astral voyages, if you accept that kind of thing, which I maybe do. At the very least, while you're inside the dome, time and space are temporarily destroyed. I've been hitting it a lot, on my way in and out of Giant Rock, which is the basis of my current project. You heard of Giant Rock?"

"In Landers, you mean?"

"Sure. Survivalist Central."

"I've *been* to Giant Rock," I heard myself brag. "I've hitchhiked around those parts, in fact."

"Well, I want to have it moved," said Wild Edge.

"Sorry?"

"To Griffith Park."

"Have what moved—the Integratron, or Giant Rock?"

"Giant Rock."

"The whole thing? Isn't it, like, five million tons? And broken in two pieces?"

Wild Edge shrugged, suddenly taciturn. Stephanie leaped in. She spoke soothingly, in jargon. "Moved, or reconstructed. Kurt's exploring the logistics. The idea is to push it to whatever extent is possible. The enterprise itself is the artwork, in the vein of Turrell or Noteless or Smithson."

"Have you heard of Hammertown?" I asked. Heist looked at me strangely now.

But Wild Edge's eyes widened. "Sure, the King of the Hammers, the off-road race, cool beans. I want to go there." I'd earned his respect.

I explained to Stephanie, doing my best to dredge up the nonsense Laird had filled my ears with. It couldn't be made worse nonsense than it had been to begin with. "Apparently they have these insane desert races out there, in Alpha Force Vehicles, which are these special vehicles they've hand-blacksmithed for months before the race begins."

This embellishment puzzled but also fascinated Wild Edge. Stephanie, I saw, wasn't wholly pleased. I kept on.

"It's like a ceremonial thing, of course, but the winner has to go live without any provisions on the top of a mountain until he makes his way back to civilization." I could vomit out such stuff until Heist had to drag me from the table—it really might be simpler to unsash my robe and streak my way free. "Needless to say, they're all insane fucking Trump supporters but they're also really into tripping on datura seeds so that's kind of cool." It struck me as I said this that I'd blundered into a truth I could have offered to the Bears, could have whispered to Shockley if I hadn't been so busy pretending to command a fleet of black helicopters. The truth was this: The Bears weren't wrong to think a flood pursued them, but it wasn't a flood you could take to a mountaintop to avoid. It took the form of conceptual artists and all-terrain-vehicle buffs and suburban preppers, whose activities posed a more urgent threat to the desert communities than the global warming for which they prepped. Gentrification, the flood before the flood.

In her consternation, Stephanie turned to Heist. Her void-steeled nerves failing her, she reverted to the Manhattan Question: "So, what do *you* do?"

"I find people," he said. Charles Heist forever freely exhibited his dead-flat unironic koan-generating self; it wasn't just for my benefit, if I'd ever been tempted to believe it.

"In what sense?"

I raised my hand. "He's totally, like, running a shuttle for runaways, back and forth between various death cults and off-the-grid white slave organizations," I said. "It's kind of a cool project, I think." *My shitty elusive boyfriend is so much more bad-ass than yours, Steph, you can't possibly imagine.* "It's dangerous work. Here, Charles, show them your scars." I reached for Heist's collar, to tug it loose to display his shoulder. Firm and adept, he caught my arm. "We actually had to kill the guy who did this. Can I try your green juice?"

"Uh, sure," said Stephanie.

I drained it. "*Mmmmmm.*" Heist stood, and seeing as how he gripped my arm just below the bicep, I stood too. "Listen, this has been great, but we've got to get back to the room now. Did I mention that we killed a man? Maybe two men, it depends on how you count. Also, I'm totally outlandishly great in bed, though no one ever seems to mention it. Maybe I just seem to need to hear it too much, I don't know! But Charles and I are driving back tonight, he's got to get home to feed his dead possum, and he needs me to drive the Jeep—it's a rental, and it's only in my name, plus there's a chance he's slowly succumbing to internal injuries, so I'm sure you understand. It was nice to meet you, Mr. Edge."

77

I REMEMBER WISHING MY MOTHER WOULD DIE SO I COULD BE ALONE WITH my father. This was when I was eleven or twelve, but it wasn't a sudden feeling. It was a recognition, one that didn't evaporate upon recognition, nor did it vanish in guilt. I knew enough to audition it as *oedipal*, but it didn't feel oedipal to me. It felt like my dad was gentle and fun, and my mother was harsh and a drag. It wasn't as if my wishing killed her—she was still alive.

Then there came the moment when my mother's harshness was what I needed more than anything. I'd gotten into colleges easily, a lot of them. I was about to go to Columbia and refuse the others so that I could live at home. My mother forbade my doing so. She'd looked at me and seen a coming misery, but she hadn't troubled to appeal to my self-sympathies. She said just one thing, speaking levelly, without her usual caustic grain, and asking no sympathy for herself: "Don't worry, when you're gone he'll find another movie friend." The words released me from an insufficient home in the world.

Heist's retrieval of me from the restaurant called Essence— at that moment he became, temporarily, my mother.

78

THERE WASN'T MUCH TO PACK. WE JUST CHANGED OUT OF THE ROBES into the same crapped-out clothes that stank of the yellow dust. Before we left the room I glanced at the bed where no one had slept. I tossed the key card onto the pillow, not wanting to deal with explaining at checkout. I suppose that even without an invoice for his person-finding services, I'd paid for the sex with Heist, if I chose to think of it that way. I'd try not to.

I was pretty sure I hadn't lied to Stephanie and Wild Edge in the middle of my nervous breakdown—Heist really did need me to drive him home. He couldn't have done it himself. Making love, then frog-marching me through the door of Essence, he'd willed himself to uncommon strength, as in his climb on the Ferris wheel. But now, like some opportunistic predator, a lion napping between hunts, he was asleep again in the passenger seat before I'd even gotten on the freeway heading west. He was too weary to notice when I drove through a McDonald's for a couple of Filet-O-Fish and a shitty coffee to replace the surely terrific one I'd never touched at the restaurant. Heist was a sick man healing. He was also needed in the place to which I'd be returning him, home. He had a project. I hadn't lied at all about that.

Looking at him now, asleep crushed against the passenger door while I gobbled mayonnaise sandwiches and drove with

one hand, keeping us at seventy in the slow lane of the fiend-
ish interstate, Heist looked a little bare. He was denuded of his
protective cloak of dogs, that's what it was. Well, he'd have them
back soon enough. Maybe I'd shaved him a little much too, a tad
aspirationally, but his sideburns would grow back. The question
was whether I'd be around to see him redogged and reburned.
It was a question that didn't need answering until we reached
Upland.

Heist might have to navigate some police and social work-
ers, he might have to run a few feints, but he still had his project,
a living family of rescuees installed here and there, like Laird
and Melinda. I was the one in trouble. As when I'd been on
the verge of living at home during my college years, I'd without
fully noticing become bare like a stone. Unworlded. A glimpse
of it at the table with Stephanie and Wild Edge was all Heist
had needed to make his intervention. He'd been quick on the
draw, seen me better than I'd seen myself. So he'd roused himself, just long enough to rescue me from my rescue of him.

Maybe we could go forward on that precarious basis, what
the hell. I might return with Heist, into his game of tiny res-
cues, of not asking questions larger than who needed pulling
out of which family or cult on any given morning, or I might
not. But I wasn't going back to op-eds and conceptual art instal-
lations and *Paris Review* parties and scrolling outraged updates
interspersed with pastry photography, any more than I was going back onto that couch with my dad to watch *The Philadelphia
Story* for the umpteenth time. Better no world than that one,
sweet as it all had been. It was gone.

79

AROUND REDLANDS I SAW HER AGAIN, MY GOLDEN GIRL, THE BLOND MOTOR-cyclist on the chrome-gold Harley with the golden helmet and goggles. She pulled up in the fast lane, and I kept pace with her for a while, though it made me jealous to imagine Heist waking and seeing her there, emblem of a freedom I'd never known and could never pretend even to understand. Plus, she looked really hot. Heist didn't wake. The biker girl guided me westward a certain distance, then peeled off ahead and took an exit ramp, to whatever fabulous nowhere she called her own. I had a ways to go.

ACKNOWLEDGMENTS

THIS BOOK OWES A LOT TO SAM SOUSA, BRIAN KRAATZ, JOHN AND SCARLETT Ellis, Alix Lambert, Sean Howe, Daniel Lanza Rivers, Charles Long, Mimi "Splain" Lipson, Anne Boyer, Dorna Khazeni, Anna Moschovakis, Dana Spiotta, Julie Orringer, Mandy Keifetz, Jeena Trexler-Sousa, and Cobra Becerra. Thanks as well to the ensembles that propped me up: Dan, Zack, Miriam, Sonya, Laura, and Emma at Ecco; Eric and Raffaella at WME; Pomona College; Kate's Lazy Desert; the below-zero faithful of the East Blue Hill Library, particularly Steve Benson, Lee Lehto, and Jen Traub; above all, Everett, Desmond, and Amy.